Thunder in the Night

Kate Fellowes

CRIMSON
ROMANCE
Avon, Massachusetts

Published by
Crimson Romance
an imprint of F+W Media, Inc.
10151 Carver Road, Suite 200
Blue Ash, Ohio 45242

www.crimsonromance.com

ISBN 10: 1-4405-4535-9
ISBN 13: 978-1-4405-4535-1
eISBN 10: 1-4405-4533-2
eISBN 13: 978-1-4405-4533-7

Dedication

For Joan Giencke
Every line of my pen, every beat of my heart is for you.
I miss you, Mom.

Chapter One

Not far away from me, two men were arguing in low voices.

I sat still, leaning against the bus window, trying to locate them, trying to hear, but it wasn't easy. The hotel shuttle was loading and all around me people were talking and laughing and bumping their luggage into the rows of seats.

The men weren't here, on the bus. They were outside, near my open window.

"What are you playing at? This isn't a game, you know."

"Just shut up and follow directions," a harsher voice snapped. "Think you can manage that for seven days?"

"I'm not talking about this trip." There was anger in this voice. Frustration, too. "I'm talking about—"

My seatmate jogged me with her elbow. She'd talked almost nonstop since our plane left the States and headed for Belize. I'd tried to be polite, but even feigned interest glazes over after a while. At least it was only a twenty-minute ride from the airport to our hotel.

"Excuse me. Mrs. Underwood has a question for you." She pointed to the elderly couple just behind us.

I gave up any attempt to eavesdrop and turned awkwardly in my seat. I was here on assignment and that was to do a puff piece on this tour, nothing more.

"Aren't you that new writer with the *Breeze?*" the older woman asked, leaning forward with genuine interest. "We saw you on the *Wake Up Show* last week. But you're much prettier in person."

"Oh, don't go embarrassing the girl, Elaine," her husband chided.

My cheeks flushed. It hadn't been my idea to go on the local morning show. That had been the brainchild of my editor. The *Rochester Breeze* was a monthly, with a very local flavor. Now that I'd come aboard, it was time to meet the community, and in Rochester that meant drinking coffee and being chatty on the *Wake Up Show*. I'm not at my best at five in the morning, but I couldn't look much better now after hours in airports and airplanes.

I stretched my hand back. "I'm Allison Belsar and you're right. I just started last month." She gave my hand a gentle squeeze. Her husband's shake was much firmer.

"I'm Dan and this is the missus, Elaine," he said. "You're fresh out of college, hmm?"

I shook my head. "I've been a few other places," I said, which was true enough. "Now, I'm really happy to be at the *Rochester Breeze*." That was also true.

"And you're getting a free vacation right out of the gate. I'd call that lucky," Dan said.

"A working vacation," I said and he nodded, but not like he believed me.

"Rain Forests and Ruins," sponsored by the local zoo and billed as educational, was the latest in a series of weeklong "zoo treks." With attendance capped at about a dozen and the emphasis on sights and amenities, the treks had proven so popular that the magazine decided a story was in order. Through my article and on our blog, the *Breeze* would share the experience with those who couldn't afford the trip.

Armchair travelogues hadn't been my beat, but they were now. Just for the time being, I told myself. Just until I proved my skills and got back to hard news and investigative journalism. Although what there could possibly be to investigate in Rochester I couldn't imagine. Still. . . .

"Who's that up there?" I asked, watching two men climb aboard. They weren't arguing. In fact, they were quite pointedly not speaking as they took seats at the front of the bus, one behind the other.

From behind me, Dan gave a hearty laugh. "You really are new here. That's Clark Webster, the zoo director."

"And the other man," his wife said, "the younger one, that's—"

"Lawler. Mart Lawler." My seatmate interrupted in a voice like a purr. "Tall, dark, and everything else," she said, winking her approval.

"He's the assistant director," Elaine explained, her brow furrowing. "Kind of makes you wonder who's minding the store!"

She laughed a cascade of lilting notes and we all chuckled at the image of the animals running free in happy abandon, like some television commercial.

The bus started up, pulling out onto the main road in a slow lumber.

"So . . . those two work together?" I returned to our topic and lifted my eyebrows. "I just heard them arguing."

"They don't see eye to eye, dear. Everyone knows that." Elaine paused, adding, "At least that's what I've been told."

"I've got it on good authority that they don't share the same 'mission statement,'" my seatmate said, putting finger quotes around the words.

"The zoo has a mission statement?" I made a mental note to check the website.

"Doesn't everyone?" Dan sounded amused as the bus bumped along, hitting every pothole, as buses seem to do all over the world.

May as well get to work, I thought, and pulled a notebook out of my backpack.

I looked first to the woman beside me. "I feel I know so much about you from our conversation on the plane, but I never caught your name."

"Didn't I mention that? Sorry! I'm Jen Carlino," she said.

About forty, color coordinated, her blonde hair in a geometric cut, Jen fit the image I'd expected of my fellow travelers. As did the Underwoods.

Their names had rung a very little bell earlier, as if I should recognize them. It took me a few moments—after all, I'm new in town—and then the information slipped into place.

Dan Underwood was Rochester's biggest philanthropist, a regular figure at every society fundraising event. He even attended charity runs, handing out water and awarding the prizes since his running days were long over. His plentiful gray hair had been mussed during the plane ride and stood up around his head now, like snow swirled by a winter wind. His eyes, watery blue, had a spark that seemed permanent. This was a cheerful man.

"You've been on these junkets before, right?" I asked the Underwoods.

"Gosh, yes. We've been all over." Elaine held up her hand, ticking off locations as she named them. "There was Namibia and Kenya and Alaska and the Amazon."

Her voice was high pitched and thin, suiting her small frame. Her hair, cut short and fluffy, had been colored an unlikely shade of silver that was almost pink. All this together gave her the appearance of a delicate bird, just the right size to fit in the palm of a hand or a teacup.

"You're going to love it," she assured me, reaching out to pat me on the arm. Several rings glistened on her fingers. Elaine didn't appear particularly wealthy in her comfortable knit traveling outfit, but the chunky gemstones belied her husband's affluence.

"It's not a bad deal," Jen put in. "You learn a little something. See the sights. Get away from the husband for a while."

"I got away from mine permanently last summer," I said, glad I could say that without feeling a pang of remorse or disappointment or inadequacy.

Jen got it in one. "Good for you!" she said. "Clear the decks."

I liked that image. Me, alone on the deck of a ship with my hands on my hips, mistress of all I surveyed.

"Let's just hope," Jen went on, glancing at the back of Clark Webster's head, "that our trek doesn't end like the last one and everyone gets home alive this time."

Chapter Two

"What are you talking about?" I asked, staring at Jen and clicking my pen on and off. My reporter radar tingled. "Someone died on the last zoo trip?"

"That was an unfortunate incident," Elaine said in apparent agreement. "But hardly our concern."

"What happened?" I pressed.

"The less said, the better," Dan brushed my question aside. "Young men sometimes do foolish things." He gave Jen a quelling look.

From the front of the bus there was a bit of commotion and I wondered if the two men's argument had resumed. Then the younger one, Mart, stood up, bracing himself as the bus swayed along. He reached for a microphone and turned to face us.

"We'll talk later," Jen promised in a stage whisper. "My friend was on that last trip. It's quite a mystery." She glanced again at Clark and I heard Dan harrumph behind us.

You bet we'll talk, I thought.

"Hello, fellow trekkers," Mart called. "Could I have your attention for just a moment, please?" The group immediately fell silent.

What I could see of him was appealing. Brown hair that just brushed his collar, square chin, dimples when he smiled.

"First off, I'm Mart Lawler and I'd like to extend the official welcome to this zoo trek," he began, sending a look in every direction. "We're going to have a fantastic journey and see many wonderful, beautiful things. As you know, the rain forest is in great danger today. Unless we take steps immediately to stop the destruction, soon there won't be any left. With that in mind, we're going to show you some of the marvelous things that could be lost. I'll go over our schedule for the rest of the day and listen up, because we'll be hopping."

I pulled out the printed itinerary I'd received in advance of the trip and reviewed it as Mart went on. We'd spend seven full days in Belize, which lies east of Guatemala and south of the Yucatan. From that base, we'd trek to the ancient ruins in Tikal and elsewhere, exploring the rain forest with an expert as our guide—touring caves, visiting conservation sites, and soaking up local atmosphere in the marketplaces.

"So, we'll check into our hotel soon," he concluded, "but don't get too comfortable because this afternoon we're heading to one of the area's wildlife sanctuaries to do some bird-watching. We'll take a guided tour by boat. I've been here before, folks, and it is spectacular!" Mart spread his arms wide, radiating enthusiasm. "We'll watch for macaws, parrots, and egrets. A magnificent creature called the snake bird." He swirled his hands in the air, mimicking a snake's motion. "Boat-billed herons, storks—"

He seemed set to list every species in the country, but Clark Webster rose from behind him, grabbing the mic and interrupting with an impatient sigh.

"And I'll just put in a reminder—since Mart hasn't mentioned it—that the welcome party is tonight in the casino lounge. It's a great chance for all of us to get to know each other a little better. I realize some of you have been along on other treks but for many of you this is your first Rochester Zoo adventure."

I shifted in my seat, craning my neck for a better view of the director. A rangy six feet or so, he was in his early fifties and clearly worked to keep himself in shape. His blond hair, liberally sprinkled with gray, was cut short and tapered. When he spoke, his voice held just a trace of an accent. I couldn't place it and made a note to find out later where he'd been raised. Outside the States, I'd guess.

Now Clark tipped his head in my direction. "For those of you who don't already know, we have a celebrity in our midst. Ms.

Allison Belsar of the *Rochester Breeze* will be sending dispatches home every day."

Caught off guard by the introduction and wishing I'd thought to comb my hair, I waved to the group.

"I'm sure she'll be eager to speak to each one of you during our journey," Clark went on, looking to me for confirmation.

"Definitely," I said, beaming my biggest, most welcoming smile, and trying to look at everyone at once.

Next, he gestured to the well-dressed woman in coral in the seat beside his. Unrumpled, lipstick in place, and with her hair sprayed into a casual tumble, she looked fabulous.

"I'm lucky enough to have my dear wife, Sylvia, along for this trip," Clark said. "You may already be acquainted with her from other zoo functions."

Sylvia rose slightly and lifted a slender arm in casual greeting, smiling and projecting an aura of showmanship.

"We're both looking forward to seeing you this evening. In the mean time, if any of you have questions or concerns, please feel free to come see me. The bus should be arriving at the hotel in just a few minutes."

There was a polite smattering of applause as he sat down.

"That's interesting. Sylvia hardly ever comes," said Elaine from just over my shoulder. "She's very busy with her charity work, you know."

"Kind of like your husband," I said.

Elaine nodded. Dan, adjusting his hearing aid, frowned in concentration and said nothing. The backs of his hands, I noticed, were covered in faded blue tattoos. I squinted, then recognized the symbols. He must have been in the Navy.

The bus turned another corner a bit too sharply and I slipped sideways a little in my seat.

No one back at the office had said anything about these treks being dangerous. Certainly the editor had neglected to mention that a death occurred on the last one.

I tapped my pen against my chin and the part of me that's always curious, the part of me that always wants to know why, sat up a little straighter. Probing, getting to the heart of things, was part of my journalism training. Something here on this trip called for closer examination and I had the whole week.

Chapter Three

When we reached our hotel in the city, I drooped with disappointment. The place, sitting on the waterfront, was part of a worldwide chain and looked familiar from numerous television ads. While I hadn't anticipated or wanted anything too rustic, I did expect at least a bit of local flavor—an older hotel, with period architecture, maybe a veranda. Instead, I followed the others through double glass doors, across thick carpet into a tastefully appointed but unexceptional lobby. The only concessions to locale were the prints on the walls featuring dramatic photographs of ancient ruins and lush scenery. The upside of such modernity, though, meant that every amenity would also be ours. The chlorine scent of a swimming pool prickled my nose.

Our marching orders left no time for scoping out the place or unpacking or flopping onto the big bed in my single room. I did spare a few moments to stand at the window and look out on the water, though. Thinking about the soggy, gray scenery I'd left back home made me appreciate the curl of sunlit blue even more.

"Thank you, *Rochester Breeze*," I said aloud then kicked back into high gear. Within the allotted half hour I was heading back downstairs, camera in one pocket, cell phone in the other, eager to be off.

Instead of taking the elevator, I opted for the stairs. I was only on the third floor and while there might be time to hit the fitness room or the pool later for some real exercise, a quick sprint downstairs would revive my travel-weary body.

Spinning down the steps and landings, I came to an abrupt halt at ground level. This stairway ended at some back entrance to the hotel. Through the glass of the door, I could see the parking area. And in the parking area, I could see Clark.

He was leaning up against an older, shabby-looking car, conversing with a driver I couldn't make out clearly. There was someone in the back seat, too, but from my vantage point I couldn't tell if it was a man or a woman. Only one thing was obvious from Clark's serious, dark look. He wasn't asking for directions.

As I watched, Clark reached for his wallet, pulled out an impressive wad of bills, and thrust them through the window at the driver. He looked around the vicinity.

Checking for observers? I wondered, shrinking back a step and fumbling for my camera. I snapped a few quick pictures of Clark and of the car, even as I asked myself why. It was the money thing that made the transaction furtive. The money and the beat-up car and Clark's anxious expression. Was he up to something? If so, what?

In the space of a few seconds, I thought, *this job has gotten a lot more interesting.* I'd go bird-watching now, but I'd keep one eye on Clark. He might prove just as intriguing as the boat-billed heron.

*

Mart came to stand next to me on the sidewalk as we prepared to head out. I'd hustled down several long corridors to find my way to the front of the hotel and had managed to arrive with time to spare.

"Ready for adventure?" he asked, his manner relaxed and matter-of-fact.

Some of my tension—the stress of travel, spying on Clark, rushing to get here—eased away.

"Yes, indeed. That's why I'm here."

"Well, we're really happy to have you along, Ms. Belsar," Mart said. I could see ginger highlights where the sun glinted on his hair.

"Please call me Allison, Mart," I said with a smile and he nodded.

"Deal. You know, the zoo uses these trips for several purposes. Of course it's for publicity, but it's just as important that we shine a light on the problems and ongoing dangers animals face in our world." He reached out, touched my arm for just an instant.

"Would you be willing to hear about that? Incorporate it into your articles somehow?"

His dark eyes were intent on my face and I knew whatever he wanted to share with me would be heartfelt.

"Sure, that sounds great. I thought I'd look for the tie-in between zoos and the jungle—if there still is one."

He smiled, as if I'd passed a test, and nodded. "There certainly is. Protecting the endangered. Serving as sanctuary," he began and I thought at once of the zoo's mission statement. "We can talk about all that later," he said, looking around at the crowded sidewalk. "It looks like everyone is here."

But when we pulled out for the drive north, Clark was not among us. Had he gone off with the guy in the beat-up car? Did Mart know where he was? No explanation was offered for the director's absence.

As we got underway, Mart had each of us introduce ourselves to the group and give a one-sentence biography. It was a great way to put names to faces and there were plenty of both. I knew some names by now and caught a few more. With luck, I'd get to know everyone by the time the trip was over. Some folks used way more than one sentence to sketch their backgrounds, but the exercise was still a good mixer.

Soon enough, we reached our destination and clustered into an excited bunch, ready to board the boat that would take us down a jungle stream. The hot sun, combined with high humidity, brought a sheen to my forehead as I waited my turn to hop on. I swiped it away with the back of my hand.

"I'm getting really excited now. It'll be amazing in the rain forest." I didn't direct my remark at anyone in particular, but just lobbed it gently over the net. Three young women, traveling together, murmured in agreement.

"Oh, the forest is incredible," said a bookish-looking man of about forty, wearing a sun hat and shorts. Professor Sheridan

Ramsey, I remembered from our mixer. He taught science at Rochester's nearest university.

He launched into an account of his last trip to the area, delivering details in such a way that the group enjoyed listening. With his dark hair and thick dark-framed glasses, he looked smart but not nerdy.

Clapping his hands, Mart got everyone's attention. "Keep your eyes peeled, folks, because there's plenty to see along our route. Hundreds of species of birds, monkeys—even crocodiles!"

One of the young women, a redhead, gasped.

"Better not trail a hand in the water, Faith," Mart said. He winked, and I wondered whether he'd been kidding about the crocodiles or if the sun was in his eyes.

He handed me into the last of the seats, up at the front between the guide and himself.

The boats were full now and our guide began speaking, giving us a brief history of the sanctuary and describing the highlight to look for.

"The jabiru stork is quite majestic, with a wingspan of eight feet or more. They're the largest flying birds in the western hemisphere and they nest in the wetlands here," he concluded.

"That'd be something to see," Dan said. "Good thing my duck-hunting buddy's back home. No bird's safe around that guy."

The guide bristled. "This sanctuary was created to protect this nesting area," he told the group, "and the jabirus, which are an endangered species. We take our duty very seriously and your duck-hunting friend would find himself in quite serious trouble, I must tell you."

"Hunting endangered species is nothing to joke about," Mart said, not to the group, but to me. He pressed his lips together, eyes scanning the shoreline.

I heard Elaine mutter something to her husband under her breath and from his expression I could guess what it was.

"Look!" Mart called suddenly, pointing.

A huge white bird swooped low over the water just downstream, looking like something from the prehistoric world. All wings and legs, its black head and red-ringed neck clearly identified it as the stork in question.

"It's gigantic!" someone said, echoing my own thought.

"They can reach a height of five feet," our guide reminded us.

As our boat neared the point where the bird had landed, I snapped a picture. In the next half hour, we saw every single one of the two hundred species of birds in residence. At least that's how it seemed, especially with Dan doing his best to mimic their calls.

He might have continued if just at that moment a crocodile lazing in a sunny spot hadn't trundled into motion from the bank of the stream, entering the water not far off. I was ready, landing a good picture of the animal before he dropped out of sight.

"Time for dinner," Mart said. "He'll be looking for a snack. But that's nature, folks. If our zoo animals were living their natural lives, they'd hunt for chow, too, rather than just waiting for their meals at the feeding station, like we do at a buffet."

Our group being Midwesterners, the mention of a buffet set everyone buzzing about hunger pangs. Our stop at the visitor center, then, was brief and our wander through the village equally short, allowing just enough time to purchase the native specialty—cashews—for the ride home.

Back in the bus, I flopped onto a seat toward the rear.

Jen slid onto the seat beside me. "Wasn't that a marvelous place?" she asked, pushing both hands through her tousled hair. "I should have brought my camera, but I didn't have time to find it in my luggage. I got this great book, though." She flipped the pages of one of the titles available at the visitor's center.

"I got a good shot of the crocodile," I said, poking buttons to scan through my pictures.

Jen took the camera and looked. "Oh, yeah. I like how you can see that big tail. Did you get one of the stork?"

We put our heads together to see the screen. "Yes, and here are those monkeys," I narrated, pushing more buttons. "And then, oh."

"What's this? A practice shot?"

The screen showed Clark in the parking lot next to the beat-up car. You couldn't see the money in his hand, but I knew it had been there.

"Oh, it's Clark!" Jen said. She squinted then looked at me. "What's he doing?"

"I don't know." I wasn't about to let Jen know the situation looked suspicious to me. "He probably knows some local people if he's down on these zoo jaunts all the time."

"Suppose so." Jen looked at the photo again. "Huh." I could hear the question in her voice.

"How well do you know Clark?" I asked.

Before she could answer, Dan hollered across the aisle. "Did I hear you got a shot of that stork? Can I see?" He extended his hand and waggled his fingers.

Dan took my camera from Jen, who had cued up the stork picture. He made appropriate noises of appreciation then scrolled through the rest of the sanctuary pictures.

As he scrolled further, I got nervous. He was bound to see my series of Clark photos. What would he make of them? Would he tell Clark I had been spying on him? Not that I had, of course. Not really.

Reaching across the aisle, I held out my hand and smiled my request. Dan passed the camera back without comment. Shoving it into my backpack, I looked away from him, scanning the scenery.

"I need a nap," Dan announced.

"Especially if you don't want to miss casino night," Elaine said.

Casino night. The welcome party. Would Clark be in

attendance? He had seemed enthusiastic about both earlier in the day. And if he always carried around wads of cash like he'd handed over in the hotel parking lot, he might look forward to rolling the dice. No, he wouldn't miss tonight's event the way he'd missed this one. I'd be willing to bet on that.

Chapter Four

I fingered my last silver token, blew on it for luck, and then dropped it into the slot machine. A whoop went up from my neighbors when bells rang, lights flashed, and what seemed like hundreds of tokens poured out. A big win, it sent my spirits soaring and I jumped up and down. Laughing, I turned to the trekkers around me, accepting their hugs and claps on the back.

"That's it for me," I announced, sweeping up my winnings. "Quittin' while I'm ahead."

"You can't do that. You're on a roll," Alan, a math teacher on his third zoo trek, urged.

"Yeah, quite a roll, too!" his wife, Maria, echoed.

The room was full—full of people, full of noise, full of color as everyone paraded their resort wear. Tourists made up most of the gathering, but there were plenty of native sons and daughters trying their luck in the casino, too. Tables ringed the outside of the room, surrounding the rows of machines like wagons around the campfire.

Jen's table was the noisiest one, drawing the youngest people on the trip and featuring bursts of laughter at regular intervals. I wondered what could be that funny, wishing I'd been in on the start of the jokes. I'd hoped to get a chance to speak with her somewhere quiet but that definitely wasn't here.

Across the room, Dan and Clark sat beside each other, not speaking. Each man studied the cards he held as if the future of western civilization depended on his next move. Dan's pile of chips was larger than Clark's, I noticed. Was Dan a better player or just lucky? Was Clark losing to a big benefactor on purpose? Could you even do that, playing cards?

Off in a corner, Mart was deep in conversation with a woman I couldn't identify. Admiring the breadth of his shoulders, the bulge of his biceps beneath the fine knit of his shirt, I let my eyes trail down him in lazy inspection. Lean hips, long legs. I swept my gaze up again. Hair still damp from the shower, he was smiling now, then laughing at his companion's remark. In one hand, Mart held a glass of something amber. The other hand clasped the woman's narrow waist as he leaned close to whisper in her ear. His grasp made creases in the fine silk of her vibrant blue sari. When she tipped her head, her long cascade of smooth black hair fell off to one side. From my vantage point, I could see the intimacy of their body language, feel the crackle in the air between them.

Mart was a fast mover. We'd only checked in a few hours ago and already he'd made a conquest. Of course, just as I figured Clark knew people in Belize from his travels, the same could be true of Mart. Old friend. No, old lover. Obviously.

When I heard my name, I blinked, coming out of my brown study. The three young women I'd mentally dubbed the career girls stood in a cluster behind me. Twenty-somethings, they all wore variations on a sundress similar to my own, colorful jewelry, and tousled long hair. Each held a glass, half full or half empty, depending.

"We're heading to the roulette wheel and we thought we'd ask you to join us for a while," one of the girls said.

"Thanks. Sounds great." As we headed that way, I glanced to where I'd seen Mart and the woman, but they were gone.

For the next half hour or more the four of us lined the table, watching fortunes rise and fall. Faith, the woman who Mart had warned at the waterfront earlier, was a serious-looking redhead who would have a serious hangover come morning. Kiran was a brunette with full cheeks and deep dimples. They worked together at the biggest corporation in town, Patty, the dark-haired one, explained when I asked.

"Usually, we just go flop on the beach in Mexico for a week," Kiran told me. "Maybe meet some guys."

"But we sure don't have to worry about that on this trip," Patty said, with a groan. "What's the male-female ratio here? Like one to two?"

"That's what we get for doing something educational!" Kiran laughed.

"Yeah, educational," Faith said, knocking back the last of her drink. There was the just slightest hint of a slur in the word.

"I hear there's a cabaret," Patty said. "Let's go see."

I stifled a yawn. The day had been long and all I really wanted was sleep. Sound sleep, preferably, for a full eight hours.

"Maybe tomorrow night," I begged off, knowing I still wanted to make some notes on our journey before hitting the hay.

"Oh, c'mon," Kiran groaned, taking my arm and tugging. "Just for half an hour."

She led us to a table up near the stage and alongside the dance floor. Glancing at the crowd, I saw some trekkers gyrating to the music. Onstage, a five-piece band played while several young women in feathery costumes danced among them.

When the song crashed to a halt, I clapped and peeked at my watch. I really needed to update those notes for my first article and get to bed.

"I think I'm going to—" I began then stopped.

The guitarist was introducing a singer. The long black hair and peacock blue gown of the woman approaching the microphone were familiar. She was Mart's companion.

"So, give it up for Ishani!"

With a grace I could only envy, Ishani acknowledged the applause of the audience, stepped forward, and opened her mouth. The song she sang was slow and romantic, emphasizing the rich alto of her voice. Her eyes swept over her listeners, drawing them into the song of love lost and found. One elegant hand lifted, she smiled down at the table nearest the stage. Mart sat rapt, his head tipped up to watch. He raised his drink in salute.

"Wow, she should record a CD," Faith said as the song ended.

The dance floor began to fill again as the band segued into a mix of popular songs. I joined in and soon spotted Sylvia Webster, in an eye-catching graphic print mini, dancing with the professor. Mart, working the crowd now, was with Maria.

At the end of the medley my second wind propelled me to the bar for something cold to drink.

"What's your pleasure?" Mart asked, joining me.

He placed our orders and we leaned against the bar, watching the others. I tapped my purse against my leg in time to the music.

"Ishani has a beautiful voice," I told Mart. "Faith thinks she should record an album."

Mart smiled, nodding. "I've told her that, too, but she wants to focus on her work. Singing's just her hobby." Looking over the crowd, he asked, "Wanna dance?"

Ishani was at the microphone again. The music had changed to something slower and the lights dimmed accordingly.

"Sure."

I let him lead me the few steps to the floor and moved into the circle of his arms. His hand at my back felt warm through the thin material of my dress. Mart hummed along to the song, his breath tickling the top of my ear in a provocative way.

Closing my eyes, I followed his movements without effort. Up close, he smelled faintly of coconut. Up close, his eyes were more green than hazel. Up close, I could see a little white scar on the bridge of his nose. I gave a sigh of pleasure.

"You're a great dancer."

He tipped his head. "Thank you. I'll pass the compliment on to Mom. She paid for the lessons, way back when." Showing off, he gave me a spin then tucked me in close. "Graduated top of my class."

I laughed out loud then had to stifle a yawn.

"And now I'm boring you," Mart teased.

"Not at all. It's just been a busy day."

"Wait until tomorrow. We're touring the ruins at Tikal. Then on Wednesday, after the early morning nature walk, you can go snorkeling. Or there's tubing on the river. And some caves to explore."

"Whew! Sounds exhausting. It'll make for some great articles, though, and that's what matters."

Mart gave me a thoughtful look. "What brings you to our humble zoo trek when you could be covering some art gallery opening or fancy society wedding?"

I wrinkled my nose and looked off over his shoulder. There had been plenty of those in the last few weeks. "I'm climbing my way back to real news. I hope."

Mart spun me out again, turned another circle. "You hope?"

"Fervently. I want to report on important stories. I want to investigate issues, put them on the front page." I was talking too much, I knew, but I couldn't seem to stop. "I want my work to matter!"

"Music to my ears," Mart said. "Why do you have to climb back?"

My sigh was long and deep. "I was low man—or woman—on my last job. When the staff cuts came, out I went." I shrugged in dismissal.

Mart waited a second, two. "That can't have been easy."

"No."

The tune came to an end. Mart released me and I smiled. "Thanks for the dance. It was lovely."

"You're welcome. I have to say, I'm glad you lost your old job," he said. "Because now Rochester has you." He gave my hand a squeeze, ran his thumb over my fingers.

"If I do a bang up job with this trip, Rochester could have me for quite a while."

Mart hesitated, seeming to choose his next words with care. "This could be a very important story, if you ask me."

"Oh?"

"Sure, depending on your angle. It's all in the angle."

I yawned again behind my hand then apologized. "I'm so sorry. It's not you, it's the hour. Can we talk more about this, when you have time?"

Mart nodded. "It's a long ride to Tikal. Maybe then."

"Yes, then. And now, goodnight."

Mart lifted a hand in farewell.

In the elevator, I leaned against the back wall and watched the doors slowly close, reflecting me in their mirrored surface. I looked as tired as I felt, but at least my hair was still tidy in its chignon and my dress hadn't wrinkled too much in my suitcase. I closed my eyes, still feeling Mart's arm around me, still smelling his scent.

Too bad about the girlfriend, I thought sleepily.

The elevator doors opened to take on another passenger. I stood up straighter when I saw Clark, sans Sylvia. He was looking down, frowning and reading a text on his cell phone, so he didn't see me at first. When he did, he made a move to pocket the phone, but missed. It slid across the floor of the small space, landing squarely up against my right ankle.

He bent to retrieve his phone then hesitated. He could hardly reach for it there himself.

"I'll get it," I said.

The cell phone had settled face up, so I could see the text message he'd been reading. I didn't really mean to read it, but put words in front of my eyes and it's hard not to.

The message said:

Thursday's shipment—twenty five airborne, thirteen grounded. Delay arrival. Uncle visiting.

I frowned. What could that mean? Shipment of what? Whose uncle?

Quickly, before Clark could think I'd read his mail, I handed the phone back and smiled.

In a minute, in my room, I'd write those sentences down and puzzle over them.

"I heard about your big win at the slots tonight," he said, taking the phone I handed to him. "Nice way to start your vacation."

"Yes," I agreed. "Very cool."

I noticed a ruddy tone to his cheeks. Sunburn, perhaps, or the result of too many drinks in too little time. He led the way off the elevator when it reached the third floor, lifting a hand by way of farewell.

Slipping my room card from my purse, I mentally recited the odd message from his phone then jotted it down on the hotel notepad almost before I turned on the lights in my room.

After a quick, warm shower, I sat on the bed with my cotton nightgown tucked around my feet, braiding my damp hair and reading. The message was a mystery. From the look on Clark's face, it had not been good news, but it was all Greek to me. Eventually, I filed the slip of paper away and spent a few minutes looking over our itinerary for the next day. Then, I made notes for my first blog entry and sent the pictures from my camera to my online account. I wanted every megabyte available to me tomorrow, at the ruins. And, if I were being honest, I didn't want anyone else to see the shots of Clark in the parking lot. Dan may or may not have already. Jen definitely had.

The photos probably didn't mean anything sinister. Maybe Clark was just paying off a taxi, or arranging for one later. Later, when he wasn't along on our trip to the sanctuary.

The ding of the elevator sounded faintly from down the hall. I could hear the low drone of two people talking, their voices growing more distinct as they approached. From the room next to mine came the muffled closing of a door. One male voice, one female, laughing now.

My mind instantly conjured up an image of Mart and that woman. Could it be? I wondered then shook my head. None of my business, that's what that was!

Snapping off the light, I settled back against the pillows. The hum of conversation continued faintly from next door, but within minutes, I was dead to the world and dreaming. Dreaming of placid pools of water where crocodiles swam just beneath the surface and monkeys shouted from the trees along the bank and Dan Underwood said, "Young men sometimes do foolish things."

Chapter Five

The dining room was a hubbub of excitement when I arrived there early the next morning and looked for an empty seat.

Breakfast was served smorgasbord-style and several folks passed me with laden plates as I ambled along, my eyes sweeping left and right. I was just about to give up and eat leaning against a wall when I spotted Mart tucked at a tiny table off in one corner. He had dishes spread all around him, like everyone else, and was concentrating on a stack of papers.

The chair across from him was vacant and inviting. If he was hard at work, preparing his speech on the rain forest, say, I could just sit silently and read my guidebook. I marched over.

"Excuse me, is this seat taken?" I inquired, lowering my backpack onto the chair.

He looked up, a scowl creasing his forehead. In an instant, though, it cleared away. "Oh, hi, Allison. Go ahead. I'll clear some of these dishes away."

He stacked some plates and gave them a shove off to one side. "There."

"Thanks." Glancing over at the buffet, I realized I hadn't eaten in ages.

I'd only taken a few steps in that direction when Mart's voice called out. "Wait a minute!" When I turned, he smiled, his cheeks dimpling in quite an attractive way. "Would you please bring me a few more slices of fruit?"

I nodded. "Sure."

Hotel staff kept the buffet well stocked with standard breakfast cuisine, although a few unusual items were also on offer. Taking a tray, I was happy to see pancakes, a bit rubbery-looking from the heat lamp. I added a bowl of cereal and a glass of juice then put together an assortment of fruits.

Mart looked surprised when I returned, as if he'd forgotten about me.

I slid the tray onto the cleared spot of the table and smiled. "I brought a whole bowl of fruit," I said, gesturing at the colorful, juicy display.

He nodded. "Thanks. It looks great."

This morning, he wore an ivory camp shirt, open at the throat to reveal a patch of dark hair. Long, khaki shorts came to his knees and he'd paired them with hiking boots. His socks were scrunched down over the tops.

"So, have you written your first blog entry yet?" he asked me, lifting his coffee cup and sipping.

"Yes, as a matter of fact." I looked up. "Pretty straightforward. Who's here and where we went."

Spearing a piece of melon before answering he said, "You have to start somewhere."

I didn't answer, concentrating on pouring syrup over my pancakes.

Setting aside his papers, he propped his chin in his hands. "I just wish this trip emphasized the need for people to take action before the habitat is destroyed and the animals are gone. But it's more of a see-it-quick-before-it-disappears sort of thing. Like a tourist attraction, or a wonder spot, you know? I just hope this sort of trip doesn't do more harm than good."

"What?" My hand stopped. My fork hovered over my plate, dripping syrup. "According to the literature, this trek is supposed to promote understanding of and concern for the rain forest."

Mart sighed, pushing a hand through his hair. "The rain forest doesn't need tourists any more than Antarctica does. I can understand that that's sometimes the only way to get people to care, but I'll always say it's the wrong way."

My eyebrows drew together as I frowned, pondering his words. "Then what are you doing here?" I asked bluntly.

"It's my job," he stated. "And I live in hope." Leaning one elbow on the table in a casual manner, he went on. "Hope that it's not too late for the forest. Hope that attitudes about zoos will change. Evolve."

"You'll have to forgive me, Mart. Zoos aren't my regular beat. I didn't know there was so much to ponder about them."

"Tell me about your regular territory," he said.

"I've been covering all sorts of topics—from club functions to charity events to a couple of really boring committee meetings. But what I really want to do is investigative reporting." I set down my fork and let my mind conjure up a vision of what I hoped the future might be.

"Like Woodward and Bernstein?"

"Exactly!"

"That sounds like a tall order to fill from Rochester," he said.

"But you have to have goals. They're what I keep in mind on the days I cover humdrum stories, you know?"

He nodded. "Yeah, I know."

He went back to shuffling papers around as I finished my pancakes and I assumed our conversation was over. When I pulled my cereal bowl closer, however, he spoke up.

"Be sure you try some of the local cuisine as long as you're here. Take a flavor break." He surveyed my bland-looking bowl of cornflakes. Obviously, he was of the when-in-Rome school of thought.

I poured my grapefruit juice over the cereal. "Yes, but it's familiar and I like it."

"You put juice on your cereal!" Mart leaned forward. "I don't think I've ever seen that done before."

"You should try it sometime. It's wonderful," I assured him, lifting a heaping spoonful of flakes. They were light and crunchy in my mouth and the juice gave them a tangy, citrus flavor that always reminded me of summer.

I'd dressed for summer as well, pulling my hair back and braiding it so it hung just past my shoulders. According to the guidebooks, the temperature would be well over eighty degrees, so I wore loose-fitting khaki walking shorts and a light, airy shirt with an apricot tank underneath. I knew the colors went well with my fair skin and the blue of my eyes. In my backpack I carried sunglasses, a baseball cap with an oversized bill, tanning lotion, and enough bug spray to stop a cloud of locusts. Be prepared, that's what I always say.

Mart had bent his head, returning to his papers, whatever they were. I munched through my cereal, watching him concentrate.

"Will you be giving us a presentation on Tikal?" I gestured to his papers.

Mart tilted the papers away from me, so I couldn't see any of the writing and tidied them into a stack. "No, no. This is just some personal research." He rolled the papers into a tube shape and slipped a rubber band around them. "Clark will give a brief talk on the ruins before we leave this morning." He glanced at his watch. "Very soon, in fact. Then, the group will split up for the ride to Tikal. It's lucky there hasn't been much rain or the roads would be impassable."

"Then what? We'd miss the site?"

"No, then we'd have to be flown in. It wouldn't take as long to get there by plane, but it would be a bit more expensive, of course."

"And this way, we'll get to see some of the country," I said. "Some of the forest, too?"

He smiled, pushing back his chair and rising. "You'll see plenty of forest, Allison. I promise you that."

For an instant, as I sat looking up at him, our eyes met and I felt the welcome stirring of attraction. I lost this game of chicken and looked away first, back at the plates and bowls spread across the table.

"You'll excuse me, but I need to speak with Clark before we get underway." Mart tapped his rolled papers against his temple in a jaunty salute. "It was nice breakfasting with you, Allison. I'll see you in the lobby."

I nodded and watched him thread through the maze of tables and chairs in the dining room. It had been an interesting meal in plenty of ways. Not the least of which was Mart himself, and those deep, dark eyes.

I almost laughed out loud, listening in on my own thoughts. Here I was, at the beginning of an assignment, wasting valuable time thinking about someone's eyes. I'd been sent here to do a job and, right now, that job entailed gulping the last of my coffee and joining the others headed for the hotel lobby.

I followed the sound of chattering voices to where our group was gathered. The Underwoods waved and I returned the gesture, but didn't push through the throng to reach them. Scanning the group, I noted Clark's position near the wall. As I watched, he waved his arms overhead in an appeal for quiet.

"This morning," he began once the group hushed, "we'll be journeying to the fantastic Mayan ruins of Tikal. I guarantee you will find the site fascinating and utterly, utterly unforgettable." He closed his eyes on the second "utterly" and reopened them now to direct his warm smile at each of us. "We'll be traveling in four-wheel-drive SUVs, so we'll break into small groups momentarily. I'd like to share a bit of Tikal's history with you first, however."

I fished rapidly for my notebook so I could jot some of this down.

"Tikal is the largest city ever built by the ancient Mayan Indians and served as the capital. When I say 'ancient,' that's exactly what I mean, too. There is evidence Tikal was occupied as far back as 2500 B.C. and had a population of at least forty thousand. At the site, there are remnants of more than three thousand buildings. The University of Pennsylvania spent years working to restore some of these, cutting back the jungle growth to reveal the structures, but such work is a colossal undertaking."

He turned, gesturing to a picture on the wall nearby which showed the flat-topped pyramid with steps down the front. "Some of the temples are as tall as a modern-day skyscraper," Clark told us. "This one, for instance, is probably fifteen stories high. That's about one hundred and fifty feet. The tallest, which is still pretty well covered by the jungle, is two hundred and twelve feet high."

There were whistles and gasps from the crowd as we tried to imagine an ancient civilization constructing such massive buildings without the aid of modern machinery.

"For reasons no one fully understands, Tikal was abandoned before 900 A.D. and not rediscovered until the mid-nineteenth century. Today, restoration work continues, so we may all admire and respect the wondrous achievements of the people referred to as 'the Greeks of the New World.' On the way to our vehicles, I urge each of you to pick up a copy of this fact sheet on Tikal, put together by our own Mart Lawler especially for this group."

Clark held up a green sheet of paper. "It will give you plenty of further information to help you enjoy the ruins. We have a beautiful day for the trip and our transportation is just outside, so let's get started."

The people nearest the door began the migration and slowly filtered through the hotel's entryway. As I had last night, I hung back, letting the others break up into clusters of friends who wished to ride together.

Clark and his wife, Sylvia, stood curbside, directing traffic. Clark was outfitted in bona fide safari clothes today—khaki from head to foot. Sylvia wore a variation on the theme—short-sleeved cotton shirt in white, a scarf at her neck, and a dark green, slim-fitting skirt that draped to the ankle. Her sneakers and socks looked comfortable and coordinated and very, very retro. Glossy brunette hair peeked out from beneath her straw pith-style hat. Chunky gold earrings glittered in the sun. Obviously, she felt one didn't need to sacrifice style merely because one was about to enter a jungle.

I felt like a tourist, in comparison, and took a few steps in the opposite direction. But as I approached the only vehicle whose door still stood open to indicate a vacancy, Alan streaked past me. He smiled an apology. "Have to sit with my wife," he said as he climbed inside. The door closed, leaving me on the sidewalk with only Clark, Sylvia, and Mart as company.

"You'll be coming with us, Miss Belsar," Clark said, walking up beside me and sliding his arm around my elbow. He steered me toward the lead vehicle, where the other two waited. "It's best like this, I think, because you'll be able to ask all the questions you want on the ride out."

"Sounds great, Clark. Please, call me Allison."

"Do you mind taking the rear seat?" he asked, holding the door. "Sylvia gets carsick if she isn't up front."

"Not a problem." I gathered my pack into my arms, ducked my head and climbed inside.

From my reading, I knew we needed to travel in high-bodied vehicles because of the poor roads. As Mart had mentioned, during the rainy season the roads turned into muddy ruts. Improvements were taking place all the time, but the literature I'd consulted before we left warned me that a bumpy ride lay ahead.

The sun shone, bright and glorious, in a sky of deep, vibrant blue. A few enormous white clouds hung overhead, adding to the picture postcard appeal of the scene. Old buildings constructed of wood shared the blocks with newer concrete structures. We passed a two-story structure Mart said was the courthouse and I had to admire its charming veranda bordered by wrought-iron scrollwork. It wasn't an especially busy day at the market, so the square opposite wasn't very crowded.

"There will be plenty of time for shopping and exploring the city, Allison," Clark assured me, twisting around in his seat to face me. "Our trekkers enjoy the marketplace almost as much as they do the ruins," he added with a smile. Sylvia echoed his expression but, since her eyes were carefully hidden behind sunglasses, I couldn't tell if her smile reached her eyes.

I wriggled in my seat, trying to get comfortable. It was a long road to Tikal and I figured we were in for a tense time with Mart and Clark in such close proximity. But as mile after mile passed, I began to relax. Clark answered a few of my easy questions about the zoo trek program and a few more about how he came to the Rochester Zoo. I tried to ask Sylvia about life with the zoo director, but she seamlessly tossed the question back to Clark without really answering. It's a trick I've seen politicians use on occasion, and I had to admire the skillful manner in which she'd deflected attention. I gave up being a reporter after a time and the conversation turned all small-talky.

That's what made it even more startling when Sylvia said, "Mrs. Underwood told me something interesting about you last night, Allison."

Chapter Six

"Oh?" I said. "What's that?"

"She said your father was a journalist, too. That he even served as editor in chief of your magazine for a while."

Apparently, Sylvia hadn't gotten up at the crack of daylight to watch my appearance on the *Wake Up Show*. I'd talked about Dad, in response to the host's questions.

"That's right. He was a brilliant journalist and he did run the magazine." I smiled, remembering Dad with his sleeves rolled up. Sitting at the typewriter, a cigarette dangling from one corner of his mouth, he was the picture of industry. "That was a long time ago now. He inspired me to become a reporter," I confessed.

"I'm sure you'll do an excellent job with this story, Allison, and do him proud," Clark said with certainty, verbally patting me on the head. "You know these treks are pretty interesting events— and I don't say that just because they were my idea." He paused. "Although they were."

Then, he started telling tales about other treks the zoo had sponsored. Funny things that had happened. Food disasters. A love story. I didn't really think he'd bring up whatever had happened on the last trek—the "unfortunate incident" Elaine had called it—since that would mar the image of the treks. And he didn't.

So I did.

"I heard there was some trouble on the last trek to Belize. What happened?"

I didn't imagine the immediate silence and the tension that filled our vehicle like an electric charge.

"An accident," Clark began, overly interested in the view all of a sudden.

"Elaine called it an 'incident,'" I pressed, keeping my tone questioning.

"Incident, accident," Clark waved away the semantics. "All of our trekkers were safe. That's what matters."

"Someone was . . . hurt?" I soft-pedaled. "In the jungle?" I pictured a snakebite or a fall off a cliff.

Clark sighed then spoke. "Someone was killed. Accidentally. There were drugs involved."

"I see," I said, recognizing the bad public relations connotations in the tragedy.

"Yes. Please don't dredge up the story again, Allison. It would serve no purpose."

"I won't. Thanks for telling me," I said, making plans to check local newspaper archives for the original coverage.

There had to be more to the story. A drug overdose, no matter how tragic, wouldn't cause the flash of energy I'd felt, like a breath held, in the SUV.

Shifting gears, I asked Clark about that accent I could hear in his voice on certain words.

"Oh, I was born in Austria," he explained. "My parents brought me to the States when I was just a boy, six or seven. I'm American, now, through and through, but that accent," he stopped to wave a finger at me, "it remains with me. We still travel back to see the relatives every once in a while," he said as Sylvia nodded. "Maybe we can have a trek there one day."

And he was off again, thinking out loud, making big plans, which seemed to be the only sort of plans this man made.

He went on and on as the vehicles bucked and jumped over the ridges of earth, jolting us about. The week before our arrival, the rains had been moderately heavy, deepening the ruts in the road. Now, the ruts were at least a foot deep and some were still filled with water.

Several times, my head made contact with the window at my side. A few more times, I bounded in the opposite direction, up against Mart, who gallantly righted me.

"Have you been to Tikal before?" I asked Mart as the SUV continued to creep, rock, and bounce along at about fifteen miles per hour.

"Oh, three or four times, I guess," he said, screwing up his face to think back. "Four, actually, but this is my first time here with the zoo."

"Oh, really." I found this—and him—interesting. "How long have you been at the zoo?"

"Too long," Clark muttered from his seat in front of me, but Mart didn't hear.

"I've been at Rochester just over a year now," Mart told me. "Before that, I worked more directly with animal conservation and protection." At my puzzled look, he elaborated. "I'd been working with a rhino relocation program in Namibia."

"That sounds fascinating," I said, my mind conjuring up romantic scenes from *Out of Africa*.

"Yes," he nodded. "It was."

"Why did you stop?"

"Grant money ran out," he stated. "No money, no rescue missions. The end." Before he looked away, his eyes became huge, dark pools, unfathomable and distant. I knew he must have been recalling the animals.

I didn't know what to say, so I clammed up. Lifting the camera from around my neck, I pointed it out the window and snapped a few frames.

All around us, the jungle pressed in, a hundred shades of green. I craned my neck, trying to see the tops of the trees, but couldn't. I'd read some grew to more than one hundred feet. A light mist hung within the foliage, brought on, I assumed, by the combination of moisture and heat.

We were well into Guatemala now, forty miles beyond the border of Belize. Picking up the sheet of information Mart had compiled, I read it over for the fourth or fifth time and felt a surge of excitement course through me. This trip hadn't been my idea, but right now, in the midst of the forest on the edge of the ruins, I was glad to be here.

"Here we go," Mart said, nudging me from my studies. "Put that away, Allison. It's time for the real thing."

I looked up, gazing out the window. The road had led us to a clearing where a white, contemporary-looking, flat-roofed building stood.

"This is where our tour begins," Mart said as the SUV came to a halt and Clark opened the door. "It's the museum—and the gift stalls, of course. You can pick up guidebooks and postcards."

As the rest of the SUVs pulled in behind us and discharged group members I looked over my shoulder at the museum. "I think I'll just see what's in there."

It took only a few seconds to reach the entryway and once I stepped inside, I was fascinated.

There was a model of the city as it must have looked long ago, detailing many of the structures which, at the present time, were still covered with jungle growth. Photo displays illustrated the long, tedious process of uncovering the ruins. Most enthralling, however, were the stelae—stone monuments standing up to twelve feet high. From a plaque nearby I learned one was believed to be the oldest from Tikal, dating back to 292 A.D. Standing next to it, I tried to imagine what the world had looked like 1700 years ago. What had these forests been like then? When no SUVs drove into its depths with tourists? When no planes flew overhead? When pollution of water, air, and land was unheard of?

Gingerly, gently, I reached out and touched the relief carving on the stelae, thinking of the history recorded there. Moving on, I saw other artifacts from the site—beautiful stone statues and other objects made from wood, bone, and jade.

There were also books and postcards available for purchase and I chose a few, paying for them with quetzales, the local currency I'd gotten at the hotel.

Out in the hot sun once more, I wandered over to the stalls where many of our group had already congregated, joining crowds of other tourists. Colorful woven textiles of all varieties spread on shelves and draped over wooden framework.

I ran my fingers over the nubby texture of a shirt done in tones of orange, red and blue.

"That's a huipil," a voice came from behind me.

When I turned, I saw a native Guatemalan about my own age. Her long, dark hair fell past her shoulders and I noticed she wore an outfit like those up for sale, this one in vivid shades of blue and green. Despite the temperature, she looked cool and comfortable. She smiled as she approached, her teeth gleaming white against her darker complexion.

"These are all handmade by local people," she explained, "woven in a method that dates back many generations." She gestured and I noticed for the first time two young girls working on looms. A bright, patterned material, the basis for the huipils, stretched before them.

"Now, remember, you told me you'd take it easy on the souvenirs this time."

"Yes, yes, dear. I know."

I smiled, recognizing the Underwoods. Gruff Dan Underwood sounded determined to keep an eye on Elaine's spending. Recalling the jewelry that had flashed on her fingers, I wished him luck.

More trekkers crowded into the stalls. While I hemmed and hawed over my choice, other shoppers snatched up blankets, belts, and tops at an amazing rate.

I stepped back, out of the fray, and came smack up against another body. I knew it wasn't Dan. I'd have bounced off his ample mid-section.

"Excuse me," I apologized, turning.

"No problem," Mart said. "Can't be helped in this crowd. We'll be starting the walk to the ruins in about ten minutes. If you're planning to make any purchases, you'd better do it now so you can get them stowed in the truck."

I held up my guidebooks and postcards. "I've just got these for now. But I want a huipil." I trailed off, considering.

Mart surveyed the clustered Americans and sighed. "These folks don't care about the ruins, the antiquities. They're more interested in getting a few goodies to take home."

Watching the shoppers pick over the merchandise, I had to wonder if he was right. The scene did resemble the opening minutes of a white sale.

Mart moved into the thick of the group and I heard him relaying the message about the tour. Inside of ten minutes, we were once again assembling.

The ruins, we were told by Clark, were a twenty-minute walk away. He pointed at a path leading into the forest and informed us he would lead the way, while Mart brought up the rear.

"I hope you have all applied your insect repellent. Conditions are always right for mosquitoes in Guatemala," he told us. "The path here is clearly discernible, so no one is in any real danger of wandering off," he assured us. Turning on his heel, he set off at a brisk pace. A few of us took a moment to squirt a fresh coating of bug spray on our exposed skin then hurried to catch up.

Conversation dimmed as we progressed through the jungle. Like the others, I swiveled my head to try and see everything at once, marveling at the sights and sounds. Plants I'd never seen before. The breeze through the treetops. Scurrying noises of some small creature not far off. The insistent buzz of a mosquito even nearer at hand.

Brightly colored butterflies flitted nearby, dancing from one vibrant plant to another. Birds called from high up in the trees, their squawks harsh but melodic.

I was glad they were far overhead and not inquisitive about their two-legged intruders. Their lovely markings in brilliant hues were beautiful viewed from a distance and I hoped it would stay that way. Birds are not my favorite creatures, although I try not to mention it. Something about them makes me nervous. In my heart, I know that's silly; but it doesn't change things.

While I searched the immediate vicinity for birds, Jen, just in front of me, paused on the path. I came close to tumbling over her when she knelt to tie a shoelace.

"How are you enjoying the journey so far, Allison?" she asked, tightening the knot on her sneaker and rising. "I think it's gorgeous!" She gestured expansively, spreading her arms out as if to gather the whole forest up.

"Yes, it's breathtaking," I agreed. "In more ways than one!" Taking my fact sheet, I fanned my face. The forest was naturally quite humid and even the little bit of exertion we'd done had brought a slick of perspiration to my skin.

"Good for the complexion. Helps the pores breathe."

The people behind us were beginning to grumble at the human roadblock we made. Jen took a few running steps to catch up on the trail, the full sleeves of her purple top floating out around her. The red sash at her waist flopped in time to her footfalls.

I trotted along in her wake, thinking she looked like some species of bird—one of those awkward but striking ones. It was difficult not to think about birds here, when the jungle echoed with their songs and the sounds of their flapping wings could be heard. But there was so much else to see, as well.

Huge, four-foot-tall cones were a frequent sight just off the path. They seemed to be made of dirt and when I wondered aloud what they were, the answer was quick to come.

"Those are termite nests," the professor spoke up from behind me. He shifted his glasses back up his nose, which was slippery with sweat, and enlightened everyone within earshot. He had done his reading and was more than happy to share his knowledge, as he did the day we arrived. "Just one acre of the forest can have up to a thousand of these nests," he told us. "And each one—each one—contains as many as ten million termites!"

The next time we passed by one of the cones, I thought about the swarming insects within. Back home, termites were considered a nuisance. Here in the jungle, it was obvious they were an important part of the ecosystem, the web of life.

Oh, Mart, I said to myself, see how wrong you are about bringing tour groups here? I've only been in the jungle half an hour and I'm already reconsidering termites!

Suddenly, there was a rustling in some trees on our left and everyone froze. From the looks on some faces, I'm sure we expected King Kong to emerge, even though this was a different continent. Instead, a marmoset monkey rocketed out, his long tail waving like a banner behind him. The contrast between what some of us had pictured—a hairy ape of some kind—and the foot-long, five-pound reality caused relieved laughter among the crowd.

This world of the jungle was totally different from my urban world. So natural, so pristine—at least in this area—it was like paradise. Except a little too warm.

I forgot all about the temperature when we broke through the forest, into the clearing.

Lying peacefully under the blazing sun, the ruins of the city spread all around us. I stopped in my tracks and hardly noticed as others pushed past me, fanning out over the area.

"Pretty spectacular, hmm?" Mart said as he came up behind me, crossing his arms over his chest. He rocked back on his heels, turning his head to look in both directions. "You know, I think I could see this sight every day and always be amazed by it."

I didn't answer. I couldn't answer, struck dumb by the sheer size of the sprawling city. Towering stone structures stretched up to meet the clouds, massive monuments to the ingenuity of humankind. Steps cut into the front of these Mayan pyramids were dotted with tourists braving heat and height to climb well over one hundred feet up.

Lifting my sunglasses, I blinked into the glare, half expecting the vision to disappear when I opened my eyes.

Mart, watching me, gave a laugh. "Hard to believe it's real. And that it's thousands of years old."

I found my voice. "Are you used to people just standing and staring, then?"

He nodded, reaching up to run a hand through his hair. "Oh, yeah. And who could blame them?" He looked away, squinting. Something across the smooth lawn caught his eye and I could sense him tensing. He straightened up, craning his neck and narrowing his eyes. "What the—" he broke off.

Catching his mood, I tried to follow his gaze, but couldn't see anything amiss. Our group had joined other tourists and scattered over the site. We'd been instructed earlier to rendezvous at a specific time, and as a result, no one seemed to be sticking together. At a distance, I couldn't discern faces, but obviously Mart could.

"What?" I prodded. "What?"

Mart came back quickly, giving his head a brisk shake. "Nothing. I thought I saw someone I knew."

I shrugged. "Well, that could be. You said you've been here before."

"Hmm? What?" He hadn't been listening. "Look, Allison, I've got to go," he said briskly, reaching out to put his hand on my arm. "Take a good look around. Use your guidebook." He smiled, dimples creasing his cheeks. "I'll see you later." With a brief squeeze to my shoulder, he loped off across the grass in the direction he'd been studying.

I watched him leave, puzzling over his abrupt departure. He'd seen something he didn't like. But what? None of my business, I knew, and certainly nothing to do with my magazine article. And yet, I was intrigued.

I couldn't very well follow him, though. He'd already disappeared across the way. Opening my guidebook, I readied my camera and began exploring.

*

A short time later, I plunked myself onto the low stone steps near an area that must have served as an arena. It felt good to sit down, even if it was in the sun.

"Heat getting to you?" Dan Underwood asked, climbing slowly up to flop down nearby. He lifted his hat, swabbed his brow with a handkerchief and sighed. His face was red and glowing with the beginning of sunburn.

"It's warm, all right," I agreed. "Where's Elaine?"

Dan pointed a chubby finger at the Temple of the Giant Jaguar. "Climbing."

"All the way up?" I was astounded. It seemed like quite a feat for the tiny little woman to attempt.

"Oh, yes. She's a heck of a gal. A real adventurer. You gonna try?"

I hadn't planned on it. It was so high, the steps were so narrow.

"Maybe," I said, surprising myself. I looked at the temple, at all the others scrambling up and down. "Probably."

"Well, good luck." He leaned back against the next step. "If you see Elaine, tell her where to find me."

"Okay." I hitched my pack firmly onto my shoulder.

Setting off toward the temple at a leisurely rate, I realized I was not very far from where Mart had headed. My steps paused then stopped, and I considered the jungle just beyond. What had he seen? Who? I hadn't encountered Mart since he'd walked off. Hadn't noticed him milling around the area either.

Looking both ways, as if someone would see me veering off and call me back, I moved into the forest.

Chapter Seven

There was no clearly etched path here. The ground was covered with plants and fallen greenery, which ants would scavenge. Far from silent, the forest seemed still as I crept along. Feeling foolish, I glanced at my watch. Five minutes. If I didn't see someone or something in five minutes, I'd head right back.

I didn't have to wait that long.

Surrounded by the sounds of nature, the sounds of man stood out, ringing through the air like an alarm. I heard the jangle of keys or something metallic and the unmistakable sound of laughter.

A huge tree with buttressed roots was just in front of me and I slipped behind it, resting my palms against its trunk. It was difficult to see through the dense foliage, but some judicious bobbing and weaving brought my quarry into view.

Standing about twenty feet in front of me were Clark Webster and a man I'd never seen before. A native of the country, that man wore traditional Guatemalan dress—bright colors rivaling the plumage of the birds I'd seen earlier. Clark was smiling and nodding, clapping the other man on the shoulder with enthusiasm.

"It went well, then?" he asked and again I caught that slight accent in his voice.

"Yes. It is done."

"Good, good. And next week?"

"We are ready." The Guatemalan's English was accented, too.

Slowly, silently, I raised my camera from where it hung around my neck. My hands shook as I lifted it into position. I had no idea what I was witnessing. I only knew I wanted to capture it.

Just as the shutter clicked, my pack slipped off my shoulder, smacking against the tree trunk with a notable thud. Both men froze and I dropped down low so they wouldn't spot me. Clark muttered a few words in Spanish and the underbrush rustled as they hurriedly parted.

I stayed where I was, crouched among the plants, barely breathing, for a full five minutes. Apparently, Clark wasn't going to investigate.

Moving swiftly, I retraced my steps and emerged into the clearing of the Great Plaza, not far from where I'd left it. A row of stone monuments stood just before me and I took a moment to lean against the closest one. My hand rested in a protective fashion against the camera around my neck as I scanned the groups of people nearby, anxious to locate Clark.

When I spotted him, he was standing in a cluster of tourists and seemed to be giving an impromptu lecture. He turned, extending an arm to gesture at the stelae. Was it my imagination or did his eyes rest on me too long? Did he pause for an instant in his oratory, or was it just my guilty conscience?

Casually, I moved away, snapping a few pictures and waiting for his hand to land on my shoulder. But there was no way he could know it was me in the woods. And why would he care if I took his picture, anyway?

I puzzled over what I'd seen as I headed toward the looming temple, but when I approached it, the imposing structure demanded all my attention.

How tall it was! The stones were black and gray and white with steep narrow steps cut in the front leading up, up, up. At the top was a three-roomed chamber where rituals had been held all those years ago. An arched carved piece, called a roof comb according to the guidebook, topped the pyramid off.

A little boy of seven or eight brushed past me in a hurry and proceeded to scale the steps like a mountain goat. Unafraid, he scampered quickly to the top, turning to wave and shout at his parents, down on terra firma next to me. When that couple began the climb at a more sedate pace, I followed, shucking my arm through the other strap of my pack and settling it between my shoulder blades.

Hand over hand I started up, clasping the steps above for balance. Each step was only five inches wide, so I was forced to turn sideways to advance. Is this how the Mayans climbed, I wondered, breathing heavy and falling behind the other couple. Or were their feet smaller than ours? Now, there was a question for the zoo director, I thought, stowing the idea in a mental file.

My pack kept bumping into my back at each step and I wished it wasn't so large. Its cumbersome weight made my balance precarious. I was only about twenty feet up, but it felt like more with nothing around me but blue sky.

The rocks were rough to the touch, chipped and worn in spots over the centuries. Gamely, I continued climbing. The steps were wide enough to permit others to pass me quite easily, and several folks already had when I heard steps approaching behind me. I moved closer to the far side of the steps, out of the way, my eyes still on the step just above me. This time, though, the climber didn't go around but hit me straight on, colliding roughly with my shoulder. The next few seconds happened in slow motion, the way car accidents always do.

The bump threw me off balance and I leaned to the left, rough stone digging into my palm. I made a grab for the climber's bare ankle as I tried to keep my footing, but I missed and those narrow steps did me in—once one foot slipped off, the other followed almost immediately.

I pitched forward, into the steps, my right hand grasping at stone, my left scraping roughly as it dragged against the edge of the step. My upper body hit each surface with a thud and my brain dimly registered the noise my camera made as it, too, clunked along.

I only fell about ten feet, I realized later, but it was ten very agonizing feet. By some miracle, I managed to get both hands clasped around a protruding bit of stone, the heavy bulk of my stupid backpack making the motion both awkward and treacherous. Then, I stretched my toes out behind me, feeling for the next step.

Once I found it, I planted my other foot firmly beside it, taking deep, calming breaths and holding on for dear life. I had barely reached this position—bent over to form the letter "C"—when two firm hands found me, coming rapidly around my waist.

"Are you okay?"

It was Mart. My hero, about ten seconds too late.

I nodded, shaking, and he steadied me on the steps. "Did you see what happened? Someone smacked into me!" I was indignant now that the danger had passed. "I could have been killed!"

He agreed solemnly. "Whoever hit you was certainly careless. This is no place for rough-housing. Did you see who it was?"

"Not really. Bare legs and sandals. Then, just—boom!—and I was falling."

Shielding his eyes, Mart looked up the stairway. Several people had paused to watch me tumble, but there were at least a dozen people on the steps. Plenty more at the top. "Everyone's got bare legs and sandals," he said. "I wish I'd been paying more attention. We'll probably never know who hit you."

"Right now, I don't even care," I said. "Just get me off this thing."

"Sure." He held out his hand. "I'll spot you. I'm right here."

Under his watchful eye, and knowing his arms were there to catch me, I limped slowly down the remaining ten feet of stone and reached earth with quivering knees. Mart pushed me gently onto the grass and sat beside me, holding my hands and turning them palm side up.

"Whew!" He let out a whistle and I winced at the sight of scraped and bloody skin. "Ouch," he said. "That must hurt. Do you have any disinfectant in here?" He indicated my backpack.

I nodded. "There's a first aid kit. I always carry it everywhere, but I've never needed it until now," I babbled as he rummaged.

"Well, that's smart thinking, Allison." Mart opened the kit. "You're pretty resourceful, aren't you?"

I knew he was trying to distract me as he dabbed on the lotion. When it hit the damaged skin, I let out a hiss of pain and then the worst was over. After the injuries had been cleaned up, they really weren't too bad. I'd skinned my knee and rapped an ankle, but those aches were minor.

"You'll be stiff for a few days and these'll be bruised, too," Mart told me, indicating my hands. "All in all, though, I'd say you were very lucky."

"I could have been killed!" I repeated, more convinced of it now than ever.

"No, Allison. I would have caught you. I saw you start up the steps and decided to tag along. I'm only sorry I wasn't there a few minutes earlier to prevent the accident."

I gave an unladylike snort. "You and me both, pal."

He smiled. "Do you wish you'd stayed at home?"

"No." My answer came fast and unwavering. I paused, took a breath. Now that I was on terra firma and safe, I could focus a bit better. "It's been thrilling here—and amazing," I told him. He nodded, smiling, as I went on, "And I've already done plenty of thinking about the jungle. You know, what the average person can do to help save it. I'm planning to stress that in my articles, too."

His smile faded and he lifted broad shoulders in a shrug. "Well, I'm glad you think it helps. . . . Have you seen the building they call the Acropolis yet?" When I shook my head, he said, "Then, if you're up to it, come on."

He rose, towering over me, and extended his hands. I took them gingerly and he pulled me up. Shucking my backpack onto his shoulder, he led the way. I couldn't help looking over my own shoulder at the temple.

"I could have been killed!" I muttered, turning quickly away.

Mart's bright chatter didn't pause as we crossed the plaza. For him, the incident was over. I knew I'd relive it in nightmares for a long time to come.

Chapter Eight

At the end of the long afternoon, our group assembled at the foot of the temple as planned and retraced our steps back through the forest to the museum.

All the trekkers looked tired and sweaty, hair straggling, noses sunburned, skin glowing. Still, happy and excited conversation filled the humid air.

My scraped knee was beginning to ache and I walked along silently, content to enjoy the high spirits of the others. The way back seemed shorter and, before we knew it, the museum and SUVs came into view.

I didn't relish the idea of another ride with the Websters, especially after seeing Clark in such mysterious circumstances.

Determined not to end up in their SUV, I elbowed my way up to another and climbed in, looking around at Jen, Alan and Maria. Watching the other vehicles load up, I saw Mart join a group nearby. I had to stifle a laugh when the Underwoods got aboard the Websters's SUV.

Oh, what a ride they'll have, I thought, picturing the pair arguing good-naturedly or just talking, talking, talking. I hoped Sylvia had some headache pills along because she was going to need them.

*

Hours later, I took the elevator to my room and indulged in a long soak, lying back among the bubbles and letting my mind wander. When the water grew cold, I scurried into bed, expecting to sleep soundly. But slumber was fitful that night.

I dreamt of the jungle, of birds swooping low over my head, screeching in my ear. I dreamt of the temple and the fall I'd taken. In this version, I was much higher up, near the top, falling straight out, arms spread wide, screeching like the birds. I woke with a jolt and a whimper, not sure where I was or why my heart was pounding. Sitting up in bed, I pushed my hair out of my eyes and blinked.

The room was dark and silent. It was well after midnight. Moonlight filtered through the window across the room, throwing silvery slats of light against the wall. The shadows of trees swaying in the courtyard beyond loomed and receded with each gust of air.

My own breath sounded harsh to my ears and it took me a moment to collect my wits, taking deep breaths to banish the horrific images of my dream.

Lifting off the light cotton sheet, I made a trip to the bathroom, rinsing my face with cool water and staring at my haggard reflection in the mirror. Before returning to bed, I double-checked the lock on my door. It was bolted fast. Sinking back against the pillow, I tried to think calming thoughts. I closed my eyes experimentally and they stayed that way.

*

I couldn't tell you what woke me a while later. If it was another dream, I forgot it upon waking. I knew instantly where I was, this time, and I also knew I wasn't alone. Lying in bed on this endless night, I froze, my body stiffening. I held my breath, trying to sense what was wrong.

It was several long seconds before I heard the stealthy movements near the doorway and the dresser where my things were stored. My back was to the window and I faced the area where an intruder lurked. If I opened one eye, I could see him. Or her. Or it. If I opened one eye. . . .

I was afraid. In a foreign country. Alone. In the dead of night. I was terrified. Irrationally, I thought if I didn't look, it wouldn't be real. If I didn't see it, it wouldn't be happening.

My nerves grabbed hold of my body and I started to quiver. The noise had increased in intensity, as if my intruder couldn't find what he was rummaging for. What did he want? I hadn't brought all that much money. Losing my passport would be a burden, but not a tragedy.

The burglar stopped and gave a low grunt of triumph. I slid one eye open and saw the outline of a man bent over a dresser drawer. He was just a dark smudge in the shadows of the room, his face tipped down and indistinct. When he straightened up, I could see the silhouette of my camera in his hands, its lens poking forward.

I was still paying off that camera. As with my laptop, I'd charged my purchase, figuring I could deduct it as a business expense. Okay, they weren't top of the line equipment, but they were darn near it and I couldn't afford to lose them. The laptop was loaded with personal information, too. Visions of identity theft flooded my brain and outrage overran my fear. Opening my mouth, I shrieked at the top of my lungs. I bolted from the bed, my feet scissoring the sheets away. My hand found the light switch on the wall and I slapped at it.

He could have shot me, if he had a gun, but I didn't think of that. As light flooded the room and footsteps pounded in the hall, I just kept on screaming.

The man—short, dark, and startled—whirled around. His eyes were wide with panic at being discovered. Making an angry gesture, he moved toward the door at a run, still clutching my camera. He turned right, into the corridor. I took off after him, rushing out into the hall only to crash into Dan Underwood. Mart was right behind him.

He took one look at me and guessed what had occurred. "Where?" he asked and I pointed. With a muttered oath, Mart shoved Dan aside and set off in pursuit.

"Are you all right? What happened?" Dan asked. He was wearing what must be his usual sleeping attire—a t-shirt and boxer shorts. He put a hand on my shoulder and looked into my face. "Can you tell us about it?" he prodded gently.

In halting phrases, I stammered out my story. A hotel employee went to fetch the manager and I repeated the incident for him, while curious onlookers hovered in the doorway, listening.

The manager apologized profusely. "Nothing like this has ever happened here before, miss," he assured me, but I didn't believe him. "We have a safe hotel. Very, very safe," he insisted. Across the room, open drawers dangling my rumpled clothing mocked his words.

About ten minutes after it all began, Mart returned. I heard him before I saw him.

"Okay, folks, the show's over. Let's all get back to bed, shall we?" He came into view, making shooing motions with his hands, urging the gawkers on their way. He wore only a loose pair of blue-checked pajama bottoms, slung low on lean hips. When the spectators had gone, he joined us, crossing the room with concern stamped across his features.

He was a bit of a distraction, standing next to me that way, naked from the waist up. His chest was thickly covered in dark, springy hair and the well-defined muscles of his arms were smooth beneath the skin.

"He got away outside," he said flatly, sounding frustrated. "I nearly nabbed him in the stairwell, but once he made it outside, it was as if the shadows just swallowed him up."

"Did you get a look at him?" Dan asked and Mart shook his head. "Not well enough to identify him, I'm afraid."

"I'll get a police officer, if you'd like," the manager offered.

"Yes, thanks," I said and he left the room at a trot.

Turning to Dan, Mart said, "Thanks for holding down the fort here." He clapped the older man on the back, making him beam with self-importance.

"Glad to do it, Mart. Anything for a damsel in distress." He smiled at me and I returned the gesture weakly. "If you don't need me anymore," he fished.

"Go back to bed. I'll stay until the police arrive."

"Right, then." Dan pointed a finger at me. "I'm just down the hall, Allison, and I'll be listening up, so don't you worry, okay?"

I nodded. "Okay."

He ambled from the room, socks drooping around bony ankles.

When he'd gone, Mart collected the chair from over near the balcony's open door and sat down. Clenched hands dangling between his knees, he said, "Sorry this happened, Allison. Did the guy take anything?"

"My camera. But I think that's all. I haven't checked yet." Now that the danger and excitement had faded, I felt self-conscious clad only in my thin cotton nightgown.

Mart noticed. "Shall I get your robe?" he offered and I nodded.

I felt better once I was attired more conventionally, and perched on the edge of the dresser without disturbing the evidence.

"Good thing you woke up so early," Mart said, "before he could get your money and your computer. You can buy another camera tomorrow."

I nodded forlornly. "It was a good one. Kind of expensive. Maybe that's why he wanted it," I said.

Mart caught his lower lip between his teeth. "He probably couldn't even see it that well in the dark," he said, one hand moving up to push through his hair in a gesture I was beginning to recognize. "No offense, Allison, but plenty of other people on this trip have more elaborate camera set-ups. And your laptop is worth a lot more money."

"Maybe the burglar didn't know that."

Mart was shaking his head again. "If he was a burglar, he'd know," he said with conviction.

"Well, maybe he was in the wrong room, then?" I suggested, hoping it was true.

Mart sighed, all his breath coming out in a long rush. "Look, I know you're upset and you've got good reason to be, but be logical. I think," he said at last, "that he did want your camera. More specifically, he wanted the images on it."

Suddenly, I recalled what I'd witnessed that afternoon in the jungle. The zoo director and the Guatemalan meeting secretly, speaking cryptically. Wide-eyed, I turned to Mart knowing he could read my expression.

"What did you see today? What did you photograph at Tikal? Anything that struck you as odd?" He spoke urgently, his voice a raspy whisper.

"I . . . I . . . ." What *had* I seen? I didn't know. How could I explain? An unexpected wave of fear rose in my throat and I swallowed hard.

Mart was on his feet in an instant, crossing the space between us and taking me by the shoulders. "Allison, what? What was it?"

I gulped and found my voice. "It was Clark. Clark and a local. Talking. Just talking."

"Talking?" Mart picked up the word. "About what? Could you hear what were they saying?"

I had to shut my eyes to recall the scene, but the words wouldn't come. "I can't remember!"

"This could be very important. You have to remember."

"I'm trying—"

There was a tentative knock on the door and we both looked up. The police had finally arrived.

I moved away from Mart, greeting the officer with a shaky smile. For the next hour, I went over old ground, repeating the story I'd already told several times and answering questions as best I could. Only one made me hesitate.

"Do you know any reason this man would choose to break into your room, Miss Belsar?"

"N-no," I spoke haltingly. "I don't know why." I wasn't lying, I told myself. I didn't know.

Finally, an eternity later, as I stifled yawns and blinked scratchy, bleary eyes, the official visit was concluded. Nothing but the camera had been stolen, a quick inventory revealed. I'd been lucky, the policeman said.

Lucky, indeed.

I closed the door behind him and turned to face Mart. When he opened his mouth, I held up a hand. "Please, no more," I begged, leaning heavily against the wall. "It's so late and I'm so tired, I can't think straight."

He shut his mouth and nodded. "Tomorrow's a free day," he reminded me, rising from the chair and stretching a bit. "Meet me for a late breakfast? Ten o'clock?"

"Yes, sure, fine."

Walking over to the balcony, he shut the opened door, fiddling with the latching mechanism. "Pretty clean work, here," he said and I heard the click of the lock.

"I'm changing rooms in the morning," I stated. "The ones on the other side of the hallway don't have balconies."

With a reassuring smile, Mart gave me a chuck under the chin, as if he were the big brother I never had. "You're okay," he told me. "You can take care of yourself."

"Highest praise, seeing that you've rescued me twice today," I said, feeling a quiver at my own words.

Opening the door to the hall, he didn't debate me. "See ya." One hand flapped in a wave then he headed off to his room.

I shut the door securely, ramming the lock home and putting a chair under the knob. With the faintest light of dawn beginning to peek through the curtain, I turned back to bed.

Chapter Nine

Mart and I met at the doors of the hotel dining room, joining a few other stragglers for our meal. Our breakfast was a lengthy event, with Mart listening in deep concern to my story about seeing Clark in the forest the day before. I could relate it coherently now, having thought about it ever since waking up.

I kept my eyes on him as I spoke, waiting for any sign of false concern. A blink of the eyes. A glance away. But he just pondered my words, chewing slowly, his eyebrows knitting together as he thought. If I expected him to give me any answers, however, I was mistaken. When I pushed gently, he evaded me.

Those broad shoulders lifted in a shrug. "Clark's a different kind of guy. I'd never claim to understand him, Allison."

I set my fork down with a clatter. "I realize there's no love lost between the two of you," I told him, "and if you're worried that I'll mention that in my stories, you can relax. The readers of the *Rochester Breeze* aren't particularly interested in personality conflicts. They just want a travelogue."

"It's not that, honestly," he began and I held up a hand.

"I don't expect you to tell me any secrets, Mart, but this one seems to concern me. My room was broken into, perhaps because of that picture I took."

"And someone pushed you down the steps," Mart reminded me.

"What? That was an accident."

I was shocked at the implication in his sentence. Until that instant, I'd made no connection between the two events. They'd been horrible parts of the same day, and this man eating pineapple across from me had been close by for both. Which might or might not be meaningful.

Now, my hand froze around my coffee cup and I leaned over our breakfast plates to ask, "What are you telling me? Do you think that was deliberate? Do you think someone was actually trying to hurt me?"

Mart blew out a long column of air, pushing out his lips and letting his eyes drift to the ceiling. "Maybe I'm wrong," he said, his voice clearly stating he didn't believe the sentence. Still without looking at me, he fidgeted with the silverware, moving it around on the tabletop.

The jangling and clanking were too much of a distraction for me. My hand shot out to cover his and halt its movement. When my skin touched his he seemed startled, but his hand went motionless under mine.

I watched his face. Watched the start of a smile edge across his lips. When he looked up, our eyes met, and the message they exchanged suddenly had nothing to do with zoo directors or burglaries or accidents.

Those dark, serious eyes were wide and warm, inviting me in. My gaze dropped to his lips. The top one was thin, the bottom full and luscious. What would those lips feel like on mine? I wondered, flicking my tongue over my own dry lips.

Mart sighed and I blinked, breaking the spell we'd slipped under.

"Maybe I'm wrong," he repeated, bringing our conversation back to its disturbing topic, "but last night, I was thinking about it. You fell shortly after taking a picture someone didn't approve of. Now, the steps of the temple aren't deep, but they're pretty wide. Even with that crowd, they're surely wide enough for someone to have gone around you without knocking you over."

I nodded and withdrew my hand. He had a point and I wasn't sure I liked it.

"So, perhaps your 'accident' wasn't an accident. It could have been—"

"An attempt to kill me?" My voice came out high-pitched and a little too loud.

"No, not necessarily," Mart hurried on. "But your camera did suffer in the fall, right? Banged around a bit on the stones?"

I nodded.

"My guess is the camera was the goal. You were just in the way."

Turning my hands over, I looked at the scratches and cuts on them. They didn't ache quite as much this morning, but the skin was still tender and bruised. "If they'd asked for the camera, I might have been persuaded to hand it over," I said wryly. "Better that than this."

"If it's any consolation, Allison, I'd say it's a safe bet they'll leave you alone now. They accomplished their task and got your pictures. You can borrow my camera for the rest of the trip."

"Thanks, I'd appreciate that. But, my pictures—when I got back to my room, I sent them to my work address."

He was silent an instant as my meaning became clear. Mart dropped his voice low. "You'd already saved the pictures?" There was no one around our table. Most trekkers had long since headed off to the marketplaces. Still, he spoke cautiously. "You can still access your photos from Tikal?"

Slowly, I moved my head up and down. "Safe and sound," I said. "I've got that blog to keep up, remember? I want to put the pictures on the page."

Mart drew his index finger down the length of his nose several times, as if that would help him concentrate. "Well, that puts things in a different light. I'd like to see those pictures later."

"Any time. And I'll just let the burglar think he got what he wanted," I stated. "But I still don't understand. Mart, what is Clark involved in? What do you suspect?" It was hard for me to picture the suave, professional zoo director as part of some cloak-and-dagger scheme, but explanations weren't exactly heavy on the ground.

"Allison, I think it's best if you stay out of this."

"Level with me. What's going on?"

"I wish I could tell you—"

"You'd better tell me!"

"But I don't really know myself," Mart finished his sentence and I bit my lip into silence. "You see, there was that bit of shake-up at the zoo recently. I don't know if you remember?"

"I just came to Rochester," I reminded him.

"Okay, then you don't know. Tommy Mendoza, the man who previously held my position as assistant to the director, he was the man killed on the last zoo trek."

Ah ha, I thought. I was about to hear the real story Jen had hinted at. I leaned forward. "How?"

"Let's start with where. Right here. In the rain forest. He didn't show up one morning to lead a tour as scheduled. His body was discovered later that day, tangled up in a zipline in the jungle." Mart paused to let that information penetrate.

Goosebumps rose all over my body at the stark words and the image they brought to mind. I shivered to drive them away.

Mart, noticing, asked quickly, "Do you want to hear the rest?"

"Yes, yes. Go on." I lifted my glass of mineral water and drained it.

Mart continued the story. "I never met Tommy Mendoza. I've heard some rumors and innuendo from staff, of course, but no one ever seemed to have any facts. None they've shared with me anyway. From what I can gather, the zoo was quick to play it down when he was killed. Emphasized it was an accident."

That would explain Elaine's remark about the incident being "unfortunate," I thought.

Mart fell silent, picking absently at a fingernail.

"But it wasn't an accident," I made it a statement.

"No," Mart said, shaking his head. "No."

My fingers itched for my pen. "Clark said there were drugs involved."

"That could very well be true. Drugs are big business. Trafficking into the States is huge."

"Trafficking into the States," I thought out loud. "Bringing drugs in." The penny dropped. "Zoo treks?"

Mart looked up at the last, a sharp point to his gaze.

"Ah."

Lifting his shoulders, Mart said, "It's a possible explanation. Mendoza may have been using zoo treks to smuggle drugs into the States. Had a falling out with one of his cohorts."

"This is all speculation," I said, sitting back in my chair. "How do you know Mendoza's death wasn't an accident? Who says he was involved in the drug trade? Where does Clark fit into any of this?" I fired off questions. "Do the local authorities have anything to say? They haven't found the murderer?"

Mart held up a hand. He answered my last question first. "It's hardly likely they will. Criminals of the drug trade are difficult to pin down anywhere. But here, where the jungle is filled with places to hide. . . ." He let the sentence trail off and I nodded.

Mart poured more water into my glass then refilled his own.

He furrowed his brow. "As for Clark, I've heard he and Tommy were kind of close, although I have a hard time picturing him being close to anyone, really. Anyway, I suspect he's trying to trace Tommy's actions on his own." He shook his head and sighed.

"That doesn't sound helpful."

"I think it sounds dangerous," Mart said. "I mean, these are criminals. This lone wolf act," he broke off to shake his head again. "I don't know."

Remembering all the big plans Clark had outlined for the zoo on our way to Tikal, his larger than life persona, his air of importance, I thought I did know. "It would be great publicity for the zoo if Clark caught a murderer," I suggested, lifting an eyebrow.

"Next stop, his own TV show," Mart said. "Fame and fortune."

"Well, it could be a motivation."

"It could be," Mart granted me the point in an unconvincing way.

"That man I saw in the jungle with Clark, he didn't seem like a good guy to me."

Mart was already shaking his head. "Since you got shoved off the steps after you took his picture, I doubt he's a good guy."

I said, "But I didn't really see who bumped into me. Not in a way I could positively identify, anyhow. So, I don't know if it was that guy." My voice trailed off. Had it been? It could have been . . . or not.

"Look, I've probably said too much already. And I don't mean to scare you," Mart said, pushing his hand through his hair. "Just . . . be careful. Don't put any of your Tikal pictures up on the blog. I'm sure everyone on the trek took some shots. Borrow those. It'll be good public relations and the thief won't know your pictures are safe. And don't leave the tour group or anything. Stick around others. But," he reached out, put his hand over mine, "don't mention any of this to them, either. No need to put a damper on their trip for no reason."

"You be careful, too." I warned. "It wouldn't look good to have two zoo assistants killed."

Mart gave a careful laugh. "No, that would be difficult to hide."

"Especially now that I've heard the theory." I looked off into the distance. "Oh, what a story it could make! Just the sort of thing I've been waiting for, actually. Something with some teeth in it. No fluff. Nothing cute. Just a real story!"

"Wait a minute!" Mart broke into my daydream as I'd thought he would. "You have to promise me you won't go poking around in this. You said yourself it's all based on speculation, anyway. Allison, please don't write about this." His eyes were wide with pleading. Deep horizontal lines split his brow.

"I won't—yet," I conceded. "That's not the job I was sent here to do."

He didn't like my answer, I could tell.

"Now, then," I said, changing the subject, "I'm heading off to the marketplace in search of a smaller backpack." I pointed at my old one, sitting on the chair beside me. "Think I'll find one?"

"You'll find something to fit the bill," he told me. "I'll just tag along."

I'd been in the process of rising, gathering my pack onto my shoulder, when he made the offer. It took me by surprise. We'd been getting along so well and now he was choosing to spend time with me. I wanted to be flattered. But did he want to stay close to keep me away from trouble or keep me away from a telephone and my editor? To cover my confusion, I shrugged and looked down, rummaging with the contents of my pack. "If you'd like to, I'd be glad to have the company. But you don't have to, you know."

"Stay around other people," he reminded me, not quite wagging a finger. "People like me."

I made a sweeping gesture with my hand indicating the door. "Since you've been here so many times, you lead the way. Take me to the bargains!"

We emerged from the hotel into the hot and brilliant sunshine. My heart lifted even though I'd suddenly found myself in the middle of intrigue, and danger seemed an all too real possibility.

Chapter Ten

The colorful sights of the crowded marketplace dazzled my eyes. I adjusted the brim of my hat and flicked my ponytail over my shoulder. Striding beside me, Mart squinted in the sun, bringing to life the creases at the corners of his eyes.

"Where do we start?" I asked.

The square was filled with merchants plying their wares. Haphazard rows of stalls covered the area and the space not filled by merchandise was taken up by shoppers. Natives and tourists mingled, bartering and haggling. Adding to the noise were the squawks and screeches of caged birds offered for sale.

Looking at the flimsy wooden cages the birds pecked with their powerful beaks, I imagined them busting out and flapping away overhead. Then, their calls would be laughter, mocking their earthbound captors.

Mart's hand fell to my shoulder and my nightmarish vision evaporated. He looked sadly at the birds and shook his head.

"These birds aren't endangered, but they could be soon if this keeps up."

"Poaching?" I questioned and he nodded.

"Happens all the time. Appalling. But, hey, let's not turn this into a depressing day. Come see what I found."

He crouched down beside a display of vibrant textiles. His bright red shirt and tan shorts blended well with the stacks of fabric and goods around him.

As I got closer, I could see huipils in splendid color combinations, plus belts and shawls and blankets strewn upon the ground.

"Look here," Mart directed. "How about this for a new pack?"

He held up a long-handled boxy tote bag woven with birds and flowers in primary colors against a black background. The geometric patterns surrounding the motifs were ones I had seen in the ruins and knew were typical of the area. The craftsmanship was exquisite.

"It's wonderful," I said, thanking him with a smile. "I'll take it. Where do I pay?" I rummaged in my tattered old pack for my wallet and signaled to the girl running the stall.

"You have to bargain," Mart scolded as I counted out the amount in the unfamiliar money. "It's expected, local custom," he told me, watching as the money changed hands.

"But it's so beautiful, and the price is already too low for all the work that went into it," I told him, transferring my belongings from old bag to new. "She deserves more than what she asked." I tilted my head, my hands full of pens and lipstick and tissues. "I put more money into the local economy."

He shrugged, his shoulders lifting beneath the bright red shirt. "Good point." For a long moment, I could feel his eyes on me as I finished stowing my stuff.

We started walking down the row of stalls and my eyes eagerly scanned the displays. Mart wasn't shopping anymore, however. He was fishing, instead. Fishing for information.

"How did you end up in journalism, anyway?" he wanted to know. "Is this what you've always wanted to do?"

Walking beside him under the sun on a relaxed and peaceful day, I wanted to answer: Yes! Yes! This is what I've always hoped for! But that wouldn't answer his question.

"Like I said yesterday, I've always wanted to be a journalist like my dad," I told him. "The magazine is wonderful and it's a great place for now."

"But—" Mart led me on and I grinned.

"But it's not my goal. It's not what I really want to do with my life." I stopped at a display of carved wooden figurines modeled after the stelae of the ruins. "I'd like to cover important things. Issues rather than events, you know. With no sugar coating or deception."

"Ah, yes. The investigative reporting," he said.

"Exactly," I agreed. "But, in the mean time, I'll cover fashion shows and open houses, I guess."

"And go on zoo treks deep into the jungle."

"Of course!" I laughed, then sobered. "And, who knows, maybe this will be my springboard."

The light went out of those deep, dark eyes and his mouth set in a firm line of disapproval. "You said you would keep out of this. It was just a quirk that got you involved in the first place."

"And nearly killed me!"

"It could have been serious, that's true. All the more reason to stay as uninvolved as possible. You did promise me." He reached for my hand, pulling me to a standstill and searching my face. Gently, so gently, he reached up, his fingers resting on my cheek as our eyes met.

I held my breath, not moving. When his hands captured mine again, I took his willingly, enjoying the feel of his skin against mine.

He gave my hand a squeeze, crunching my fingers together in a no-nonsense way. "Keep your promise, Allison," he said, his voice making the request a demand. "I might not always be around to rescue you."

The night before I'd wondered why he had been so close both times I'd needed him. My overtired brain hadn't wanted to assign scary motives, though. Today, in the bright sunlight, my fears lost some power.

I blinked slowly, and squeezed back. "I'm a woman of my word. I keep all my promises." The tingle I felt where our hands met spread like a trail of fire up my arms, then down my spine. Fighting the urge to shrug my shoulders and dispel the lovely bit of tension, I stood rooted in place.

All around us, the life of the marketplace went on. Bargains were reached and money changed hands.

What kind of bargain were we making? I wondered. It seemed to go beyond the matter at hand, if I was reading the situation correctly. *And, oh,* I thought, *I hope I am!*

"It's awfully warm, Allison. How about something cool to drink?" Mart's welcome suggestion changed the subject, defusing a potentially intense moment.

Side by side, we walked a few blocks down a narrow dirt street. It appeared to be the business district and, as we passed intriguing shop windows, I promised myself I'd explore them later.

Mart caught my wandering eye. "Thinking of adding even more to the local economy?"

"Maybe," I hedged. "And I still don't see why you object."

"To tourism in this country?" he clarified.

"Yes." I told him about how I'd felt in the jungle the day before. How, after seeing it and actually being a part of it, I was more concerned and aware than I'd been when the rain forest was just a faraway place on a map.

"That's good, Allison. I'm glad you're concerned now. But does that mean until you see African elephants on the continent you won't care about ivory poaching? What about whales? If you've never seen one swimming free in the ocean, you're not bothered by their slaughter?"

"Well—" I interrupted with a sputter.

He kept right on going without pausing for breath, gaining momentum as he went. "What about oil drilling in the Arctic? You don't have to personally experience these things, Allison. Just knowing the facts—seeing the pictures—should strike a responsive chord in you. In everyone!" As he lectured, his hands flashed in constant motion. His voice wasn't angry, just animated and fired with the strength of his convictions.

I wouldn't want to debate him, I thought, tuning out for a moment or two. In the end, I know I frustrated him enormously. Tactfully, I said, "I think both positions have merit. Tourism may do some damage, but it brings attention. Staying noncommercial may keep things pure and untainted, but it also keeps them unknown. You've heard that old saying. Out of sight. . . ."

He nodded, his head bobbing forlornly. "Out of mind," he finished, adding reluctantly, "Point taken."

He stopped at the entrance of a tiny building. Mart pulled open the carved wooden door and gestured me inside.

The interior of the little shop was dim and cool, its stone exterior keeping out the worst of the heat. Rickety tables and chairs were scattered around the floor and a low counter ran against the far wall. The decor was definitely understated. Colorful banners in the Mayan style hung from the walls and shelves held row after row of carved figurines.

Mart pulled out a chair for me and I sank gratefully into it as he went to the counter.

Using the brim of my hat, I fanned my face. It felt so good to be out of the sun. Out of the glare. Slumping a little, I gave a sigh and let my eyes close.

Thump! Thump!

I opened them again as the table jiggled under my hands. Mart was just sitting down across from me and on the table stood two tall, sweating glasses of apricot-colored juice.

Mart ran a hand over his head from front to back. Then, with a smile he reached for one glass and raised it in a toast. "Bottoms up!" He gulped deeply and I watched his Adam's apple bob up and down. His skin glistened from the heat. The crisp hair at the open throat of his shirt sparkled when the light touched it and I realized—not for the first time—how utterly alluring the hollow of the throat can be.

I sat up straighter and reached for my own drink. It was hard to keep a grip on the wet glass, but my efforts were rewarded. The cool, tangy juice made my taste buds wiggle with delight and I felt instantly relieved from the oppressive warmth.

I swallowed. "Mmm. That's wonderful," I told him. "What is it?" The mild, slightly citrusy flavor was unfamiliar.

"It's papaya. One of my favorites." He took another long drink and I followed suit.

Earlier, I'd told him a bit about my ambitions in life. Now, I wanted to hear his. "Tell me about you, Mart," I suggested. "How did you get into this field of work? Is it what you want?"

His tongue darted out to circle his lips. "Is this for your article?"

I wasn't quite sure how to answer. Some of it could be used in my story, but part of my motivation was personal. I shrugged. "You never know. I like to collect a lot of information. More than I need. Then I pick and choose what to include."

This seemed to satisfy him. "As I told you, I had been working on rhino relocation in Africa before coming here. Before that, I did other jobs in the field for various conservation groups."

"So, you've always worked with animals?"

"Oh, yes. I've wanted to for as long as I can remember. In high school, I volunteered after school with the local humane society and learned to rehabilitate wild animals."

"Rehabilitate?"

"Yes. Fix broken wings and injured eyes. That sort of thing. A hundred little tragedies every day." He sounded sad as he spoke. "After college," he went on, "I got involved with the groups in Africa. I've been at it ever since."

"This is your first zoo job, then?" I took another sip of the quenching juice.

"Yes. I don't know if all my experience in the wild is good or bad for this job, though. It's a whole 'nother world!"

"How so?"

"To tell the truth, Allison, I don't honestly approve of zoos. At least, not in practice. I understand the theory—to save and protect wild animals, so they don't become extinct, so humans can look at them and, hopefully, learn something. But all too often, zoos don't fulfill these lofty goals. In fact," his face scrunched into a look of obvious dismay, "it seems to me that some zoos are just holding tanks, warehouses. Stick the animals inside, give them food and water and that's it."

"And that isn't enough?" My statement came out as a question. "Of course not!" Mart said. "Would it be enough for you?" *Uh oh,* I thought. *Wrong question.* "No," I said.

"Allison, you saw the monkeys in the jungle, right? You saw the birds?" When I nodded, he continued. "Do you think those monkeys, who are used to living in a complex and complete ecosystem, are content with a pile of rocks, a tree, and a tire swing?"

I'd made only one trip to the Rochester Zoo since my arrival in town, but I recognized his accurate description of the monkey exhibit.

"And some animals don't even get that! No rocks, no trees, no outdoors! Allison, some animals are forced to live year-round in tiny, glassed-in enclosures. The stalls are easy to keep clean, but they're monotonous and boring for the animals."

I nodded. I remembered that, too. Remembered walking through a concrete building and trading gazes with a gorilla who sat listlessly in a cage. I'd left feeling blue without analyzing why. Maybe Mart had given me a clue.

"That's how the Rochester Zoo is," I said. "What about other zoos?"

Mart drained the last drop from his glass before answering. "More and more are beginning to recognize the needs of animals and respond to them. These zoos create natural surroundings. Acre after acre of unfenced land where many species live together, as they would in nature, like their wild counterparts." He paused. "Although it's my opinion that any time you take an animal from its natural environment, you significantly alter its behavior."

"You mean because they can't roam and hunt and interact?" I thought I was beginning to pick up on his philosophy.

"Exactly. That's what makes me continually question whether a zoo can ever truly save an endangered species."

"Like the rhinos, you mean? The ones killed for their horns?" I'd read plenty about the plight of rhinos and elephants, poached for their ivory horns and tusks. In the wild, they were in danger of dying off. Zoos were seen as a way to save the species.

"Right. A rhino in captivity doesn't behave like a rhino in the wild. I think putting them in a zoo mutates them, if that's not too strong a word."

I shifted in my chair and it bobbed to the left where one leg was shorter than the others.

"So, a black rhino in a zoo isn't a black rhino in the wild. Therefore, the true black rhino no longer exists," he concluded.

I let a silence fall between us while I pondered his comments. "If you're so critical of zoos, how can you be part of one? Doesn't it go against everything you believe in?"

His head tipped to one side. Heavy creases marked his brow and his inner struggle was quite obvious. "Because it's so wrong, I have to be part of it. I have to try and bring about change."

He rubbed a finger over a very old chip in the surface of the table, as if debating with himself. I stayed quiet, waiting. At last, he went on.

"To that end, I'm hoping to implement a plan at our zoo to make it more of a sanctuary and less of a showcase. I've applied for some grant money. Talked with some folks."

I lifted my eyebrows. "That sounds great. Like progress."

"Yeah, as long as Clark doesn't put an oar in and screw things up. He's already agitating about it. Taking it personally. It's got nothing to do with him."

Recalling their shouting match in the parking lot, I asked, "Could he derail the whole thing?"

"He's Clark Webster, zoo director extraordinaire. He definitely could. But I'm appealing to his higher instincts and crossing my fingers." He smiled and met my eyes. "And to appeal to his baser ones I'm also pitching the idea as a money maker. One of the two might work. All I know for sure is reforms are not instituted by those content with the status quo."

This man made sense, I decided, and my admiration for him increased. I may not agree with all his ideas, and I may not fully understand others, but clearly he was a thoughtful person. It couldn't be easy to spend each day in an environment you didn't approve of and found hard to tolerate. That took stamina. And determination. And a heavy dose of courage, to boot.

Leaning back in my chair, I crossed my arms over my chest. "You're a very complex guy," I stated, watching with secret delight as a faint blush stained his cheeks.

He fidgeted in his chair and cleared his throat. "If we continue this tour you may be forced to listen to more of my ramblings and ravings," he teased.

I pushed my chair back and rose, smoothing the creases from my navy blue shorts. "I'll just think of it as research," I said and he laughed.

Chapter Eleven

Several hours later, and several quetzales lighter, we straggled back to our hotel. It had been a pleasant afternoon of gentle adventure. No tumbles down stone steps, no lurking in jungles. Just good old sightseeing.

The day had been a carefree one, with only a single moment of intrigue when we'd spotted Clark's wife meandering further down the narrow little street we were on. Sylvia was alone and moving slowly but assuredly over the sandy road, as if she knew where she was headed.

Mart had stopped, clutching my hand to stop me, too. "I'd rather not run into her just now," he said, watching her movements carefully.

He turned around, leading the way back a few yards to a cross-street. Just before we turned down it I looked back over my shoulder. Sylvia was with someone now, stopped in the middle of the road, her hand on his arm. Clark? I squinted and couldn't tell. Mart was talking, so I turned my attention back to him. Soon I'd all but forgotten the incident.

Another ten minutes and we were back at our hotel. The lobby was cool and dim, a welcome haven from the hot and humid outdoors. Mart and I stood side by side at the elevator, clutching my various parcels and talking about the next day's schedule.

"Mart?" A breathy low voice spoke over our shoulders and we both pivoted.

The beautiful lounge singer I'd seen him with that first night at the hotel stood hesitantly before us. She wore a tropical patterned sundress of some gauzy material that floated around her body as if gently fanned. Her shoulders were bare and her long glossy hair cascaded around her.

"Ishani!" Mart greeted her with a grin just like the ones he'd been aiming at me all day and something in my stomach squirmed.

Ishani turned her big eyes from him to me rather pointedly and I took a step backward. As if on cue, the elevator doors opened with a whoosh.

"I'll . . . I'll see you later," I told Mart and he nodded without looking at me. I stepped into the elevator as he walked toward her and didn't mind when the doors came together, blocking them from view.

Leaning against the polished wood paneling, I let out a sigh that caught a bit at the end. We'd only spent the day together. There had been no tender words or gestures. Well, nothing blatant, anyway. Certainly there had been no promises of future outings. I had no right to feel disappointed, but I did. As I walked down the corridor to my room, my parcels weighed heavily in my hands.

In my room, I checked my text messages, returned one from my editor, and made a quick decision.

Pulling on my swimsuit, I grabbed a towel and headed for the pool. When in doubt, work it out, I always say. After a fun day in the sun with Mart, when it was difficult to ignore his attractiveness, when I liked him and it seemed he liked me, and yet there was this beautiful girl with the exotic name—well, it was time for some exercise.

Tables occupied by tourists ringed the perimeter of the pool. Some little kids were splashing in the shallow end of the water.

There was a diving board and a slide at the deep end and a few more laughing guests. I deliberately didn't look around me. Eye contact led to conversation and just then all I wanted was the feel of cool water flowing over my hot skin.

I tossed my towel to one side and stepped to the edge. A pause to gather myself and then I was off. The jolt of the cold was a tonic, fueling each stroke, each kick, each turn at the end. Letting the rhythm guide me, I swam until I felt both tired and revived.

Heading off to the edge, where the water came just to my shoulder, I hovered contentedly, drinking in my surroundings.

The career girls were here now, I noticed, stretched out side by side on the lounge chairs. Last night they'd worn variations on the maxi dress. Today they were in variations on the bikini. My own suit was a more modest one-piece, but was just as brightly colored.

The lounge chairs furthest off in one corner were occupied, too. Clark and Sylvia? No, it couldn't be. I'd seen Sylvia just a short time ago, heading away from the hotel. And apparently the man she'd met had not been Clark, because here he was, swimsuit clad, deep in conversation with some other woman. When she turned to get her drink from the table beside her, I recognized Jen. Sylvia was off with another man and now Clark was chatting up another woman. A very modern marriage, I thought.

Plunging under the surface again, I bobbed up and then out. There was another lounge chair by the career girls and it seemed to have my name on it.

*

After spending a bit too much time lying in the sun, I reminded myself I was on this trip as part of my employment with the magazine and meandered off to my room to write my next blog entry. Later, I'd expand the entry a bit, into a full article for the magazine.

I had a few false starts, but then I always do. Soon I was writing quickly about what we had seen and what we had eaten and what the weather had been like. I wanted to put a lot of description into my blog, so people could actually imagine what it was like here in this beautiful country. But one of my other goals with the magazine series was to include facts like the ones on Mart's information sheet, or like the ones Professor Ramsey had rattled off on our first day.

I bit my lip. Mart was already mentioned plenty of times, since he was a zoo employee, so I'd mention the professor. It was easy to remember his last name, but even after sitting for several minutes staring off into space I couldn't remember his first name. Admitting defeat, and not wanting to waste any more time, I opened the university's website and clicked on the faculty link.

"Science, science. He said he teaches science," I muttered, searching and clicking once more.

Then, I sat back. There was no Professor Ramsey teaching science at the university. Okay, maybe it wasn't science. Maybe it was some specific form of science. Returning to the home page, I put "Ramsey" in as a keyword search. That ought to find him.

But it did not. At first, I was just irritated at my own ineptitude. If I were better with names, I wouldn't be having this problem. My eureka moment came when I remembered I had a passenger list as part of the paperwork in my suitcase. It took a bit of digging, but at last I held it in my hand.

"Sheridan!" I said, typing the name for the third time.

And coming up blank for the third time, too.

Intrigued, I left the school's homepage and just plugged the name into a search engine. Plenty of Sheridan Ramseys came up, more than I ever would have expected. I groaned. This would take a while. On the fourth or fifth page of his hits, I came upon an entry that sounded like the right guy—professor of science, and so on, and so forth—just not at our local university. When I opened the link, I saw a younger version of our professor.

"Hmm, so he did teach at a different school," I said to myself, "but now he says he teaches here." Tapping my fingers lightly against the keys, I thought and thought. Could he be new to the university and so not on their webpage yet? Possibly. Did the university even list all the faculty on the site? "I mean, it's not like someone would lie about something like that," I said aloud.

Returning to the blog, I modified my sentence to eliminate the need for identifying the professor's affiliation and hurried on through to the end. After reading it aloud—the only way to find the bumpy bits—I deemed it worthy and posted the entry.

When I dressed for dinner that night, it was with more care than usual. I'd only brought one good evening outfit along—a silky amethyst camisole top and an ankle-length skirt in a pattern of jewel tones, cut in a full circle. Made of chiffon, it danced around me when I moved. I took a test spin in front of the mirror, smiling when it swirled around my legs.

My spirits lifted as I studied my reflection. *When I make an effort, I can look pretty,* I thought with amazement. Usually, my hair is combed straight or pulled back in a twist. Tonight, I'd done a little back combing, so it fluffed full and bouncy around my face. I'd spent some extra time on my makeup, too, adding eyeliner and lip pencil to my usual blush and lipstick routine. I patted on a dusting of loose powder to make it last.

Squaring my shoulders, I grabbed my evening bag and headed to the dining room. With luck, I'd see Mart tonight. And he'd see me, looking my best. Too bad I'd have to make it an early evening, but the *Breeze* was expecting that entire article based on my blog entry and tonight was the night to write it. *Lesson one,* I thought with a giggle. *Don't fall for your tour guide!*

*

Despite everyone's more formal attire, dinner was a casual event. There was plenty of chitchat around the tables as everyone eagerly shared stories of their day's adventures.

After only two days, the group had divided tidily into predictable groups. Somehow, I knew I'd spend the week with either the career girls or the Underwoods and the Websters. Tonight, Dan Underwood sat at my left and regaled me with stories throughout the meal. I kept pretty quiet, lapsing into my listening mode. At appropriate intervals, I laughed at his jokes and scoffed at his tales. By the time dessert was served, I pitied poor Elaine, listening each day to stories she'd heard a hundred times before.

When I leaned over to pass her the sugar for coffee, she caught my eye and gave me a secretive smile, as if she'd read my mind.

Across the room, Mart sat at a table with other trekkers. He and the Websters were acting like captains on a cruise ship, sharing their attentions with a different group each evening.

Sometime between salad and the main course, I glanced across the room at Mart, admiring the way his sport coat outlined his broad shoulders. With skin tanned by the sun, he looked like a transplanted lifeguard or football hero.

As I watched, the waiter came to his table, refilling water glasses. Mart leaned back out of the way and caught me staring. I could feel the heat rising in my cheeks as he grinned that lazy grin, raising his glass in salute.

What was I to make of this man? So opinionated and dedicated, he was also caring and amusing. A few hours earlier, he'd gone off with a gorgeous female and yet, now, he was regarding me with anything but casual interest. I hoisted my own glass, bobbed my head at him and sipped.

Mr. Underwood launched into another lengthy tale which demanded everyone's complete attention. "Allison, Allison! Listen to this! Here's a story you can use, I'll bet!"

I turned to Dan, doing my best to look interested.

Later, after our plates had been cleared away and we lingered over coffee, the lights of the dining room dimmed and there was action near the tiny stage against the far wall. Until that moment, I hadn't taken notice of the stage, set with an electronic keyboard and a microphone, not realizing there'd be entertainment in the dining room. Overhead, a mirrored ball hung, ready to throw spots of circling light around the room. A minuscule dance floor, about twenty feet square, stood in front of the stage, looking empty under the sudden spotlight.

The manager of the hotel stepped up to the mic, straightening his tie and smiling self-consciously. "Ladies and gentlemen, we are pleased to present the fabulous Ishani!" He began the applause and we all joined in.

I was glad the room was dark as the woman came into view. I looked from her to Mart, but he was just a shadow in the dark.

With a delicate nod of her head, Ishani acknowledged our applause. Behind her, a man stood ready at the keyboard and, at her signal, began to play. Tonight, she dazzled in a silver-spangled outfit. Cut slim, the dress fell to the floor and, when she moved, a generous amount of leg was revealed by the thigh-high slit. Her low, sultry voice suited the old standard she crooned with great emotion.

After several numbers, one brave couple took to the floor, dancing, and soon others crowded onto the tiny space. Beside me, Dan rose and extended a hand to Elaine. What an odd couple they made—he so big and she so tiny—circling under the dancing light.

I didn't even jump when I felt a hand on my shoulder. I knew who was there.

"Would you care to dance, Allison?" Mart asked as my smile spread ear to ear.

"I'd like that."

He held the chair as I stood, then took my hand as we threaded through tables to the floor.

I stepped easily into his arms, as if I'd done it on many occasions and not just once. Putting one hand on his shoulder, I let him capture the other with his. At first, we moved in silence, our feet matching each other. Humming along to the music, I was too conscious of the way his hand nestled at the small of my back.

"You look beautiful," he told me, looking down into my eyes. "But you already know that." He turned me rapidly in a circle, the full folds of my dress wrapping around us before gently falling.

I smiled and tipped my head to one side without acknowledging his remark. "You look quite handsome tonight, I must say. I'd never guess you usually spend your days tramping through jungle mud," I teased.

"Things are seldom how they appear, Allison," he said, his expression serious. "If you're getting back into investigative journalism, you'd better remember that straight away." Shifting the hand that held me, he drew me nearer.

I snuggled up against his chest, trying to remember the words he'd just spoken, but it was hard to concentrate in this position. As the music rolled on around us, he rested his cheek near mine and my eyes drifted shut. Lost in the moment, I forgot about Ishani and my job and my fading bruises. There was only here and now. Mart and me and the melody.

Too soon, the number ended. We stepped apart to applaud. When I turned to go back to my table, Mart's hand stopped me.

"Not yet, Allison. Please not yet." As the next tune began he swept me toward him and I went without hesitation.

This time, I kept my eyes open scanning his features under the twinkling lights. When he smiled at me, the creases deepened in his cheeks. The mirrored light seemed to be caught in his eyes, shining out at me in a way that left me blinking.

What must Ishani think? I wondered as we spun together. *What should I think?*

Nothing, I decided. Think nothing and just enjoy it. I gave another sigh, letting all the air slide out of me, and squirmed a little closer.

Chapter Twelve

"I've just posted my first full article for the magazine," I proudly stated the next morning.

By mutual, but unspoken, agreement, Mart and I had met for breakfast at the tiny table in the corner of the dining room. Soon, we'd be getting into the aging SUVs again for another journey to ancient Mayan ruins. Altun Ha was today's destination.

"That's great," Mart commented, sipping juice and studying the newspaper carefully folded up next to his plate.

"Would you like to read it?"

"Hmm? Oh, sure, sure. Love to. Do you have it with you?" He folded the paper and looked up.

I was already retrieving the five pages, covered in my legible longhand, from my new tote and handed them over with a smile. " Let me know what you think. But remember, this magazine is aimed at your average citizen," I reminded him.

He took the papers from me and began to read while I ate dry toast and watched him.

Things didn't look good. First, I noticed a tightness visible around his mouth. Then dimples appeared as he compressed his lips. By the time he'd finished reading, furrows had appeared across his forehead. He set the pages down on the table.

"What?" I asked, puzzled by his too-silent reaction.

"This reminds me of the story about the baby giraffe last summer. It was a good public relations piece. Very . . . sweet." He shrugged, handing the article back to me. "I guess I just hoped for something more."

Whatever I'd expected him to say, it wasn't that. My story was a good one, I knew. The article was lively and informative, telling readers just the things they'd find most interesting. I leaned back in my chair, feeling stunned.

Tucking the article back in my tote, I said, "Did you read the part where I say it will take more than tourism to save the rain forest?"

"That's the best part," he said.

"It's the last paragraph because it's also the lead-in for my next article," I explained. "I thought I'd suggest to my editor that the series be continued beyond the four parts already planned. Stretch it out to include some of the things you've told me about the zoo. Not just Rochester's zoo, but all of them."

"Sounds great." He reached for his newspaper. "Think you'll get the go-ahead?"

"It's all in the angle, as you said," I told him. "But I'm hopeful."

Sipping at orange juice, I thought about the pitch I could make once we were home, framing sentences in my mind. Silence stretched between us, but it wasn't a comfortable one. Today, at Altun Ha, Mart could watch me in action from a distance, I decided as we wordlessly finished our meal and joined the tour group out front.

"See you!" I called, walking away from him, toward the vehicle bringing up the rear of the caravan.

"Allison!" Dan Underwood's robust shout greeted me as I ducked my head to enter the SUV.

I jumped, startled, and cracked my skull soundly against the door frame. Wincing and cursing under my breath, I took a seat beside the professor and rubbed my bruised cranium.

Behind me, the Underwoods made sympathetic noises of concern.

"Oh, Allison, sorry to scare you like that."

"Are you all right, dear? That looked like it hurt!"

My smile was pained. "It did hurt, thanks."

"Poor girl," Elaine clucked. "I'm always telling him to pipe down. 'Use your inside voice,' I tell him. As if he were a little child."

Dan didn't seem to mind this public scolding and sat with hands folded, looking cherubic and harmless. After several minutes, however, he said, "Oh, Elaine, stop. I think the patient will live."

"I'm fine," I assured them, putting more wattage into my smile. "Looking forward to the trip?"

The change of subject was effective. Elaine launched into a lengthy but not uninteresting oratory on the background of Altun Ha which had me reaching for my notebook.

"You've really done your homework," I said as we rumbled along the sandy roads out of town.

"Oh, yes. It seems to me you get so much more out of a visit if you know the history of the place. Like knowing about the author when you read a book," Elaine explained.

"Oh, but not entirely!" Professor Ramsey spoke for the first time and we all turned our attention to him. He cleared his throat. "I mean, facts and figures have a place and a purpose, to be sure, but I think one needs to immerse oneself in a country. Soak up its culture objectively, using your own senses and your own judgment. No preconceptions. Not all guidebook philosophy."

"Well, that's as it may be," Elaine jumped in and the debate began.

I sat back against the seat, listening. This could provide plenty of flavor in my next article, I figured. I'd have to make sure I quoted lots of the other trekkers in the stories, too. People love to see their name in print.

"Yes, but—" the professor grabbed hold of the conversational ball, wrestling it away from Elaine with an effort.

I fished around in my tote bag for my notebook. Flipping through the rapidly filling pages for an empty one, I happened upon the piece of hotel notepaper containing the message I'd read on Clark's phone the other night.

Bending the corner of the paper back and forth, I felt momentarily detached. Half my mind was tuned to the talk going on around me. The other half was pondering Clark's cryptic text. The words tumbled over and over in my mind's eye and, like a difficult crossword clue, refused to go away.

Thursday's shipment—twenty five airborne, thirteen grounded. Delay arrival. Uncle visiting.

In light of what I'd heard from Mart about suspected drug smuggling, the secretive, coded language sort of made sense. At least the part about shipment. Had Clark already made contact with Tommy Mendoza's associates? Was he communicating with them regularly, as the note implied?

A tiny shiver of fear tingled in the small of my back at the thought of the potential danger. Following on its heels came another unsettling idea. Was Sylvia aware of her husband's plans? Did she know what Mart suspected—Clark's search for Mendoza's killer?

It was difficult to imagine her condoning her husband's adventurous scheme. I had a feeling she'd think dirty work was best left to professionals like policemen. "They are paid to put their lives on the line, after all," I could hear her say.

Was that why she was along on this trip? To keep an eye on Clark?

I made another note, scribbling "S?" in the margin of my paper and slipping the note back among the pages. There was more than one mystery to be solved here, it seemed, and I was determined to get some answers. I didn't stop to question my motivation, choosing to lump it under "Research for My Articles," even though I knew that wasn't true.

I wouldn't be getting any answers now, though. Altun Ha was much closer to our hotel, and was located in Belize, not Guatemala. Already our SUV, in the middle of the procession, was slowing to a crawl. Elaine, looking eagerly out of her window, broke off in mid-sentence, and leaned forward, bouncing in her seat with excitement.

"Will you be climbing any of the temples today, Elaine?" I asked, sliding my notebook into my tote.

"Count on it," Dan drawled, sounding less than pleased and Elaine gave him a poke with one pointy elbow.

"You old frump!" she scolded affectionately. "It isn't as if I make you go with me, you know. But I don't know why you even came if all you're going to do is sit in the shade somewhere. You could do that at home."

"I'm not the only one who doesn't feel a need to put my head in the clouds," Dan retorted, looking at me. "Allison won't climb either, right?"

I shrugged, recalling my last horrendous attempt to scale the steps of a temple. The thought of a repeat performance was terrifying. But I would have been all right if I hadn't been pushed. Could I screw up my courage and make the climb? My glance darted over to Elaine. Easily in her late sixties, she didn't have a moment's hesitation.

"Maybe I will and maybe I won't," I hedged.

Dan's eyes sparkled with mischief. "That's what I like. Sure and swift decision-making."

"Excuse me," the professor broke in as our vehicle came to a halt. "Would you mind if I squeezed past you?" Even as he spoke, he was sliding by me and, in a blink, had thrust open the SUV's door. He leapt to the ground and strode off.

I wondered if he'd share our vehicle on the ride home or make good his escape and avoid further verbal sparring with Elaine. Hiding a smile, I climbed out, too, stretching arms and legs and gazing around me.

Just as in the jungle near Tikal, I was astounded by the dense foliage and varying shades of green. I took a deep breath, filling my lungs with the warm, moist air that smelled of the rich, dark earth.

As I pondered how I could convey this sensation to my readers, Clark shouted for the group's attention. Obediently, we clustered together and listened as he gave us a brief synopsis of Altun Ha's centuries-long history.

"Altun Ha was named for the nearest village and is Mayan for Rockstone Pond," he told us, beaming a smile in all directions.

"It's believed people were living here by 200 B.C. and the site remained an active settlement until 900 A.D. The greatest archaeological find here so far has been a jade carving of the Sun God." He paused for dramatic effect. "It's six inches high and weighs nearly ten pounds! Solid jade!"

There were suitable *oohs* and *aahs* from the group and I'm sure I wasn't the only person wondering how much such a find was worth.

"Feel free to explore the ruins at your leisure," he continued, spreading his arms wide in a sweeping gesture. "The hotel has packed us all a picnic lunch, so let's meet back here around one o'clock."

"One o'clock," Dan grumbled in a voice meant to carry. "Where I come from, lunch is served at noon."

If Clark heard the disparaging words, he didn't acknowledge them. He'd turned and moved away from the group, walking next to Sylvia. Their heads nearly touched as he bent to hear her. Soon, other trekkers had filed in behind them and they were lost from sight.

I caught my lower lip between my teeth. Maybe I'd spend a little time with Sylvia today, I decided. We could chat a bit, maybe over lunch. It would be work, I knew, to get her to open up. She seemed so tightly bottled, shying away from conversation beyond the cocktail variety.

Pulling on my hat to insulate and protect myself from the heat, I fell into line. Apparently, Mart was once more scheduled to bring up the rear of the parade. I could see him up ahead, leaning against the huge buttressed trunk of a tree.

He might be able to make sense of Clark's coded message, but I couldn't bring myself to ask. Recalling his initial response to my article, I kept my head down until I'd gone well past him.

Once we'd begun the trek from where the SUVs were parked, it was easy to forget about Mart. The jungle closed in around us, so I had to focus my attention on watching my step, avoiding the jutting roots of trees.

Along the way, we paused several times to examine huge overgrown mounds at the side of the path. Through the line, word traveled back from Clark that these mounds were unexcavated stelae, totally covered by jungle growth and towering over our heads. I stretched out a hand and touched the thick carpet of greenery. So thick as to be almost impenetrable, it was hard to imagine that beneath it lurked one of the gigantic carved monuments.

I was trying to picture the stone hidden within, imagining the thrill of being the one to uncover it after centuries, when suddenly there was a shriek and a flurry just past my right shoulder. Something shot at me, so close my eyes couldn't focus and I fell back, sending up a shriek of my own. The other sound came again and I recognized it with fear. It was a squawk, and the flapping just inches in front of me was being made by what surely must be a gigantic bird. I got a glimpse of pointed beak and sharp talons as it hovered for the space of a heartbeat. Then, with a mighty whoosh of its wings, it rose up and up, disappearing into the treetops. But the shrieking went on and on.

It wasn't until Dan Underwood grasped me firmly by the shoulders and gave me a shake that I realized the sound was coming from me. My heart pounded in my ears and my breath was coming in short, powerful gasps. My fear had left me dazed and it took a moment for me to orient myself. When I did, it was with great embarrassment.

I'd sunk to my knees, cowering behind the shelter of the overgrown stelae. All around me, other trekkers had stopped to stare, gawking but not helping. Only Dan had stepped forward, squatting down beside me and delivering his own form of aid.

Now, his forehead creased into a hundred wrinkles of varying depth and his liquid eyes were serious and concerned. "Allison, for corn's sake! Are you okay? What happened?"

I felt like a fool. My silly phobia had been revealed to everyone. I managed a sheepish smile. "I'm sorry," I said in a voice like a whisper. "I feel so stupid. But, see, there was this bird! A huge bird!" I stretched out my hands to indicate its size, then shuddered and covered my eyes at the memory.

"You're afraid of birds? That's it? It didn't bite you or anything?" Dan pressed questions at me.

Shaking my head, I looked just at him, avoiding the faces of the others. "No, it didn't bite. It just flew."

Dan sat back, his hands dropping off my shoulders. "Well, that's what birds do, you know. Fly."

"I . . . I know. They just scare me," I finished lamely.

"So long as you're not hurt, Allison. We'll all try and keep any birds out of your way." He stood up and pulled me to my feet, then addressed the crowd. "She's fine. Just a scare. Nothing to worry about. We can all move on."

The crowd dispersed slowly and I smiled my thanks at those who expressed concern.

"You just stick with us today, dear," Dan said, putting one pudgy arm around my shoulder.

Elaine took the other side and got a firm grip on my elbow. "We'll watch out for you."

Ungratefully, I thought, *Terrific! There goes my chance to try and talk to Sylvia!*

But I was wrong.

Chapter Thirteen

We'd been wandering among the ruins for nearly an hour when Elaine announced her intention of climbing the steps of a temple. I'd fully recovered from my encounter with the bird, but Dan, in his role as my bodyguard, suggested I wait a while longer before attempting such a potentially dangerous move.

So it happened that the two of us went looking for a place to sit down for a while. And we found one. When I saw a big stone slab occupied only by Sylvia, I pushed Dan in that direction.

"Let's go keep Sylvia company," I offered generously. "She looks lonely."

Indeed, she did, sitting with her legs stretched out in front of her, straw hat resting on her knees and eyes intent on examining some pebbles at her side. *The caption to that picture would read "Bored Rigid,"* I thought with a trace of humor.

She looked up when we approached and her expression rapidly changed from blank as a post to one of minor irritation. Then, with resignation, a thin, tight smile appeared.

"Hello," she greeted us as we made ourselves at home.

"Hi! Hope you don't mind if we join you?" I asked. "We needed to get out of the sun and you seem to have found just the right place." I looked around me with a great show of interest.

"So, Sylvia, how are you enjoying our journey?" Dan removed his canvas fly-fishing hat and flapped it in front of his face. "Sure is hot enough."

No one could argue with that. Sylvia bobbed her perfectly coifed head. How did she manage to look so put together when the rest of us were falling apart? I wondered.

"It's okay, here, I guess," she answered Dan, lifting her shoulders in dismissal. "I mean, it isn't Paris, is it?"

Ah, Paris. That would suit her, I thought. *Museums, shopping, civilization.*

"Don't ask me," I chuckled. "This is my first big trip."

Sylvia turned and looked at me for a long, silent moment, as if she were assessing me and I came up lacking. "Poor you," she drawled. "Starting here."

How on earth had she ever linked up with Action Man Clark? He of the jungle and safari suits. She of the country club. Only one way to find out.

"So how did you and Clark meet? Childhood sweethearts?" I suggested.

She uncrossed her ankles then crossed them again the other way. "Years ago. At a fundraiser for the symphony. We were both on the organizing committee."

"And it was love at first sight," Dan put in, a big smile spreading across his face. "I know because I was there," he told me in an aside.

"Really?"

"Why, sure! Elaine and I had been season ticket holders for years. We're quite active with the symphony, aren't we, Sylvia?"

"Oh, yes. Quite." Her tone implied she was less than thrilled by their activity, and, for a moment, I could sympathize. A little Underwoods would go a long, long way.

"It was the wedding of the year, of course," Dan adopted a socialite's clipped voice. "At least, that's what all the ladies told me."

"I'd imagine it was," I put in, picturing the incredibly thin Sylvia as a radiant, perfectly groomed bride.

"Ancient history now," Sylvia spoke matter-of-factly, slamming the door on that topic.

I pressed on. "So, Clark's been at the zoo for quite a long time, then?" This was information I could easily obtain from the zoo, but it made a good lead-in.

Sylvia sighed and I knew she didn't want to answer. Didn't want to talk about anything, at all. But her social training shone through and I was graced with another flash of smile.

"More than ten years. My husband has seen the zoo through plenty of changes, Miss Belsar. When he took it on, it was heavily in debt. Now, it turns a profit every year and has never been more popular with the public."

I recalled Mart's words and his criticism of Clark for being totally consumed with making money at the expense of other equally important issues. "Plenty of fundraising and special promotions, right?"

Her eyes narrowed the tiniest bit, as if she knew what I was getting at. "That's right," she said curtly. "It's been a very successful approach."

I nodded. "That's what I've been hearing."

"I'm sure that isn't all you've been hearing."

I shifted on the hard surface of the rock before answering. "Lots of people tell me lots of things."

"Ooh, I'll say!" Dan interrupted with a hoot and we both gave a start. He'd been sitting so quietly, I'd forgotten he was even there. "I know I've done my share, eh, Allison?"

"That's for sure," I quipped, only half in jest. "You've given me enough information for a year's worth of articles." I turned back to Sylvia. "Seriously, though, I have heard other opinions regarding zoo management."

"From Mart Lawler, of course."

I shrugged. There seemed no need for an answer. As a journalist, it's my job to examine both sides of an issue and present them to the public in a balanced, unbiased way so they can then make educated decisions. That's a responsibility I take quite seriously and one I shouldn't have to explain.

Sylvia looked away, off into the trees, her hands bending the brim of her straw hat back and forth.

All around us, the sounds of the forest pressed in. The rustle of leaves as unseen animals scurried hither and yon, the sighing sound from overhead where the breeze was able to penetrate the forest's canopy. Closer, the sounds were very human—talking, laughing. Dan had distanced himself from our conversation when it took on a confrontational tone and now sat facing the opposite direction, whistling a Broadway show tune.

"You have to understand, Miss Belsar, Mart is a young man," Sylvia said. "Idealistic. Brash. Arrogant. He hasn't worked in a traditional fashion before. There are no time clocks in the wilds of Africa. No bosses, either. I think he's used to playing by his own rules. Doesn't recognize authority." Her eyes snapped back to mine and she continued. "He has answers to all the world's problems, if only people would listen."

Even though I was currently annoyed with the subject of our conversation, this unqualified critique of Mart was difficult to swallow.

"It seems to me he brings a great enthusiasm to his work," I said. "He's very dedicated to those ideals you dismiss."

"Well, we all see what we want to see," Sylvia's cold words were meant to put me in my place.

But I wouldn't go.

"I'm sure you'll be pleased to know I'm planning a series of articles when we return. I'll be exploring Mart's views—as well as the more traditional ones. Consulting other sources and examining the role of a zoo today. What it is and what it should be."

In a swift move I wasn't expecting, Sylvia stood. From her vantage point towering over me, she said, "Good luck with your work, Miss Belsar. I'll be ever so anxious to read it." With a few rapid strides, she marched off around the corner of our shady nook to join the others. Her arms moved in steady cadence, her hat dangling from one hand.

"Well, you've done it now." It was Dan, tuning back in to the encounter. "Couldn't help hearing all that." He spread his hands to plead innocence and I nodded. "She looks like a cool cucumber, that one, but she's actually a real fiery gal. If you weren't already on the wrong side of her, I'd warn you not to end up there." He shrugged. "Too late, now."

No kidding, I thought, pressing my lips together tight to keep the words back. "She shouldn't be so touchy. She must love Clark very much to get so defensive."

Dan closed one eye in concentration. "Don't know if it's him she loves so much these days."

"What?"

That head of white hair shook. "No, no. I shouldn't tell tales out of school." He gave my hand a paternal pat of reassurance, which I tolerated with a smile.

"Let's go find Elaine," I suggested.

Easing himself up from the stone, he said, "She should be to the top of the temple by now."

With my mind elsewhere, I followed the elderly man. It would feel good to get out of the cool shadows. They were beginning to chill me straight through.

Chapter Fourteen

The next several hours were magical ones, much to my surprise and delight. At the base of the temple that dominated one end of Altun Ha's plaza, Dan and I stood with our hands shielding our eyes, gazing up, up, up.

Our search was rewarded with a shout of "Yoo hoo!" Little Elaine stood at the top, waving both arms enthusiastically over her head. Once she had our attention, she yelled "C'mon! It's an easy climb!"

Beside me, Dan sighed deeply, as if he knew when he was beaten. "I suppose I'd better do this," he said with resignation. "I like Elaine to be happy." He nudged me. "What do you say?"

This temple wasn't as high as those at Tikal, but it still rose awfully far overhead. Standing in front of the steps, I looked up and swallowed.

Dan read my expression with little trouble. "We'll do it together, Allison. Let's be brave, eh?"

How could I say no to the overweight, elderly gent ready to risk life and limb?

"After you."

He stepped back, hands up and head shaking. "Oh, no, dear. Ladies first."

I scowled at him and he laughed in a great bellow.

Cautiously, slowly, we made the climb, one chipped, ancient step at a time.

"I think the key is to not look down," Dan puffed from behind.

"Could be."

"Because, if you look down and see how high up you are, well, that would be frightening," Dan prattled on, to cover his nervousness, I figured.

I didn't answer anymore, but the monologue continued. The distraction must have helped because it seemed like only moments later we were standing upright at the very top of the temple. We were on the platform just outside the walled room where sacrifices had taken place hundreds of years ago. The gaping, dark hole of the entrance loomed before me, but I turned away. And caught my breath.

Oh, we were high! And all around us, the blue sky stretched off to the horizon. The green canopy of the forest top ran parallel, an unbroken carpet of foliage.

Dan let out a long whistle, sweeping off his hat and mopping his brow.

"Well? Was it worth the effort?" Elaine practically danced over to us, sliding an arm around her husband's paunchy middle and beaming.

"It's magnificent!" I agreed, turning to look in each direction.

We weren't alone at the top, of course. Plenty of other tourists were present, exploring the ruins, as well. Several couples had young children along. The kids climbed up and down the temple steps with no hesitation and limitless energy.

I saw their smaller feet fitting easily onto the narrow steps and wondered how I'd tackle the climb back down.

When the time came, Elaine had a suggestion. "Bump down one step at a time, dear, on your behind." She gave her own a pat.

Dan and I turned to face each other, chagrin painted on our faces. At his forlorn look, I had to laugh. With the saggy corners of his mouth drawn down even further, he looked for all the world like a basset hound.

I chucked him familiarly under the chin. "If we made it up, we can make it down!"

One white eyebrow rose in question. "I hope so," was all he said.

"We'll caravan," Elaine said brightly. "One behind the other."

In her self-appointed role of group leader, Elaine went first. She moved slowly, feeling carefully for the next slab before edging down.

Staying off to one side, out of everyone's way, our little trio eventually landed on terra firma.

Dan dropped to his knees and delivered a resounding kiss to the earth.

"Oh, Dan, honestly!" Elaine squeaked in embarrassment.

We each grabbed an elbow and helped him to his feet. He took his time dusting off his knees and pulling faces.

"That's enough of that," Elaine scolded. She glanced at her watch—a tiny sapphire-and-diamond masterpiece—and let out a gasp. "We'll have to hurry if we're going to see the reservoir!"

"Wouldn't want to miss that," Dan grumbled as his wife marched away.

This was certainly more fun than wandering around on my own, so I tagged along once more.

Elaine set a strenuous pace, her running commentary as fact-filled as a guidebook. I covered page after page in my notebook as we toured the grounds.

Later, the group reconvened for a picnic lunch. Aside from the predictable American fare, there were plenty of local dishes to try. I had grown especially fond of chile relleno, a delicious stuffed pepper, and tamales de chipilin, which consisted of cheese and tomato sauce surrounded by seasoned corn paste all wrapped in a banana leaf.

I sat on one of the colorful blankets strewn on the ground, listening to Dan describe to the others our hazardous descent from the temple. He told the tale in a hilarious fashion, and we all roared with laughter. As I chuckled at another of his wild exaggerations, I felt eyes watching me. It could be Sylvia, I thought, remembering the enemy I had made earlier in the day. Borrowing a gesture from Mart, I pushed my hands through my hair, massaging my scalp and relieving some of the tension that thought had produced.

This whole trip was getting a bit too complicated for me. Clark tracking criminals, Mart following Clark, Sylvia in a snit, and

Ishani just existing were all succeeding in distracting me from my real work. It was impossible to ignore these situations, however. It was especially impossible to ignore Mart and the undeniable attraction between us.

I swiveled around, looking quickly over my shoulder. Mart stood a short ways off, leaning against a tree trunk and looking like his photo from the zoo trek brochure. Except now, he wasn't smiling.

The noisy chatter of Dan seemed to fade away as we looked at each other. My heart set up a thumping that echoed in my ears and I could feel every muscle tense up.

His dark eyes were solemn, wide, and deep. Little wrinkles curved on either side of his tightly clenched jaw, like commas setting off a sad phrase. After a long, long moment when it was hard for me to sit still, he jerked his head to one side, silently inviting me over.

Why should I go? I thought, looking back at him, thinking, debating.

His shoulders lifted and fell as he sighed. Then, he mouthed one word. "Please."

Slowly, deliberately, I stood up and excused myself from our group. I know they all watched me leave. I'm sure they had plenty to say, too, but I didn't care. I only wanted to hear what Mart had to say.

"Yes?" I stuffed my hands deep in the pocket of my shorts in a defensive posture.

He shifted from one foot to another. "I'd like to talk to you."

"Okay." I nodded. "About what?"

"Earlier. I shouldn't have reacted the way I did, Allison," he said. "You're just doing your job and you're the person best qualified to know exactly what that means. If it's stuff like that article, well, then it's stuff like that article."

As far as apologies go, it wasn't much.

"Thanks," I said, accepting it anyway. I wouldn't forget his response to my article, but I wouldn't let that color my work, either.

"And I think your idea for a series is a good one. I'm sure Clark would be willing to cooperate on a project like that. If you want, I'll speak to him about it."

I smiled and it felt good. "Thanks, Mart. I'd appreciate that."

He smiled, too, and the commas disappeared. He looked better without them. "Let's walk," he suggested, putting his hand on my crooked elbow.

We moved away from the group and the sound of their voices faded to a murmur.

"So, what do you think of Altun Ha?"

"Oh, it's fascinating. I've had a very interesting day!" I said, launching into my own description of my travels up and down the temple with Dan. I must have told the story well, because Mart ended up laughing out loud.

He stopped laughing when I described my conversation with Sylvia. "She's a piece of work, all right," he commented, dismissing the subject when I tried to pursue it.

Further efforts on my part produced similar side-stepping, so I abandoned that topic and we lapsed into a cozy silence. I'd taken my hands from my pockets and he reached for one now. His fingers tightened pleasantly around mine and I returned the squeeze.

"You know," he began after a while, swinging our hands between us, "I was surprised to see you get defensive this morning when I didn't like your article."

"Why is that? You'd be furious if I implied you didn't do your job properly."

Bobbing his head, he agreed. "That's true." The hand not holding mine fanned the air as he went on. "Seeing you get all fired up made me realize just how seriously you take your job. Integrity is pretty high on my list of admirable traits, Allison," he continued, footsteps slowing to a full stop. Turning to face me, he took my other hand and looked down into my eyes. In a voice so

quiet, I had to strain to hear it, he said, "I'm glad you've got it."
He paused before concluding, "Gorgeous and ethical—a lethal
combination."

No one had ever called me gorgeous before and my cheeks
burned with the compliment. Plenty of folks had called me
ethical. Or stubborn. Both descriptions made me proud. But I
wasn't dwelling on that now with his face so close to mine as he
bent his head. I knew then that he was going to kiss me and that
I'd kiss him back. And, sure enough, I did.

His lips touched mine, briefly, gently, as if he was unsure of my
reaction. This was what I'd daydreamed about quite frequently, so
my own reaction was spontaneous. I returned the pressure against
his mouth, closing my eyes and breathing in the scent of his skin.
He kissed me again, firmly and with no hesitation. Our noses
bumped and then our chins and I felt the scratchy tickle of his
whiskers against my flesh.

Our hands had left their place between us. Mine were curved
around his neck, resting on his sun-warmed nape. His were settled
none too gently at my waist, the heat from them burning easily
through my blouse.

I'll never know how long we would have stayed there,
smooching in delightful abandon. At just that instant, one of
those colorful, raucous birds let out a screech from close by. I
leaped at the sound, not away from Mart, but closer to him. He
held me tight and chuckled.

"I'd heard you were afraid of birds, but right now, I can't say
I'm sorry."

My eyes moved swiftly from the offending creature in the trees
to the man who cuddled me close despite the heat.

It was good to not be angry.

Chapter Fifteen

"Yes, Mom, I'll be home in a few days," I said, checking my tote bag for supplies. "Today we're going to tour a cave by inner tube. We float down some river and go into these caves. I think we wear headlamps to see. And then we're going to a resort where we'll be staying in cute cabana huts for the night. It sounds pretty neat." I waited for her to tell me to be careful in the cave and watch out for bats in my hair.

Since it was Friday morning, I'd given Mom a call while I got ready for the day. We talked every Friday morning and just because I was thousands of miles away, that was no excuse to miss a conversation.

I hadn't told Mom about my fall or the fact that I was using a camera I borrowed from Mart because mine had been stolen. No need to give her more than bats to worry about.

"I sent you a postcard but I'll probably be home before you get it," I said. "Watch your mailbox!"

After assuring her I'd call the minute our plane touched down on U.S. soil, I tossed the phone into my bag and scurried out the door.

We were headed to one of the many caves found all over Belize. As I'd told Mom, we'd be doing our touring from the water and had been warned to wear swimsuits and bring a change of clothes. On the tour bus, I sat next to Jen, evading her questions about my growing relationship with Mart.

At the venue's headquarters, a rustic, rough-hewn lodge, I was surprised to see you could also rent ATVs and drive them along trails through the forest. This didn't seem quite the ecologically responsible thing to do. What must Mart think? Did he know?

One look at his face gave me that answer. His lips pressed tight and his jaw clenched. I wondered if he'd refuse to participate or make us all get back on the bus and go do something else. But with Clark at the head of the ticket, the die was cast. As we queued for inner tubes, I saw Mart pull his boss aside. From the arm gestures and head shaking, I could have provided the dialogue of their conversation myself.

The line inched forward and I noticed a wooden sign indicating the path to a zipline feature. Hammered into a tree on my right, the sign pointed up a hill and into the trees. Looking ahead, I saw the line for inner tubes was still moving slowly. Slowly enough for me to follow a hunch?

Just as we were staying in the same hotel as the last zoo trek had, so were we visiting the same activity center today. Was this where Tommy Mendoza had gotten fatally tangled in his zipline harness? Would an employee talk to me about it?

A long shot, to think there might be someone who remembered the event. But how could you ever forget it?

Stepping away from my fellow trekkers, I went in search of the zipline.

I could see the double cable strung through the trees once I'd gotten away from the main entrance. The excited shrieks and cries of the riders had been audible from the moment we'd left the SUVs.

I approached a middle-aged man in a bright yellow t-shirt bearing the company logo and asked a question or two about the zipline. He was busy, readying riders with an efficiency that made it obvious he wasn't new to the task. *So he might have been around last year*, I thought.

He handed a safety helmet to the next customer in line for a bit of high-speed adventure. As he watched her fasten it under her chin, I asked in a low voice, "Did you hear about the man who was killed here last year?"

The employee glanced over his shoulder at me while he finished checking the fit of the customer's harness. She hadn't heard my question, I'd made sure of that.

"Okay," he told the eager-looking teenager, "take three running steps and then you go!"

We watched her brief sprint, heard her exclamation as she took flight, suspended on the cables. Finally, he glanced at me, shaking his head.

"We are not allowed to talk about that, miss," he said, and I got the clear impression the discussion had ended.

"Were you working here when it happened?" I pressed.

Looking over his shoulder, he shrugged my question away, again shaking his head.

"Please, miss," he said. "All I can tell you is a man was killed. I don't know who shot him."

"Shot him? I thought he got killed on the zipline."

"No, no. The zipline is quite safe. Someone shot that man." He put his index finger to his temple in the universal gesture for gun. "Will you be taking a ride?" He pointed at an empty harness, ready for another adventurer.

Feeling stunned by his news, I backed away, holding up a hand. "Some other time. Thanks."

Turning, I headed back down the trail, reeling. Mart had been right. Tommy Mendoza's accident hadn't been an accident, at all. It had been murder.

I stumbled over a tree root and had to run a few steps, wheeling my arms to keep my balance.

Yesterday, I'd been angry at Mart, but just then all I wanted was to find him, pull him aside, and tell him what I'd just learned.

A quick sprint brought me back to headquarters, where no other trekkers were in sight. I stripped down to my swimming suit, stowed my bag in one of the lockers against the wall and was issued an inner tube and a headlamp like a miner's. Rushing out of the building, I slung the inner tube across my body like a beauty queen's sash. Pulling on my headlamp, I saw Clark heading back toward the lodge.

"Shake a leg, Miss Belsar," he said, his eyes roving over me, stem to stern.

"Which way?" I asked, hands out in question. There were signs all over the place directing to one path or another. I could have taken the time to read them, but why?

Clark pointed off to the right. "Just there," he said. "I'll be along in a minute."

There'd been a light rain the night before, making the ground dark and damp now. The clouds gathering overhead spelled more rain to come, if I were any judge. I just hoped it held off until we were indoors again.

It's awkward, walking with an inner tube. Especially big ones like this which insisted on bumping into my leg with every step. I took the trail Clark had pointed to and was instantly surrounded by the familiar green of the jungle. The path ahead of me was empty and I couldn't hear anything like the usual chatter of conversation our group made. How had they gotten so far ahead of me so fast?

I broke into a trot but had to stop when I came to a fork in the road. Which way? Left? Right? No useful signs were pounded into trees here. And Clark had only said, what? "Just there." That was no help now.

Turning around, I checked the path behind me. Clark had said he'd be right along. Shouldn't I be able to see him? Grinding my teeth together, I stomped on, taking the branch to the left. I hadn't gone far when I was faced with another fork, another decision.

I had just decided to turn around and go back to the lodge when I heard sounds of someone coming up behind me on an ATV. At last! It must be Clark, planning a grand entrance, and I must be on the right trail. Arm wrapped around my inner tube, I waited for him to appear. Maybe I could hitch a ride with him.

But the person who motored into view wasn't Clark. Wasn't anyone I even should have recognized. And yet I did, in that instinctive, pit of the stomach sort of way. It was the man I'd seen with Clark at Tikal, the one who may or may not have pushed me down the stairs and broken into my room.

From the way he narrowed his eyes when he saw me I knew I didn't have to wonder anymore if my fall down the temple steps was deliberate. Oh, yeah. It so was.

I took a step backward, off the path, trying to act calm. Maybe he would just pass me on the trail and disappear up ahead.

But, no. Slowly and without breaking eye contact, he spat out the stub of cigarette he'd been smoking and ground it firmly under one heel. The smell of it, cloves, filled the air. Revving the engine on the ATV he aimed it in my direction.

I took a few rapid backward steps, pulling my inner tube in front of me. Not much of an airbag, it would be no protection against being hit by the four-wheeler. Another unfortunate accident, people would call it.

"Back off!" I shouted. Then added, "Help! Help!" in case Clark was in earshot. "Fire!" That was supposed to make people come more quickly, I'd read a long time ago, never imagining I'd ever need to use the idea.

In answer, the man gunned the engine, inching forward, straight at me. He never spoke a word, making him even creepier, scarier. Deadlier. That last thought was enough for me.

I spun around and took off. My water shoes pounded down the damp earth path and the inner tube bumped against my thigh. I should have abandoned the thing, I realized immediately. Now it would take too long to slip it over my head and down my arm to toss aside. Way too much concentrating required there.

My breath puffed out heavy but shallow and I could hear him just keeping pace there behind me. He didn't need to make me run. I was already doing that myself. Pushing branches out of my way with one hand, I shoved at the stupid light strapped to my forehead as it began to slip, then yanked it off altogether.

The paths forked this way and that and I chose at random whichever way looked less traveled. Maybe he'd get mired in some mud or the undergrowth would be too thick for the vehicle to get through.

But, no. And no, again.

I heard him laugh once, just before he stepped on the gas and twisted the handlebars, spurting close enough to send dirt flying against my legs.

"Help! Fire! Help!" I tried once more, but my shout lacked confidence even to my own ears.

Then, abruptly, I didn't hear the engine so close at hand. Had he given up, having put a good scare into me? I slowed from a run to jog to a stop around another curve in the path. My chest heaved as I gulped the air.

This was worse. I could hear the ATV idling just out of sight. Was the man still on it, or was he on foot now, in silent pursuit?

Ahead on the path, there seemed to be a break in the trees. The sun was brighter there and I could hear—yes, I could hear voices. Many voices. And laughter.

With one last deep intake of breath, I sprinted forward, toward the light and the laughter. I'd gone perhaps fifty feet, no more, when the roar of the engine coming full bore filled the air all around me. I didn't need to look back to know he was tearing up the trail with me in his sights. The game he'd been playing was over apparently, and it was time to get serious.

Inner tube over my shoulder, headlamp in my hand, I ran as if the hounds of hell were nipping at my anklebones.

I burst out of the dense jungle growth and into a tiny open space—twenty feet above the river.

Chapter Sixteen

I might have stopped running when faced with that cliff and the water below me but the ATV also shot from the jungle cover. Wheels churned up earth as the man braked. He spun wildly sideways toward where I teetered at the top of the cliff.

I had only enough time to look out and down, to see the source of that laughter—our tour group floating peacefully down the river—before I was off and over the edge. The headlamp flew from my hand as I gripped the inner tube and pinched my eyes shut.

Then came the shock of cool water against my skin and I was safe. Safe and away and alive. I shook the water off of my face and looked around at the startled faces of my fellow travelers. When I glanced up at the cliff, I saw dirt settling to earth. My tormentor had vanished.

"Woo-hoo!" Jen hollered, applauding. "I give that dive a ten!"

"Yeah, like those cliff divers we saw in Mexico," Patty added.

"Except they didn't have inner tubes!" Kiran said.

"And they were, like, graceful," Faith commented, in a teasing tone.

Of course they had no idea what had just happened. Or very nearly happened. And they were in jolly holiday mode.

Mart paddled toward me. He wasn't smiling or laughing or cheering me on.

"Are you all right? What happened? Where were you?" he asked, helping me adjust my rubber ring. "You're shaking." He chafed his hands up and down my arms and looked directly into my eyes.

"I'm okay," I assured us both. "It's okay. We need to talk." The panic in my voice made my breath come in short gasps, but they hitched up when I saw Clark go drifting innocently past us.

"That was a spectacular dive, Miss Belsar," he called over. "I did wonder if you were going to catch up with the group. But I had no idea it would be in such dramatic fashion. Bravo!" He put two fingers to his forehead in salute.

Mart looked a question at me again, but I realized now was hardly the place or the time.

"Please don't let me out of your sight today," I begged Mart. "Promise."

He didn't hesitate. "Promise!"

We intertwined our fingers and kept them that way as the river current swept us along.

I couldn't hear what our guide was saying about our surroundings and could not possibly have cared less. There was still a rushing in my ears, in my brain, it seemed, preventing coherent thoughts.

Mart didn't press me for explanations but I did see him look from me to Clark and back again. I gave him a shaky smile and squeezed his hand. Eventually my heart rate slowed to something close to normal. I took a few long breaths to steady myself, to lessen the quaking in my veins.

As our inner tubes drifted into the mouth of the first cave and the sunlight dimmed, my excitement from fear was replaced by a different sort of excitement.

We had entered a small cave. I could see sunlight at the other end and I was glad. My headlamp was at the bottom of the river, so Mart's light would have to be mine, too.

There was plenty of oohing and aahing at the beauty of the craggy, cavernous space. And Dan had to yell to see if there would be an echo.

So it went, down the river, into caves big and small. In one spot we had to portage our tubes. In another we went through rapids. The physical activity made my mental static recede into the background—at least momentarily—and my tension drained away.

Even as our guide told us about the ancient relics and equally ancient bones found within the caves, I was calm. Ancient people didn't worry me. It was someone very much alive who actively disliked me. Someone here and now who was out to get me. Ancient, no problem. Contemporary, big problem.

Mart tugged me closer, bumping his tube into mine.

"We get out now," he said, having listened to the guide, "and get to explore a while."

"Cool. But is that safe?"

"They wouldn't let us do it if it weren't," he assured me.

We pulled up toward the walls of the cave, where sand-colored rock made a flat landing surface.

Mart hopped nimbly out of his inner tube and I did the same. Our entire group was really geared up, with spirits high and energy levels about the same. I saw the career girls scrambling up rock outcroppings as if they'd been born to it.

"The rock climbing wall on their last cruise ship?" Mart guessed when I wondered where they'd learned their method.

Dan and Elaine were taking it easier, sticking to a path with Alan and Maria. They'd become chummy over the length of the tour, I realized now. I never saw either couple with Clark and Sylvia for very long. In fact, I rarely saw Clark and Sylvia as a couple.

It was a surprise then to see them now in the dim half light of the cave, with Professor Ramsey. Sylvia, a few feet in front of Clark, seemed particularly stiff in the spine.

I gave Mart a poke with my elbow, tipping my head in their direction. "What gives?" I asked.

He squinted then shrugged. "Don't know. Clark looks angry."

I looked again, trying to read the body language he had seen. Our zoo director did give a very intense impression, leaning forward with formidable jaw jutting toward the equally tall figure of the professor.

Ramsey made a gesture with both hands, as if shaking water from them, and broke his gaze from Clark's. They had to be whispering because voices definitely carried in the hollow chamber.

"Maybe Clark is—" I began, speculating aloud.

"Who cares about Clark?" Mart interrupted. "I want to know what happened to you earlier. How did you get so far from the group? And why did you end up making that jump off the cliff?"

He put both hands on my shoulders, steering me around a curve in the cave wall which was actually an opening to another chamber. He pushed me gently down onto the nearest flattish rock and joined me.

"What happened?"

And I realized that way down below me in the river, the group hadn't seen the man on the ATV, hadn't known I'd been bolting frantically through the jungle, hadn't guessed I'd been frightened and panicked.

So I told him in a low voice about Clark's really vague directions and feeling lost and being chased by a nameless man whose face I recognized. As I related my story the damp of the cave made me feel shivery. When Mart put his arm around me and pulled me tight, the warmth and comfort of his body went a long way toward righting my world.

"I'd no idea," Mart said in my ear. "I heard an ATV, but we heard them all along the river."

"But listen to this. Here's what happened first!" And I told him about the employee at the zipline, about what he'd revealed so casually. "You were right!" I grabbed Mart's arm, pinching hard. "Tommy Mendoza's death wasn't an accident. He was shot in the head!"

To my surprise, Mart nodded. His lips pressed together and he looked decidedly grim. "I know."

"You know? You know he was shot?"

Mart pulled his arm from my death grip, then applied one of his own to my hands.

"I heard about it, yes. But I couldn't tell you. Endanger you further."

"Endanger me!" I quoted. "Forewarned is forearmed, Mart. It might have been a good thing to know!" The news about Tommy Mendoza had been startling enough, but to find out Mart had kept that news from me was nothing short of stunning.

"I've kept you safe, haven't I?" he countered. "Look, you can be angry at me about it later. Right now, we need to think."

"This isn't over," I told him. "How could you not tell me?"

Not playing fair, he leaned in, kissing me quickly, soundly, thoroughly.

"Okay," he said, pulling back. His gaze roamed my face, assessing me. When he got to my eyes, the corners of his mouth softened.

Something at the core of me warmed and melted with that look, even though I tried to fight it. For the space of one heartbeat, then another, then another, we were silent. Then, it was back to business.

"Who told you Tommy was shot? Is there anything else I need to know?" I asked.

Mart gave a swift bob of his head, not in answer to my question, but as if making a decision. He dropped his voice even lower, practically whispering.

"There's a federal investigation underway. I didn't know, you have to believe me. I didn't know until we were here in Belize. But—" he stopped, took a breath, hurried on, "they've contacted me about helping them. Working with them to find any clues linking smuggling to our zoo treks."

I sucked in a breath. "That sounds dangerous."

"I'm supposed to keep my eyes open and report. That's all. No James Bond stuff."

Looking down at my shoes, trying to process this latest newsflash, I wriggled my toes against the sandy rubble of the cave floor.

"Have they approached Clark, too? Is that why he's looking into Tommy's death?"

That made sense. Clark would go in for James Bond stuff.

Mart shrugged. "I don't know all the details. I was told not to discuss this with him."

"But shouldn't one hand know what the other is doing?"

"Allison, I don't know anything about this sort of operation. I rescue rhinos! This is all uncharted territory."

He seemed and looked sincere. But he'd kept one secret, already. . . .

"Who was that guy on the ATV? Where does he fit?"

"Certainly it's obvious he and Clark are in cahoots one way or another," Mart said. "We've never seen the Guatemalan unless Clark is more than close at hand." He rubbed a palm over his hair, fingers scratching as he thought. "If Clark is probing Tommy's death—on his own or at government request—that would explain the proximity."

"I don't ever want to be in that guy's proximity again!" I said, giving a shudder. "I think he's way too dangerous to tangle with. Frankly, I'm surprised Clark would do anything while dragging all these innocent citizens along for the ride. What if someone got hurt? I mean, really hurt?" I clarified when Mart dropped his eyes to my scabby knees.

"We'll be home in a few days, Allison. We just need to stay sharp until then. I'm sure even Clark wouldn't be stupid enough to endanger the zoo group. Can you imagine the bad press?"

"And the lawsuits!" I added.

"Yes, and—" Mart broke off in mid-sentence, sniffing the air and scowling. He was looking past me, over my shoulder to where the unexplored cave curved off into inky darkness.

"What?"

He gave his head a shake. "I don't know. I thought I saw a light back there. Behind you. And I smell smoke."

I whirled around at his words, narrowing my eyes to peer into the cave, lifting my nose to test the air. Yes, there it was, the faintest smell of cloves, of cigarette smoke.

Mart reached up, switched off his headlamp, deepening the blackness. Then I saw a light, too.

Chapter Seventeen

Far, far away and faintly, a tiny orange dot of light glowed brightly then faded. Brightly, then faded, as if in time to a person's breathing.

"What the—"

"My thoughts exactly." Mart stood up. "You'd better wait here."

"What? Wait here! Alone? I don't think so."

"You're right," he said, pulling me to my feet. "We need to stick together. But, listen!" He tugged me even closer so he could whisper straight into my ear. "Keep quiet and hold my hand. I'm going to keep my lamp turned toward the ground. We should be able to see where we're going without throwing too much light in front of us."

I nodded without speaking and then we were haring off down a dark tunnel to investigate the smell of cigarettes. If it were that man from the jungle, would he and Mart fight it out in the back of the cave? Our mission was definitely unclear here, but when Mart squeezed my fingers, I squeezed back. If it were that man from the jungle, the fight would be two against one.

Mart did more than direct his light down. He shielded it with his hand to concentrate the beam about three feet in front of us. Our feet crunched softly on the sandy earth littering the floor of the cave.

"Do you think it's the man who chased me?" I asked.

"Don't know."

"I think it must be," I persisted, "to be right here, right now, by our tour group."

"Could be."

Still holding his hand, I pressed. "What will we do? Beat him up?"

"Let's not get ahead of ourselves," Mart said, sounding calm.

"He could be gone by now," I whispered. "I can't smell the smoke anymore. There must be plenty of other tunnels and ways out of here."

The whole situation was unnerving. The darkness, the warm dampness, the scent of the river, the eerie almost-silence.

"Do you always talk so much on when you're nervous?" Mart asked, not unkindly, but as if he really wanted to know.

My breath whooshed out of me. "It's already been kind of a trying day," I reminded him. "I mean, I'm as up for adventure as your next girl, but—"

"Ssh!"

He squeezed my hand, then let it go, advancing on the chamber where we had seen the glowing end of a cigarette. Or, at least, that's what we thought we had seen. I slipped my finger through the belt loop on his shorts and followed. No way was he going to leave me halfway down a dark tunnel alone. No way was he going to confront the guy without me.

I bumped into Mart when he came to an abrupt halt. Looking past him, I saw an empty alcove. The scent of smoke lingered in the air and when Mart turned his lamp to the ground, we could both see the stubby end of a cigarette butt, smashed into the earth.

"Rats!"

Mart turned this way and that, looking off into tiny dark spaces that must be tunnels to other chambers, other exits. "Let's look around. See what else we can find," he said. "I wish we had a map of these caves to show the feds this exact location." He'd already begun scanning the ground around us for clues.

We could see a lot with just three feet of light, which surprised me. I found a few coins that must have slipped from someone's pocket, and plenty of other cigarette butts. Right up against the wall of the cave, I narrowly avoided stepping in a pile of dog doo while checking out some crumpled sheets of paper. Stained with grease, they must have wrapped up someone's lunch.

"I wonder if they shared their lunch with the dog," I said, pointing.

Mart aimed his light to look and his eyebrows knit together.

"And look here. Looks like drag marks," he told me. The surface of the ground had been disturbed all around. His finger followed a path which ran from where we stood out of the circle of light and off to where the headlamp couldn't reach.

"Storage?" I guessed. "They use this cave for storage before the drugs are smuggled out of the country?" I guessed.

"Well, the whole of Belize is peppered with caves. They could make a convenient transfer point, I suppose."

"But not for the long term. There must be other warehouses in a town or village."

"Count on that," Mart said. "They'd have to ship the contraband from somewhere nearer roads and airports."

When I heard that word, "ship," I quit looking down and looked up instead, as the entire text of Clark's odd phone message popped into my brain like a well-loved phrase. Mart hadn't been the only one not telling all he knew and now it was my turn to blurt out a secret.

"Clark dropped his phone in the elevator our first night here," I said, which must have sounded like quite a change of subject.

"Oh?" Mart was still scanning the cave for clues.

"And I picked it up for him. He'd been reading a text."

Now, Mart stopped. He looked up swiftly, his headlamp pelting me in the eye with a piercing light.

Shielding my eyes, glad I couldn't see his expression, I repeated the phrase about shipments and uncles coming to call. "I don't know what it means. But it's obviously connected to the smuggling."

"That's definitely something else the feds will want to know," he said after a moment's ponder. "Thanks for telling me."

I'd expected him to ask why I'd kept the note to myself, but he didn't. Putting his hands on his hips, he said, "Wish we had a camera."

I thought of my tote bag, filled with the borrowed camera and my cell, far away back at the lodge.

"There's got to be a map of these caves in the brochure for this trip," I said. "We can amend it to add this branch." I indicated the tunnel we occupied. "That should be close enough for the authorities to investigate."

"We can't do much else right now," Mart said. "And we'd better get back before we're missed."

He reached for my hand again and we stepped carefully back the way we'd come into the central part of the cave where a few of the group were already back in the water.

I saw Clark give a sharp glance our way as Mart handed me into my inner tube. On this river voyage Mart had definitely been shirking his assistant director duties, but that's what the guide was for.

"Thought we were gonna have to come in after you," Dan teased, giving me a broad, knowing wink.

Elaine sighed mightily and stretched his name into three syllables. "D-a-a-n." She looked to me. "Never mind him. He has no romance in his soul."

Even as I smiled the heat of a blush warmed my cheeks. Elaine should only know how romantic it had been in the dark, avoiding dog doo and food scraps.

"But he does have a dirty mind, I think," Mart quipped in a tone so light I had to look over to where he bobbed beside me. His smile, which did so much to enhance his good looks, was genuine. Really, he was mercurial, slipping easily from off duty to on. Or from on to really on.

"It's always the ones you don't suspect," Jen piped up, splashing water in every direction as she paddled by.

Our river guide clapped his hands, calling for our attention, to explain the last leg of our journey.

It was easy to just float along in the chain of inner tubes, trailing a hand in the water and thinking. After I'd mulled our interesting discovery over in my mind for a few minutes, though, I let it go. It would be a shame—and a disservice to my blog readers—to not pay full attention to my surroundings now. Then, too soon it seemed, we were floating into a wider spot in the river and the trip was over.

"You are welcome to swim around as long as your time allows," the guide told us, indicating the path to the car park. "A five-minute walk and you will be back at your starting point," he explained, leaping up onto the bank beside the river.

Clark looked at his very expensive waterproof watch and told us we had a full ten minutes to splash around in the water if we were to remain on schedule.

"So hurry up and relax!" Patty shouted and there was laughter all around. Even Clark didn't take offense when the remark came from a pretty woman who wasn't his wife.

I flipped out of my tube, ready to be free of it again. Mart was ahead of me, floating lazily on his back. If he were thinking about anything important, you'd never know it from his blissful expression.

When athletic Clark engaged in a strong crawl directly in my path, I took the opportunity to let him have it.

"Hey, Clark, thanks for those great directions you gave me before. I was lost on those trails in about ten seconds," I said and I didn't smile.

He interrupted his stroke just long enough to say, "I encourage you to keep up with the tour group in the future."

I opened my mouth to respond, but never did. Mart was beside me, giving my arm a squeeze firm enough to leave marks.

"Let it go," he said in an urgent tone. "Until we can talk and figure things out, just let it go."

He grabbed me playfully around the waist with both hands then and swept me in a circle through the water, first one way then the other. I laughed, shaking water from my eyes.

"Race you!" I challenged, seeing others in our group head to shore.

"You're on!" Mart dropped me like a hot potato and headed off.

But I'm a strong swimmer, so I caught him easily and we called it even as we emerged from the water, laughing.

I didn't get lost on the short path back to the lodge since it was a straight shot and we were lined up like grade-schoolers on the playground. After a brief stop to retrieve our gear and change into dry clothes we all ended up in the parking lot clustered around the bus we'd come in.

According to our itinerary, we were in for another scenic ride north to the resort where we would spend the last two nights of our trip. Storm clouds were gathering on the horizon as I snagged a window seat. Chucking my tote bag onto the floor between my feet, I unfolded the promotional brochure I'd picked up on my way out of the lodge.

Color pictures touting the thrills and views of the river journey filled the front of the flyer. On the back, a simple map of the river was labeled with landmarks. One of the landmarks was the dry cave we'd been able to explore, the cave with the turning which led us to the signs of recent habitation.

I circled the spot with my pen and sketched in the darkened branch we'd gone down. Then I passed it over to Mart, looking for approval. He motioned for the pen, added an arbitrary line or two and nodded.

"That should do it," he said, folding the brochure and handing it back. "I'll get this to the authorities as soon as I can."

In less time than I would have imagined we were driving along the coastline, pulling into our new home away from home. As with our hotel, this was not a rustic old place steeped in national tradition. Instead, it was newer construction catering to the all-inclusive crowd.

From their seats at the rear of the bus, I heard the career girls crowing with pleasure at the sight of the fabulous and elaborate pools where they could swim straight up to the bar.

I gave a sigh of my own when I saw the cabanas we'd be staying in, sprouting on the shore like mushrooms on a forest floor. Up on stilts with thatched roofs and screened porches on the side facing the water, they looked cozy and exotic at the same time

"What a sunrise view!" I said, anticipating a few great pictures for the blog.

Some of them were capable of sleeping two, while others held four. Those of us on our own got the smaller huts at the end of the row, which suited me just fine. The group splintered as we each headed to our assigned hut, bags in tow.

As I walked, I saw lumpy gray clouds off to the west, making quite a contrast to the calm blue of the water. It looked like more rain was in store, but not anytime soon.

Stepping inside my hut, I dropped my suitcase and tote then took a look around. A big squashy chair filled one corner and one of those hanging basket chairs filled another. The smooth wooden floor was cool beneath my feet as I headed over to the big double bed. Separating the netting that hung over the bed from a ring in the ceiling, I stretched out to full length and sighed. Not for the first time I thanked my employer for giving me this little vacation—I mean, assignment. I pointed my toes, stretching my legs, and reached my arms over my head.

"Anyone home?" A few sharp raps on the doorframe accompanied the question.

I sat up, my heart giving a leap. Had I locked the door? "Yes?"

Mart strode in as if he belonged there. He took a long look at me, sitting in the middle of the bed, and raised his eyebrows.

"Why wasn't your door locked?" he said, jerking his thumb at the object in question. "With all that's going on, you've got to be more careful."

I pulled the netting apart and emerged from my cocoon.

"I was just going to," I said. "I wasn't expecting company quite so soon." Then I asked a question. "Are you unpacked already?"

"Unpacked?" he repeated. "We're only here for two days." He flopped into the squashy chair.

"Of course. Just let everything wrinkle," I said, smiling.

"And the rest of today is a free day to lie around or shop or whatever. I have 'whatever' on my list," he said, "and I wanted to invite you along."

I crossed my arms, tipping my head to one side. "Can you define whatever?" I made finger quotes.

Sitting forward, clasped hands between his knees, Mart said, "A long time ago, when I knew I'd be on this trip, I made arrangements to meet this guy. He's working with a conservation group here in Central America and has been instrumental in developing guidelines for what zoos can do."

The reporter in me came to life at his words. What a great interview that could be, dovetailing perfectly with my proposed series.

"I've e-mailed him and we've had a few telephone conversations, but I've never met him before. I'm really looking forward to picking his brain."

"And you're inviting me along to pick it with you?"

"Indeed I am," he said. He gave one of those big smiles, the kind that gave me an idea what he must have looked like as a boy. "You game?"

Did he expect me to beg off in favor of more swimming or shopping?

"Oh, yes! When?"

"Tonight, after dinner. I'm driving over to meet him about eight o'clock. So, let's leave at seven-thirty. Bring your notebook and at least two pencils," he teased, "because he's got a lot to share with us and I'm hoping he won't leave out a single word."

"Sounds great!"

He rose to leave, giving me a hug and a peck on the cheek.

"But not a word to anyone," he cautioned. "I don't want Clark to get wind. He'd only try to come along or ruin it somehow."

"Who would I tell?"

"I don't know. Jen, or maybe those giggly girls."

"As if they'd care!" I scoffed.

"Just—" he made the zip-your-lip motion, "okay?"

I didn't reply. I just made the zip-your-lip motion back.

Chapter Eighteen

Hours later, I had my arms around Mart, holding on tight. He felt firm and warm under my palms and I rested my cheek against the plane of his back. We were roaring along some bumpy road on a rented minibike just big enough to hold us both. Mart tried to steer around the potholes, I think, but there were so many he could only be so successful.

I was very glad I'd worn capris and not a skirt on this jaunt. Glad, too, that I'd brought a small notebook which fit in a pocket. My other pocket held only one pencil—and a lipstick.

"How much farther?" I shouted into my driver's ear.

"Not much!" he shouted over his shoulder. "We should be there in—"

I saw him take his eyes off the road to check his watch and gave him a pinch.

"Never mind. Just be—" a jounce from another rough patch interrupted my sentence, "careful," I finished.

At least our path was straight, not requiring many twists or turns. After my travel through the forest above the river I didn't want to see any forks in the road.

I'd been busy in the time Mart and I had been apart. The resort had a terrific internet connection, so I'd spent a good hour or more searching the archives of local newspapers for any coverage of Tommy Mendoza's "accidental" death. Only a few papers had noted the bit of news and even those were the briefest of entries. In the days and weeks immediately afterward, there were no follow-up stories.

Jen had said earlier, on one of our bus rides, that her friend had been along on that tragic trek. Shocked by the way Tommy Mendoza's absence went unacknowledged by Clark, she'd heard news of the zoo employee's death from their bus driver on the way to the airport.

What a buzz that must have caused, I'd thought now, clicking from the newspaper sites to my magazine's blog.

Clark had shifted attention away from Tommy and I had had to do the same. It was time for another blog entry. Time to post a few more snapshots. Time to do my real job. As usual, once I'd begun I became immersed in the challenge of finding the right words. The next time I'd looked up, I'd been amazed to see hours had passed.

As I'd hurried to shower and change, my heart skipped a beat faster at the thought of the evening to come.

And now, on the beach road, Mart shifted down, turning away from the coast, heading inland. We hadn't gone more than a mile or so when he pulled the bike onto a patch of gravel behind a two-story house surrounded by scrubby grass.

"Here we are," he announced into the sudden silence.

The house looked like a lot of houses I'd seen this week and the neighborhood did, too. The door opened before we had a chance to knock. A tiny little girl dressed in a pair of bright blue pajamas looked up at us with wide eyes.

"Umm," Mart faltered.

And then from just out of sight came a deep, booming laugh. "Teresa, I told you to wait for Papa."

The man who appeared swept the toddler into his arms and smiled at us. Just past thirty by my guess, he had very dark, very wavy hair. The tee shirt and shorts he wore showed off the impressive results of his workouts.

Shifting her so he could hold out a hand, he said, "Mart? Allison?"

So he knew to expect me, I thought, pleased.

"I'm Ricardo," he said as he shook my hand. "It's a pleasure to meet you. Mart's told me of the series you're doing for your magazine. It sounds wonderful. The animals need all the help we can give them."

He gestured us into the little house, saying he'd just tuck Teresa into bed and we should make ourselves comfortable.

Mart settled right down on the sofa along one wall, one hand instantly reaching into the bowl of cashews on the coffee table, but I wanted to look at all the pictures displayed opposite.

Family groups, a formal wedding portrait, and plenty of snaps of little Teresa filled nearly the entire space. There were black and white shots, circa the 1940s and 1950s, side by side with colorful panoramic views, making the wall a genuine collage.

"Ah, I see you're intrigued by people," Ricardo said, re-entering the room. "As I'd expect from a reporter."

"Can't resist a photo wall," I confessed, crossing the small space to sit beside Mart.

"My wife's handiwork," he said. "I'll pass along your approval when she returns. She would have enjoyed meeting you, I'm sure, but it is her night at school. She teaches reading through our church." Then, as he turned to Mart, the smile dropped off his face. "Let's get down to the brass tacks. Tell me how I can help you."

For the next ten minutes, Mart explained his desire to turn the Rochester zoo into a sanctuary, a haven for abused or endangered animals of every species. With his hands, he sketched in natural habitats, with people kept out of the way, as Ricardo nodded and murmured in agreement.

"An excellent plan," Ricardo said. "You present it well and that's important because you'll need to present it again and again."

"To benefactors?" I guessed. "To secure funding?"

"Yes. Have you looked into grants? Made any moves in that direction?"

Mart heaved a big sigh, glancing at me. "I've made a few forays but our director is definitely not on board with the concept and he's capable of making things difficult."

"Webster, correct?" Ricardo waited for Mart to nod. "I'm familiar with your boss. He's quite a force in the field."

"That's putting it mildly," Mart said, pushing his hand through his hair. "There are days—" he broke off and smiled.

"Ah, but public support is much more important." Ricardo turned to me. "That's where you could be essential."

"But I'm not an opinion journalist," I told him. "I just present the facts and people can reach their own conclusions."

"An informed and educated populace can change the world, Allison," he said. "Your facts, your articles, can do both—inform and educate—without leading readers by their noses."

I nodded. Information is power, I knew.

"And you are acting at the right time, Mart," Ricardo said. "Never have animals been as endangered. Not by the mere destruction of their homes and the pollution of our planet, but also by a growing criminal element, I'm afraid."

"Poachers?" I asked. "Trophy hunters?" I'd seen a few programs about that on public television.

"Yes, to both those. Plus, our animals are killed for their body parts. Fur. Organs. And then there are the smugglers, who treat rare species like bootleg liquor."

He made a soft but menacing growling sound, which was echoed almost immediately by a rumble of thunder from outside. Glancing out the window, I could see the dark clouds that had been on the horizon were now on the doorstep.

"There are more tigers in private homes than there are in the wild," Mart said.

"An excellent illustration. Every year hundreds of smuggled animals are confiscated by authorities. Some may still be alive, but many are not. And how many are killed to obtain the few who survive? It's devastating the already endangered populations of many, many species all around the world."

I'd pulled out my notebook and was scribbling now. "These crimes are on the increase?"

"Definitely. There is money to be made and no shortage of consumers."

"Just like the drug trade," I said.

"Just like," Ricardo agreed. "And of course some of the players of these dangerous games overlap."

Beside me, Mart straightened up. I could feel the electric charge of his attention like a crackle in the air. He leaned forward, elbows on his knees, hands clasped.

"Criminal corporations," he said. "I'd wondered about that."

I hadn't. I scratched another note.

"Are you talking globally or locally?" I asked.

"Think globally and locally, my dear," our host said with a humorless smile. "There is no animal without a price on his—or her—head."

I let my breath come out on a whoosh. Not a sigh of despair, but an overwhelmed exhale. Turning to Mart, I lifted my eyebrows. How could one little zoo make an impact on a global problem? I asked as much.

"Oh, it isn't just Mart's zoo taking action," Ricardo assured me. "While there is a bad trend toward animal trafficking, there's a good trend toward greater awareness and responsiveness to animals' needs. Why, just a few years back, no one blinked at the idea of elephants in zoo settings. Thirty or forty years standing in small concrete enclosures. Sometimes all alone! For decades! The physical and mental deprivation were never considered." He gave his head a brisk shake. "But, now, facilities around the world are closing or reconsidering elephant exhibits. And that's just one example."

"The journey of a thousand miles and all that," Mart said, reaching into the bowl of cashews again.

Another rumble of thunder filled the air around us. I darted a glance at the clock I could just see in the kitchen. Would we have to wait out the storm here before heading back on the minibike?

"I'd like to hear more about animal trafficking and its tie to drug trafficking," Mart said. "Are you aware of specifics? Any details you can share? I have a good reason for asking."

It took Mart a good five minutes to tell the tale of Tommy Mendoza and the suspected drug smuggling on zoo trips, and even I was surprised by the end.

"So just this morning we were in a cave with evidence of human and animal occupation," Mart concluded. "And it made me wonder, just for an instant, if the feds need to expand what they're looking for." It was his turn to raise his eyebrows at me.

The shiver that crawled from my neck to the small of my back had nothing to do with another sudden flash of lightning. It had everything to do, however, with the memory of my fall down the temple steps and that wild dash through the forest earlier in the day. The face of my attacker flashed before me and I widened my eyes.

"You mean Tommy Mendoza's drug smuggling turned into— or included—animal smuggling, too? While he was working at the zoo? While the zoo was sending him here on these educational junkets?" I asked. "But, that's monstrous!" My hand flew up to cover my mouth. I'd wake little Teresa if I didn't keep my voice down.

"Is that what you're suggesting, Mart?" Ricardo asked.

"Suggesting. Wondering. Proposing. None of the above?" Mart shrugged his shoulders. "Certainly I'd never had the thought before today, to my shame." He reached up to rub at his jaw. "I feel now like the idea should have at least crossed my mind!"

Ricardo reached across the space between them and gave Mart a hearty slap on the knee. "Do not beat yourself up about it, old man. Good people can't always imagine one horrific crime, let alone two."

"Let alone one like that!" I said. "To use zoo treks to smuggle— what? Animals? Animal parts? Or both?" I shook my head. "You're blowing my mind here."

"A gruesome irony, to be sure," Ricardo agreed. "If it's true."

"How will we know?" I asked.

"How will we prove it?" Mart clarified. He looked to Ricardo. "I know you have experience rescuing animals from bad situations. Any experience with types like these? Criminal types?"

In answer, our host lifted his shirt, revealing a long, shiny scar running from his ribcage down to the drawstring on his shorts.

"Just a bit," he said with a grin at our startled expressions. Letting the fabric drop, he said, "It looks worse than it is. We were confiscating some exotics—with the blessing of the law, I will add—and the owner of the facility was reluctant, shall we say, to relinquish control. It got a bit messy." Another smile. "But it did leave me with a story to tell. And best of all, the animals were removed to safety."

Mart swiped a hand over his mouth. "I'm glad the federal authorities are already on board with us."

"Tell them all your thoughts, Mart. And be careful who you trust. Think before you act. Think before you speak. Remember," Ricardo pointed a finger in emphasis, "your main purpose, where you will be the most useful, is helping get animals out of danger and to your sanctuary. No one can do it but you. You know you feel that's so, here." He clenched a fist, held it against his chest.

This man was a powerful speaker. So full of quiet confidence, exuding strength and determination. Looking from him to Mart, I saw the similarities in their expressions and knew it mirrored their commitment to, well, to changing a bit of the world.

Ricardo broke the tension in the room by rising. "I have something for you," he said, crossing the room to a desk off in a corner. The drawer gave a squeak as he opened it and removed something small enough to fit in the palm of his hand. "I've put together a list of contacts and background information on this," he said, handing Mart a flash drive. "Basically, it's a road map to everything I've learned on this journey to sanctuary. You may find it helpful."

Mart took the drive as if it were made of gold. To him, I knew, it was just as valuable.

"Thanks. I'll keep you posted on my progress."

Ricardo nodded. "Please do. And I'll be watching for your articles, Allison," he added.

My fingers tingled, wanting to type, to do my part, as I saw it. "May I e-mail you if I hit a snag and need an answer?"

"Of course." He turned back to the desk and retrieved a business card.

I tucked it into my pocket with thanks.

Taking a look out the window, our host gave us the boot. "I don't mean to rush you along, Mart, but if you want to beat this storm, you'd better head back." His eyes went again to the clouds and he assessed. "I'd say you've got about fifteen minutes."

"Will do."

Ricardo stood in the doorway as we climbed on the minibike, waving as the engine roared to life and we pulled off, into the night.

Pressing my cheek against Mart's back I held on tight. No one had patched any of the potholes in the hour we'd been gone. If anything, they felt deeper now. I could see Mart's face in the tiny mirror attached to one handlebar. His lips were tight with concentration and I wondered if he was thinking about all Ricardo had told us or just on getting back to our lodgings before the storm hit.

Off to my right, flashes of lightning put on a show obscured by tumbling clouds. The first drops of rain hit just as we gained the main road.

"That wasn't fifteen minutes," I said in the direction of Mart's ear and felt him chuckle.

"I'll be able to put the pedal to the metal now," he said. When I instinctively stiffened, he laughed again. "Only kidding. There's no speeding on roads like these."

The rain peppered our path, at first, but I knew that was merely the preamble to a big storm. And sure enough, just as the lights of the resort came in view the sky opened up. It was like standing under a faucet, the rain coming down hard and heavy. I pressed tighter against Mart, as if he offered some protection from the storm.

The wheels of the bike skidded coming out of one depression in the road and we lurched sideways. I would have let out a scream, but there wasn't time. Mart twisted the handlebars, put a foot down, twisted us back the other way.

Eventually, as we wheeled into the covered rental area of the resort, I let out the breath I'd been holding and released my death grip on Mart's shirt. When he climbed off the bike, I could see the crumpled mass of fabric around his waist, evidence of my tightened grasp. He helped me off then gave a smile to the attendant as he handed over the keys.

Turning to me he said, "Ready to sprint?"

The rain poured down undiminished. My little hut at the end of the row looked a very long way away across the sand. But I wasn't made of sugar and my adrenaline was high from the tension-filled travel.

"Race you!" Without looking, knowing he would take up the chase, I dashed out into the storm. My feet slapped against the sand in steady cadence. I could hear Mart just behind me as another rumble of thunder vibrated the air all around us. For a while it seemed I was running without making progress. The hut stayed just as far away, but then time caught up and we were side by side, chasing down the last few yards.

He laughed as we clattered up onto the tiny porch, stretching out an arm to touch the door first. "Ha!" he said. "I win!"

My breath came fast, my heart thumping. From the race? Or from the fact that he stood so very close and was so very wet and looked so very, very good that way.

"Claim your prize," I said and saw his eyes darken.

He dipped his head. I kept my eyes open until I felt his mouth warm on mine. The kiss lasted through the fumble over the threshold, into the room. I ran my hands up the soaking wet fabric of his shirt, cupped the back of his head in my palm, marveling at the jolt of desire surging through me.

His hands traveled down, leaving their own burning caress. My clothes were as wet as his, I could tell. Not only from the way they clung to my body, but also from the way he looked as he stepped back, sweeping his eyes over me. He made a sound like a cat's purr.

I intercepted his hand when it moved toward the buttons on my blouse.

"Is this all right?" I asked, a bit later than I should have. At his puzzled look, I hurried on. "I don't want to step on any toes. You know, you and Ishani."

Mart frowned. "Ishani? Why would—" he broke off, shaking his head. "Don't worry about Ishani. You are definitely not stepping on anyone's toes." He moved closer.

I moved back, my hand on his chest. I could feel his heartbeat under my palm. "You're sure?"

"I'm sure. It's nothing. Nothing special."

"Does she know that?" I had to know.

He gave a laugh. "She told me," he said. "Allison, trust me."

Some women might have hesitated even then. Might have waited, questioning. Might have turned away, uncertain.

But I, well, I gave my trust.

Chapter Nineteen

Chug. Chug. Chug. The noise of the boat's engine filled the air around us. It was the afternoon of the next day and our group was scheduled for a ride in a glass-bottom boat. The sun was shining high in the blue, blue sky and the turquoise water of the sea made the scene a tropical paradise.

Leaning back against the side of the boat, I inhaled a deep breath of fresh, clean air.

Mart, sitting beside me clad only in a pair of plaid swimming trunks, grinned. The engine racket made it difficult to talk so we contented ourselves with warm glances.

As we'd waited to board the vessel, Mart had taken the time to find Clark, giving him a news flash from my morning's e-mail. I'd gotten the okay from my magazine to do a series on zoos upon our return.

Clark hadn't looked pleased at the news, keeping his face stiff and immobile. Then, he had nodded and beamed in his best public relations fashion. "We'll be seeing plenty of you, then," he said. "I'm sure Mart will keep an eye on you, Allison." His eyes traveled swiftly from Mart to me. "He seems to be doing plenty of that already."

"I'm looking forward to the assignment," I said rapidly. "It's a great opportunity."

"Well, good luck with it." Clark gave a brief salute and moved off.

"Don't mind him," Mart remarked. "He's awfully . . . distracted lately."

"Truer words," I agreed, lifting my eyebrows.

Clark wasn't distracted now, however, as he stood near the glass panels cut in the floor of the boat. As trekkers took turns leaning over to view the magnificent spectacle of underwater life, he regaled us with facts, figures, and plenty of anecdotes.

During the week, he'd tanned to a smooth, even brown and, as he laughed, his teeth flashed white in a bright, seemingly carefree smile.

The boat anchored off the coast and, once the engine had stopped, the sound of the waves slapping the side of the craft beat a rhythmic tattoo.

Mart and I shared a window to the depths, our shoulders touching as we gazed deep into the water. A few minutes of that proved to be enough for him.

"C'mon, let's swim!" he suggested, pointing at several of our fellow tourists bobbing in the surf.

We were moving to the ladder at the side of the boat when one of the crew hauled up a net containing several starfish. He held it aloft and caught the attention of the group.

Mart froze and I nearly collided with him. "Just a minute," he told me and strode rapidly over to the net.

"Folks," he called out, "in the bad old days, this gentleman might be offering up these beautiful starfish for us to take home as souvenirs." He pointed at the net filled with the golden sea creatures. "He would also have known how to inject them with formaldehyde and kill them so they died with their arms straight. The better to sit solidly on our coffee tables back home." He beamed a smile which contrasted his harsh words, letting a poignant silence grow.

Even the crew member was stunned into silence, watching Mart carefully as the net dripped water onto the deck. The tour group was listening with rapt attention, all eyes riveted on that net, dangling heavy with the stacked starfish.

"Even now, these creatures are destined to be on live display for an afternoon or a day or a week. But since our purpose on this trip is to learn about conservation and protecting our natural resources, we'll just return these animals to their home," Mart went on, taking the net from the seaman. Walking to the side of the boat, he lowered it, depositing the starfish back in the water.

I started the applause which followed this compassionate gesture. Sudden tears filled my eyes when Mart brought the net up empty.

"Good work, Mart," Dan called out, making a thumbs up motion which several others repeated.

Humble, Mart bobbed his head in acknowledgment then returned to my side.

"That was a noble thing to do," I said, putting my hand on his shoulder.

"No, it wasn't," he told me. "It was the only thing to do." His cheeks were still flushed with anger as he bent and stretched, pushing off of the boat and arching gracefully out over the water. He entered with barely a splash and popped up a few seconds later, shaking his head like a dog.

I shucked out of my shorts and t-shirt, stripping down to my swimsuit beneath. Then, grasping my nose firmly, I stepped off into the water. As the sea swallowed me up, I had to stifle a giggle. Not for the first time on the trip, I was truly in over my head.

*

"So far today, I've been on terra firma and under the sea. Now, this!" I gestured at the helicopter sitting at the ready, just waiting for us.

The hour-long tour of Belize from the air came as an expensive option on this trip. Lucky for me, the *Breeze* had popped for it. I'd never been in a helicopter before and while it had all the unattractive aspects of plane travel—up high, close quarters, and no escape—it was only for an hour or so and I was sure the views would be well worth it. With only four passengers, we'd all have a window seat.

Back at the resort, I'd found our traveling companions were to be Jen and Elaine. They led the way to where the helicopter sat in the exact middle of a big circular target.

Mart was as excited as a little boy at Christmas. "This should be fantastic!" he said, eyes wide.

We were wrapping up our trip with nonstop activities today—the boat trip all morning and this in the afternoon. Tonight was the farewell dinner as one big happy family. And then, it would be off to bed. One way or another. I glanced at Mart from the corner of my eye and deliberately bumped my hip up against his as we walked. He bumped back enthusiastically.

The helicopter was bigger than I thought it would be when we got right up to it. Our pilot—mid-thirties and slight, with dark, deep set eyes—handed me into the craft with a warm smile. Aside from the frightening incidents I'd endured on this trip, everyone else I'd met here in Belize had been friendly, welcoming, and gracious.

The pilot made sure we were observing all the safety rules and gave us each a headset to wear so we could communicate.

"You can imagine it's pretty noisy in here," he said, pointing a finger up to where the rotor sat on the roof. "This way we'll be able to talk with each other. You wouldn't want to miss my running commentary," he said, winking.

In the seat just behind the pilot, Elaine bobbed up and down, her hands clasped together. "I don't want to miss anything!" She spread her arms wide. Well, as wide as she could in the enclosed space.

The minute we left the ground, incredible new scenes were revealed to us. The bird's-eye view was so completely different from our earthbound one, it was as if they were two worlds.

First, we traveled over the city, where the orderly rooftops and roads were at odds with the tumbled edge of the shoreline. Then, we zoomed off over the coast, where the water was a dozen shades of blue, just as the forest was a dozen shades of green. Riding low over the waves, we could see ruffle after ruffle of white curling water rushing in to shore. To our left, the view was endless azure water. To our right, the sweep of land.

We were heading for a place called the Blue Hole. I'd read about it online, preparing for the trip and our pilot repeated some of the same facts now. The ocean sinkhole was, at one thousand feet in diameter, the largest in the world. It would take us a while to get to it, since it was sixty miles east. I thought it sounded like one of the wonders of the world—I mean, imagine it! Indeed, I learned now it had been declared a national monument in 1999.

Flying low over the water, the helicopter cast a shadow on the tiny islands called cayes as we passed and once the pilot pointed out a pair of dolphins racing along beneath us.

"Oh, wow!" I said, pressing my nose closer to the glass. I knew I sounded like a little kid, but I felt like one.

In the seat before me, Elaine seemed as revved up as I was. We both had the same forward-leaning posture and barely contained excitement.

Mart said something, but I wasn't tuned in enough to hear it. Jen answered him in a nonchalant tone that didn't fool me. You couldn't be up here in this clear air on a bright afternoon, zipping over that mosaic of blues and whites, and be nonchalant.

"I wish Dan were here," Elaine said. "He would have loved this."

"Yeah, he really missed out," I agreed without taking my eyes off the swiftly moving scenery. "Why didn't he come?"

"He said he had enough of helicopters when he flew them back in the service," she said.

Then I remembered the tattoos on Dan's hands. Navy anchors, faded to a bluish green over the years.

"I said to him, 'But this will be different. Over the water and then over the forest.' But, no." She paused. "He can be stubborn," she said and I think we all knew that must be an understatement.

"Chance of a lifetime," Jen said, sounding a bit less casual. Then, she gave a gasp. "Look!"

And off in the distance, rapidly approaching was deeper, darker bluer blue, perfectly circular and surrounded by reef.

"Look at that!"

"Check it out!"

Mart and Jen spoke at once and our pilot chuckled. He must hear a lot of exclamations, I thought, and wondered if this view, this job could ever become monotonous. When we landed, I'd ask him. Squeeze in an interview. It would make a terrific blog entry.

The helicopter took a turn around the Blue Hole while we ogled at the windows. I snapped off a few pictures but they would never be adequate.

Gazing down into the navy blue of the hole, I asked, "How deep is it?"

"More than four hundred feet," the pilot told us as we took another lap around its perimeter.

Then, we were moving away from the wonder, heading inland.

I relaxed a little, sitting back in my seat. Mart put a hand on my knee.

"That was really something," he said, giving his head a shake. "I've never seen anything like it."

"What do you suppose caused it?" I asked our guide. "A meteor? Is it a crater?"

He shook his head. "It's a collapsed cavern."

"When did it collapse?" I wondered and he laughed.

"You have me there, miss. That answer, I do not have."

"Asking a lot of questions is her job," Elaine told him.

"Would you have time for an interview when we land?" I pushed Elaine's opening remark into a request of my own.

He nodded. "Certainly."

Looking out the window as we flew over the forest I noticed occasional breaks in the canopy of the trees. Down below us, squiggles of trails meandered here and there, like disorderly spider webs. If paths like those wove from cave to cave, connecting the underground cavities, how easy it would be for smugglers to move goods undetected, I thought.

Once we were back on earth, the others were more than willing to sit with the pilot and me over a cool drink for a bit of conversation. I took a bunch of notes, of course, and promised to send him a copy of the magazine when the article appeared.

Driving us back to the resort, Mart said, "I think you were right, Elaine. Dan should have come along."

"Yes, I mean, it's not like he couldn't afford it," Jen said, surprising me with her candor.

Elaine gave a chuckle. Over our time in Belize, her fair skin had tanned up a bit and the look suited her. Today, she was wearing a white top with bold floral splotches of color. Her capris were bordered in the same pattern. It was a casual outfit, but I had no doubt it would have cost me a day's pay.

"Oh, yes, we could have afforded it," she said now and I noticed her choice of pronoun. "But sometimes a woman has to give a man his head." She laughed again. "Poor Clark. My darling decided to tag along with him this afternoon and, well," she broke off, seemed to think about the wisdom of continuing and then hurried on, "when a major benefactor wants to tag along—"

"He tags along," we all chorused.

Mart and I exchanged a look when he took his eyes off the road just long enough to frown over at me for an instant.

"What was Clark doing?" I asked. "Must have been exciting."

"More exciting than our ride?" Elaine scoffed. "I don't think so." She turned her head to look out the window. "Some museum or other, I think."

We hadn't seen too many museums on this trip, so I was sure Elaine had the information wrong. Clark's last free afternoon to pursue his own interests—whatever they might be—and he was saddled with the blustery old rich guy. That would surely slow him down.

"How did you two meet?" I asked Elaine to make conversation.

Elaine blinked, as if trying to recall. I suppose when you've been married years and years that memory dims.

"We met at a peace rally back in the swinging sixties."

"You have got to be joking," Jen said, incredulous.

"You don't need to sound that surprised," Elaine said. "Dan came back from the war ready to work for peace. That happened to lots of our boys. As for me," she shrugged. "I considered it the very best of Good Works." Her tone gave the words capital letters.

"What do you mean?" I asked as Mart slowed the car for a series of potholes.

"Oh, back in the day, we debutantes did all sorts of community-minded things. Debs still do, of course."

"Debutante." Jen said the word as if it were encased in filmy pink tulle. Had we unearthed the romantic dreamy part of her personality?

"Yes. Daddy expected it and Mama insisted. I've got the pictures at home. Long, white gown. Long, white gloves."

Jen blinked now, looking at the tiny older woman. Seeing the younger version? I know I could.

"You can imagine what they thought of Dan!" Elaine said, smiling in memory. "Such a cliché we were—the rich girl and the boy from the wrong side of the tracks."

"Sounds like a romance novel to me," I said, a sucker for a great story. I made a note to check the magazine's archives for their original wedding announcement. Throughout this trip, I'd tried for a few quiet moments with each trekker, to get their story, so my articles would show personalities. This could prove to be a terrific angle for theirs.

Elaine turned her gaze on me. "That's what I always thought, too. Just like a novel. I've read my fair share of those books over the years and my favorite ones always had the couple starting out as imposters. You know, pretending to be engaged for her high school reunion or so he can inherit his auntie's estate."

"And then they fall in love for real," Jen finished, nodding her head.

"Exactly!" Elaine said. "Well, that was us. I looked like just another college girl working for social justice and Dan looked like he'd been walking picket lines for years. Turns out we were both at our first event."

"First of many?" Mart asked.

"Oh, yes. We don't march in circles too much anymore, but we've always tried to do Mama's Good Works with Daddy's money." She laughed again.

"You've been very successful," Mart said. "The whole city owes you two debts of appreciation." He turned the car onto the road leading to the resort.

"Thank you, Mart." Elaine leaned over the seat to pat his shoulder. "Sometimes you're not sure if you've made the right choices in life. Dan struggled with joining Daddy's business—and God knows I struggled, too."

She turned her head to look out the window. None of us said anything, waiting for her to finish her thought.

"But it all comes right in the end," she said with finality.

"Happily ever after," Jen pronounced and there was only a hint of underlying cynicism to her voice.

"Something like that," Elaine said as Mart wheeled into a parking space near the door of the main facility.

"Let's get something to eat," Mart suggested. He indicated my notebook, still open on my lap. "Do you want to come or do you have work to do?"

"I think I've got time for a snack," I said, taking a peek at my watch. "It's hours until the farewell dinner."

Mart shut the car door behind me and slipped an arm around my waist. "I'd really like to skip that obligation," he said, lips close to my ear, "and take you off to that big bed in your tiny cabana."

That tingly feeling of excitement began somewhere deep inside me as memories of the night before flooded my brain.

Looking into the dark pools of his eyes, I said, "We can always leave early."

*

That night, Mart and I slipped away from the noisy dining room as planned and walked along the quiet, sandy beach. The sky was gray with twilight and palm trees swayed in the tropical breeze. It was an idyllic end to our day.

"All in all," Mart said, "it's been an eventful week."

Thinking back, I had to agree. "Do you think Clark made any progress trying to locate Tommy Mendoza's killer? It doesn't seem as if he'd been trying very hard. He's been around the group too much to go off searching for clues."

"Yeah," Mart agreed, but in an offhand way. As if, I hoped, those weren't the events he was referring to.

The light was fading and the moon had come out and it was all terribly romantic.

I began to hum a tune from some old 1940s musical, about moonlight and old lace and true love. Instead of groaning or laughing, Mart started to sing, his deep baritone a fine complement to my soprano warbling. When he ended the tune by whirling me around, dipping me low in his arms with the last note, I could have died from sheer delight. Instead, I pointed a toe in what I hoped was a graceful fashion and draped my arms at my sides.

Mart dropped a kiss on my upturned chin then lifted me back to my feet. "You like old movies?" he questioned the obvious, still holding my hands.

"Very much so!"

"What's your favorite?"

"Musical?"

"All time. All-time favorite."

"Oh, well, my all-time favorite is *Rear Window*. But there's no singing in that," I pointed out.

"There's plenty of mystery, though."

"Yes. I love a mystery," I confessed with relish.

Mart cringed. "And here you are in the middle of a real one."

"Drug trafficking, animal smuggling, Tommy Mendoza's murder," I said as Mart sighed. "I'm surprised you didn't hear more stories about him from the other employees at the zoo."

"Oh, I heard plenty. But I heard them all after his murder. Everyone was just a Monday morning quarterback."

"What do you mean?"

"They always knew he was trouble. His criminal characteristics were obvious. They'd always suspected. That sort of thing."

"But nothing definite? No one ever actually saw him with anyone or anything?" I clarified.

Mart nodded. "To the best of my knowledge, all the evidence against the guy is circumstantial. Still, he's dead now. Shot in the head and left tangled, on display."

We walked on, then turned and began retracing our steps back to the resort. My mind was working on this puzzle as if it were a word game—thinking, pondering, and finally just guessing. At last, I gave voice to the thought I'd just had.

"Wouldn't it be horrible if Clark was actually in on all this? Taking over where Tommy left off instead of helping the feds or trying to find Tommy's killer?"

"I know I said Clark would do anything for a buck, Allison, but he'd never do that." In the soft shadows of the evening, I couldn't quite read Mart's expression when he repeated the words. "No, Clark would never do that."

Chapter Twenty

Morning sun beamed onto the placid water alongside the cabana's little front porch. I should have been scurrying around, tossing things into my luggage, checking for my ticket home, corralling all the souvenirs I'd picked up over the past week.

Instead, I sat with my feet up on the railing, contemplating this day, this week, this assignment, and all it had meant—so far.

In an hour, we'd leave this place and travel to an animal sanctuary for a tour of the facilities. Then, it was off to the airport.

And tonight I'd be home—eating in my own kitchen, sleeping in my own bed. Probably alone.

I frowned. Certainly these next few days would tell me whether there was anything to this thing I was developing with Mart. If I was just his girl for this trek, I'd know it when he didn't call, or return my calls.

This morning, when he'd left me only minutes earlier, my body still felt the touch of his hands and his lips, making it difficult to imagine our affair as a fleeting one.

With a sigh, I dropped my bare feet onto the smooth wooden decking. I could sit here all day and never be able to predict my own future. Or Mart's. Best to just let it all play out.

"Loosen up on the reins," my father used to say whenever I'd felt anxious or nervous. "Ally, honey, take a deep breath."

In honor of Dad, I straightened up. Then, I took that deep breath, pulling my hands to my chest in prayer. Raising my arms overhead, palms together, I swept them back to where they had begun.

There, that felt better.

"Thanks, Dad," I said aloud, smiling, and turned to head inside. It was time to pick up the pace.

*

"Most of the animals here are rescues. Orphaned by poachers, held as exotic pets until they grew too big, displaced by mankind," Mart told us as we clustered around him at the entrance to one of the area's animal sanctuaries.

Clark, I noticed, paid little attention to his subordinate, standing off to one side and behind us, fiddling with his cell phone.

It seemed a shame we'd kept the sanctuary for last because our group seemed weary this morning, as if a part of all our minds was already back in the States, contemplating backlogs at work and in the laundry room.

That all changed, though, as we meandered the paths, at last able to see some of the native animals we'd not spotted on our travels. A jaguar slept nearly out of sight in one spot, while a wild pig, called a peccary, grazed calmly in another area. We watched for kinkajous and tree otters, which were called tayras, according to a sign posted nearby. Another creature, called an agouti, looked like a big rat with no tail.

"Three blind mice, three blind mice," Dan sang the childhood rhyme. When I looked puzzled, he said, "You know, cut off your tail with a carving knife?"

"Oh, yeah." I gave a shudder and hurried along on the chipped-wood path to keep up with the rest of the group.

"Can you see the contrast?" Mart asked as we stood watching a tapir with only a thin wire fence between us. "Here, we walk through their world, as unobtrusively as possible. Rather than," he broke off, not needing to go on.

"Well, why don't you try something like this in Rochester?" Elaine asked in genuine innocence.

"Yeah," Dan agreed. "Kids would love it, I'll bet. Big draw for the place."

If Mart could have crowed with pleasure, he would have.

Mart's boss, meanwhile, remained silent, just nodding his head when Dan looked at him. It was an unconvincing nod, anyone could see.

Continuing our tour, we circled round. I took more pictures for the blog, posing my fellow trekkers in groups, waving them to stand closer and not in a shadow.

"You remind me of my mom," Patty called out from her spot sandwiched between her friends. "Always the photographer, ordering everyone around."

"Yeah, my mom, too," Kiran agreed. "That way she managed to stay out of every shot!"

"I'm not staying out!" I said, clicking off a few more pictures. Handing the camera to Patty, I took her place at the center of the group and smiled when she said, "Cheese!"

"There's a keeper!" Patty said. "Want me to get one of you and Mart?" she asked.

I blinked, looking to him and realizing we didn't have any pictures of just the two of us.

"That'd be great," he said, stepping up and putting his arm around my suntanned shoulders. His fingers gave a squeeze and I relaxed against him. Slipping my arm around his waist, I put my finger through his belt loop.

"Smile!" Patty ordered, smiling herself. Then, "Got it!" She checked the screen on the back of the camera. "Aw! It's really nice!"

When she handed it to me, I looked, wanting it to be a good picture. One I could keep always, no matter what.

And there we were, hips together, bodies casually touching, our smiles full and real. If you saw the photo and didn't know, would you? I wondered. Did we look as if we'd spent the night just so— hips together, bodies touching?

"You make a cute couple," Faith said. "At least one of us landed a guy on this trip."

Recalling their lamentation about male to female ratio, I had to laugh. "I suppose your next trip will be back to the beach," I said.

Kiran shrugged. "But it's been really amazing here. That last resort had some guys. Maybe next time we can aim for that. Some education and some opposite sex."

"Now there's a goal!" Patty said.

I chuckled as I turned away from the group, my eyes searching out not Clark or Mart, but the restrooms. They weren't far off and I scurried on over, not wanting to miss any of the tour, since the gift shop was next.

I'd just emerged from the facilities and was advancing on the gift shop when I noticed my shoelace undone. Squatting down near the wall of the building, I dealt with it quickly, making it a double knot for good measure. I was still crouched there when I heard voices from just around the corner.

Funny thing, I overhear people talking all the time, but I can really tell when a conversation isn't meant for any other ears. This was one of those.

"For you." The voice was warm and masculine.

"Oh!" A female, surprised. "But you shouldn't—"

"No, honestly, it's okay. Open it."

That was the professor talking! But, to whom?

There came the sound of gift opening—no wrapping paper torn, but a box lid lifted, a rustle of tissue. Then—

"Oh! It's lovely! Thank you!" A kiss, light and quick. "Put it on for me."

Silence. Another kiss. A murmur of contentment.

"Thank you so much, darling. I'll think of you every time I wear it."

"And I hope plenty of other times, as well." A chuckle.

"Of course! Of course!" Emphatic, then, a sigh. "If only—"

"Ssh. Don't start. Let's just take what we can. This moment."

Another kiss.

My toes were getting cramped, but I didn't dare move. The last thing I wanted was for them to realize someone else had heard them, because I'd recognized the woman's voice now.

It was Sylvia Webster.

Stunned by this interesting turn of events, I totally didn't notice anyone coming up behind me.

"Hey!" Jen greeted me, managing to put a question into the word. "What are you doing?"

I stood up, squeezing my toes inside my shoes to get the blood flowing again. "Tying a shoelace," I said.

"Oh. You just looked funny down there," she went on, in a voice that would certainly carry around the corner.

"Just tying a shoelace," I repeated in a sing-song voice. Nothing to see here, people. Move along. "Have you been in the shop yet?" I asked to distract her, but she only frowned.

Pointing, she said, "I'm heading there now. Like you." She made a face as if wondering if the heat had gotten to me.

"Oh, great! Let's go!" I took a few quick steps in that direction, certain she'd follow.

And she did. We'd taken about three steps when we encountered Sylvia and the professor, now standing about six feet apart and looking self-consciously nonchalant.

"Hey!" Jen greeted them casually with a lifted hand and kept walking.

I lifted a hand, too, and moved my lips into a smile, but I could tell from the look on Sylvia's face that she knew I had heard the lovers' remarks.

"Can you fit another souvenir in your luggage?" I asked Jen and her answer segued us neatly into the store and away from Sylvia and the man she loved.

But dodging the zoo director's wife was not as easy as all that, which didn't surprised me.

I hadn't stayed long in the shop, just taking time to pick up a few postcards and then stuff all my remaining quetzales into the donations jar on the counter.

Emerging into the sunlight, I blinked and pondered the way back to the entrance. Sylvia came at me from a big tree she must have been hiding behind, approaching at a good clip.

She grabbed my arm hard, her long fingernails making quite an impression, and when she pulled me in the direction of the shadowy corner where I'd tied my shoes, I brooked no argument.

"Geez, Sylvia, lighten up," I whined, rubbing my arm when she let go. "What's wrong?" As if I didn't know.

"Don't give me that!" she said. Her eyes flashed with something that wasn't anger, exactly, or fear.

"Look—" I began, but she shook her head.

"No, you look. I know you were snooping before. Eavesdropping like a common gossip. And I know you heard."

She was taking quite a risk here. Maybe I hadn't heard. Maybe her guilty conscience was making her say too much. I remained silent.

"So I am going to politely ask you to forget it. Wipe it from your memory and hold your tongue."

There was nothing polite in her request and her own tongue was barbed with a poisonous accent.

"Who do you think I'm going to tell?" I asked. "Your husband? Mart?"

I shook my head. There was no way I'd take on Clark in a domestic dispute and Mart might be curious for about ten seconds and then not care. Besides, I was not a common gossip.

"Sylvia, don't worry. Your secret is safe with me." I drew an X over my heart. "Honestly. But why you'd bring your lover on the same vacation as your husband, I can't understand." Really, it defied logic.

"He wasn't supposed to be here!" Sylvia hissed at me, the irritation in her voice clearly directed at Clark. "He just came along at the last minute. If only Mart had been leading the group, it would have been easy. He's so lost in his own wild world of animals he never pays attention to anyone else." She broke off and her eyes swept quickly over me from head to toe. "Until now," she added and I felt disproportionately pleased.

"Maybe Clark suspects," I suggested, but she laughed.

"And maybe I'll flap my arms and fly to the moon," she said.

Which made me wonder why Clark had made the sudden decision to come along on the trek to Belize. To find Tommy Mendoza's killer? To keep an eye on Mart and throw a spanner into Mart's sanctuary plans? Or to keep an eye on his wife, who was having an affair with a man who was not exactly what he claimed?

"Just keep your mouth shut about. . . ." Sylvia said, trailing off to wave her hands in the direction of the spot she and the professor had occupied earlier. "Give me your word."

My word. That was easy enough. Honest enough.

I made an X again and said quite solemnly, "Cross my heart and hope to die."

Chapter Twenty-One

The hubbub at the airport swirled all around me as I stood at the airport ticket counter. I was ending my trip as I'd begun it, waiting in line.

Our little group was scattered around the open area of the lobby, holding packages, sitting on luggage, exchanging addresses.

Holding my boarding pass, I moved away from the counter, my eyes scanning the room for Mart. When I finally spotted him, my breath caught in my throat and my chest tightened.

Off in a far corner near the entrance, Mart was deep in conversation with the hotel singer, Ishani. She was standing too close to him, looking marvelous in denim shorts of an indecent length and a layered tank top which highlighted her tanned and toned arms.

My hands started to tremble as I watched them and I cursed my own weakness. Still, nothing short of an earthquake would have made me look away. Ishani was talking, urgently, intently, leaning toward him and gesturing with her hands. Mart was wearing his solemn look, listening and nodding, asking questions then nodding again.

At one point, he glanced over at the big clock on the wall then put a hand on her arm, interrupting the flow of her words. It was her turn to nod, that long veil of hair moving like a silk curtain in a summer breeze.

She reached up to place her hand against his chest. The kiss she placed on his cheek was chaste and brief; but a kiss, nonetheless. The hug they exchanged lasted longer.

I blinked, feeling stunned, and pivoted. The ladies' room was located nearby and I hurried to it, needing a few minutes alone to get my bearings.

Leaning against the sink looking at my pale reflection, I chided myself for overreacting. Mart wasn't mine. Really, we barely knew each other. Sure, we'd shared some good times this past week, and weathered a few bad ones, as well. And yes, I had thought something had begun between us. But I must have been wrong. I gave a little laugh. Must have. When I sighed, it came out as a quiver, ragged at the end.

"Oh, snap out of it!" I chided that woman in the mirror. Then I splashed cold water against my eyes and fished in my bag for some lipstick. After brushing my hair a few swift, almost painful, strokes, I felt better. Squaring my shoulders, I pressed my lips together, blotting the lipstick. I wouldn't forget what I had seen—couldn't if I tried—but it was time to pull myself together and rejoin the group or I'd miss the plane. I laughed at that image. Ishani and I standing on the runway, waving our hankies at the disappearing plane. The instant of comic relief helped and I walked outside smiling.

"There you are!" Mart exclaimed, coming toward me looking casual and happy. I resisted the sudden and very infantile urge to kick him on his exposed shins and instead echoed his phrase.

"Here I am! Were you looking for me?"

"Yeah. I wanted to talk to you." His head turned, eyes darting rapidly in both directions, looking for—who? "But it's too late now."

The call for our flight came over the loudspeaker in a tinny, garbled voice and we obediently lined up.

"Look," Mart's hand grasped my arm and his eyes burned with intensity, "I've got a lot to tell you. Things I just learned this morning, but we don't dare discuss it on the plane. We could be overheard."

I nodded and Ishani faded quickly from my thoughts.

"We'll talk once we're home. Over dinner?" he suggested.

"Sounds good."

"Okay. I've got to run. I want to be close to Clark on this flight, so I can keep an eye on things. Maybe do a spot of eavesdropping.

So, if I don't see you, we'll meet up at the airport in Rochester."

I bobbed my head and shuffled along as the line advanced.

Mart dropped a quick kiss on my forehead and was gone.

He gave kisses and he got kisses, I thought. Which meant more?

*

To me, flying is like being in my living room on a rainy afternoon. I can't go outside, so I have to curl up with a good book and settle in.

I didn't have a book, but I did have my notes and, as the hours ticked by, I composed another blog entry. This one, a teaser for a longer article to run in the food section, detailed the varied cuisine we'd enjoyed. I like to eat, but writing about food just makes me hungry.

Still, focusing on hunger was preferable to focusing on the image whirling in my mind. Mart with Ishani, looking so intense, so connected.

Well, Ishani was back in Belize and I was here with dinner plans, I reminded myself. And I was a big girl, not a teenager jabbed by Cupid's first arrow. Plus, I had a job to do and just now that meant saying farewells, collecting phone numbers, and arranging lunch dates with my new acquaintances.

In the Rochester terminal, I watched all my fellow trekkers scatter off toward home then turned to Mart, waiting for me with my suitcase as well as his own.

As we emerged from the airport entrance, I was surprised to see one of the zoo's maroon vans parked at the curb. The trendy zoo logo was splashed on the side and the engine idled as a driver patiently waited behind the wheel.

"Is this for you?" I asked Mart and he laughed at my assumption. "Oh, no. Only Clark and Sylvia get picked up. My car's in the parking garage." He pointed at the looming concrete structure. "Is your car there, too, or do you need a lift?"

I'd taken the bus out last week and welcomed the ride. "Sure, thanks! How come the Websters don't use their own car?"

"He's the director, silly," Mart kidded me. "Since the trek was technically zoo business, he used a zoo vehicle for transportation."

We moved past the van and into the crosswalk. It was much cooler here at home than it had been in Belize and I turned up the collar of my light cotton jacket. I looked over my shoulder in time to see Clark and Sylvia emerge and make a beeline for the vehicle. I kept watching while they stowed their luggage in the back and climbed inside.

Since I wasn't looking where I was going my toe stubbed on a bit of uneven pavement and I stumbled. Mart caught my elbow when I would have fallen.

"Gosh, Allison! Be careful! What's so interesting, anyway?" He shot a glance backward.

The van had pulled away from the curb and, instead of moving out onto the street, had circled around onto a service road which disappeared behind the terminal.

"That's odd, hmm?" I questioned. "Where are they going?"

Mart shrugged, trying to make the gesture come off casual. The vertical line between his eyebrows gave him away, though. He thought it was strange, too.

I quickened my pace and tugged at his sleeve. "C'mon! Let's get to your car and follow them!"

"Follow them?"

"Look, we know he's just returned from a trip to a foreign country. He came along on the trip at the very last minute. And he's been communicating with smugglers." I ticked off my reasons on my fingers.

The daylight vanished as we entered the parking garage and I blinked at the sudden change of light.

It seemed to me urgency was called for here, so I gave his arm another yank, swiveling my head in both directions as if I knew what kind of car to look for. It was even cooler in the garage. Cold, actually, and I stomped my feet to keep warm.

"If we see nothing, there is no harm done. If we see something. . . ." I let the sentence trail off, putting both hands out, implying there could be a big payoff.

He jerked his head to the right. "This way." I trotted along behind him past an endless row of automobiles. The air was heavy with the odors of oil and exhaust and I wrinkled my nose in distaste. The contrast to the land we'd just come from—with its fresh air and unspoiled landscape—was tremendous.

"Here we are." Mart stopped beside a brown, two-door compact car. As he popped the trunk and pitched our suitcases inside, I stood with my hand on the passenger door, tapping my feet.

The engine didn't start when he turned the key, but just grinded and grinded.

"It's been sitting here for a whole week," Mart said in explanation, trying again. "It'll catch this time."

Eventually, after a lifetime or two, it did.

We left the garage behind and were soon on the service road where we last saw the zoo van. When we turned the corner around the terminal, the airport's runways stretched off into the distance on our left. On the right was an area designed for loading cargo. Big gaping doors revealed a beehive of activity within. Forklifts zipped hither and yon. While men and women with clipboards and headphones stood together in conversation. And everywhere, boxes and crates rose in high stacks.

Mart stopped the car near the open doors and almost immediately a uniformed young man appeared at the window.

"May I help you, sir. This is a restricted area." He was polite, but his tone was firm.

Mart was ready with a story. "Yes. Well, I'm here to pick up the shipment for the Rochester Zoo. It was on flight 822," he said matter-of-factly, referring to our plane.

The man consulted his clipboard and I held my breath, leaning across the seat so I could see and hear better. After flipping a page back and forth and back again the security guard shook his head. "No, that was already picked up. Just a few minutes ago."

"What?" Mart feigned surprise surprisingly well. "I was distinctly told. . . . Well, never mind. I'd just better be on time for the next load. How often do the Belize packages arrive?" The question slipped glibly out, causing barely a ripple of suspicion in the workman but an inward gasp from me.

The man thought a moment then shrugged. "Once a week? Twice? Hard to say."

Mart nodded. "Thanks. I'll have to check with the director so this mix-up doesn't recur." Lifting his hand in a wave, he executed a three-point turn and we headed back to the main road, merging onto the freeway.

"Does the zoo receive shipments from foreign countries on a regular basis?"

Mart kept his eyes firmly on the road. "Hmm. Well, naturally we're constantly receiving packages for everything from office supplies to veterinary tools. From a foreign country? Produce for some of the animals. But Clark certainly wouldn't be the man to pick it up. That's hardly in his job description."

"What do you think, then? What's up?"

"I don't know what to think, quite frankly."

We lapsed into silence then Mart said with a note of humor, "Allison, I've been driving for ten minutes and I don't know where you live! Am I going the right way?"

Chapter Twenty-Two

The next day, I was back at work, struggling to turn all my notes into lively and informative sentences for readers of the *Rochester Breeze*. I was having a hard time separating all the unscheduled adventures and intrigues from the official ones on our itinerary.

When Mart and I had stopped for dinner on the way home from the airport, he'd added even more intrigue into the mix.

"You know, I forwarded your Tikal pictures to the feds," he told me.

"And I heard today they've been forwarded again, to Washington." Mart's eyes were big.

I dipped a French fry into ketchup. We were at the Big Burger Barn, eating off plastic trays. "What will happen there?"

"They'll run them through the facial recognition system," he said, faltering, "or something like that, and try to put a name to the face."

"But I didn't get any really good pictures," I said. "None straight on anyway."

"Doesn't matter!" Mart said, reaching for another fry. "So now we wait to hear if they can ID the guy."

Today, I'd spent most of the morning in idle chit-chat around my desk. My coworkers were understandably eager to hear about the trip and I was more than willing to tell them about the wonders of the rain forest and the ruins.

"And how were the Underwoods? I heard they were along," Angela, the copy editor, asked.

"Yes, they were there." I shifted in my chair, crossing one leg over the other. "Do you know them?"

"Not personally," she said.

"But everyone knows them," Steve, from advertising, said, and of course that was true.

"Dan and Elaine Underwood own the biggest industry in town," Angela reminded me.

"He doesn't seem like a captain of industry, though," I said, picturing the white-haired old man, face gleaming in the heat.

"That's part of his charm, I guess," Angela said. Her voice held all the frustration of an overworked, underpaid employee who will never make it into those upper tax brackets.

"He is charming in his own way," I admitted. "We spent plenty of time together, too." I told them all about our day at Altun Ha and the climb up the temple steps.

"I thought I might look up their wedding notice. Do a human interest story," I concluded. "What do you think?"

A discussion ensued and opinion was split. Some staff thought a feature on the Underwoods would make fascinating reading. Other folks thought the idea was awful.

In the end, of course, the editor made the decision.

"That sounds like a nice, uplifting companion piece," Brian told me when I proposed it. He smiled with his words. Knowing I didn't want to do nice uplifting articles as my life's work, the irony of my suggestion struck us both.

"But you'll cut me more slack on this zoo piece, right?" I pressed for permission and he nodded.

"Just do the Underwood thing first," he said, instructing me to set up an interview with the couple and write a short piece on their travels. Obediently, I called and arranged to see them at their home later that afternoon.

The Underwood's house was huge, styled after a French chateau. It perched on the bluff overlooking Kirkwood Lake and was approached by a gracefully curving driveway that circled around the entrance. Out front, bordered by the drive, was a carved stone fountain featuring a replica of the Three Graces.

I let out a long, low whistle as my old car rattled up the road. Good thing I'd worn one of my best outfits—a graphic print wrapdress, topped by a knee-length navy trench.

Dan greeted me at the door, taking me by surprise. I'd expected a butler. Or a maid in one of those little white hats.

"Allison!" He swept me into a friendly hug, then stepped back to let me in. "Elaine's going to meet us in the study. This way. All recuperated from the trip?" He kept up a steady stream of chatter as we walked.

"Yes, but it's good to be home, isn't it?" I said. Could you feel at home, I wondered, in a house this big?

My head swiveled from side to side as I struggled to take in the elegant surroundings. We passed a marble open stairway and on the landing, a life-size portrait of Elaine held court. In the painting, she was attired in a green evening gown, and held a single white rose.

I stopped for a closer look.

"How lovely!" I exclaimed, interrupting one of Dan's lengthy stories.

He followed my gaze up the stairs, and sighed. "Yes. The artist truly captured the old gal." His voice had gone soft for just an instant, but it was long enough to let me see how much he truly cared for Elaine.

"How long have the two of you been married?" I asked as we resumed walking.

"Forty-two years," Elaine piped from a doorway about twenty feet away.

"I knew that. I was going to say that," Dan said.

"Yes, dear." Elaine gave me a hug and a kiss on both cheeks, then waved us inside and we entered the book-lined study. A huge stone fireplace dominated most of one wall, its mantle covered with photographs.

Curious, I moved closer to inspect them. There was a picture of the Underwoods on their wedding day, Dan wearing tails, Elaine in a very plain, very sophisticated floor-length gown. Her long filmy veil swirled around them like fog. Another photo showed them with a former president, and one featured an old, gray-muzzled dog who was obviously a well-loved family member. But the one that grabbed my eye was of Dan and Elaine in the recent past.

They were standing underneath a tall tree like you see in travel brochures of Africa. Standing between them, one arm wrapped casually around their shoulders, was a young man with auburn hair and dark, close-set eyes. Like them, he was dressed in safari garb, but, unlike them, he was not smiling. His features wore a blank expression, as if he was carefully holding back any emotion, enduring the picture-taking while his mind was somewhere else.

I remembered Elaine telling me they'd gone on other zoo treks, so I thought I knew who the man must be.

"Tommy Mendoza?" I asked, picking up the picture and bringing it closer.

"Yes!" Elaine confirmed my guess. "That was taken a few years back." Her voice dropped off and she added sadly, "Before the . . . accident. Such a tragedy."

I returned the picture to its place and glanced at Dan. He didn't seem too broken up at the memory.

"He was an all right guy, I suppose. Followed orders. Did his job. Can't say I was especially fond of him, though. He used to cheat at cards, greedy bugger."

My eyes grew wide with this tidbit of knowledge.

"So you claim, dear, but you'll never convince me!" Elaine took the dead man's side.

"Well, you . . . you were like all the gals about him. Don't know what any of you ever saw in the man."

"You're just jealous," Elaine teased.

"Was he along on all your zoo trips?" I asked.

"Oh, yes. Every one." Elaine lowered herself onto a flowered sofa and patted the cushion beside her. "Sit, dear."

As I complied, I pushed on. "How did he die, again? Mysterious circumstances?"

Okay, I was pushing my luck here, but it seemed worth a try.

They exchanged a look before Dan spoke. "We were told there was an accident."

"Sounds like you don't believe that," I said, looking to Elaine, who gave a shrug.

"It's dangerous country," Dan said baldly. His finger was up at his ear, fiddling with his hearing aid. He'd had so little trouble with the device on our journey I couldn't help thinking the fiddling was an avoidance tactic.

"I suppose the truth will always be a mystery," I remarked and there were murmurs of agreement from my hosts.

We talked for a bit about their travels and I used my recorder so I wouldn't miss a quote. After an hour or so, I'd collected more material than I'd ever be able to use and brought the discussion to a close.

It had been a very pleasant afternoon, complete with coffee and homemade cookies. They might own a big fancy house, but here in the study, where it seemed they spent the most time, they had a warm and cozy home.

"We'll be sending a photographer, if you don't mind," I told them, rising from the sofa.

"Better put your lipstick on, Elaine," Dan teased. Stopping on his way to the study door, he said, "I took the liberty of having a duplicate set of our photographs made at the one hour place. When you called about doing this article, I thought maybe you'd like to use some for illustrations." He moved around me to a table near the window and opened a drawer.

He pulled out a package two inches thick. "Elaine's a little snap-happy," he said at my raised eyebrows.

"Guilty as charged!" she said, laughing. "But they're all darn good."

Taking the package, I said, "Thanks, Dan. I appreciate it. Of course, I can't guarantee they'll be used. That decision rests with the editor."

"Certainly, certainly." Dan bobbed his balding head in understanding.

"You can always keep them for your scrapbook," Elaine added.

At the door, Elaine gave me another quick hug and Dan added a fatherly pat on the shoulder.

Driving back to the office, I thought about Elaine and Dan's pictures and then about my own.

The art department had promised to print out the pictures I'd taken in Belize. They'd be ready about three o'clock, I'd been told. A glance at my watch told me it was quarter to four. I pushed down a little harder on the gas pedal.

Chapter Twenty-Three

Back at the office, I clambered down the steps to the cool recesses of the basement. Here, taking up half of the available space, was the art department. And, with any luck, my snapshots.

I knocked on the door jamb and entered. "Hello? Anybody home?"

"Yo!" A voice shouted from somewhere nearby. In a moment, the heavy door leading to the inner office opened slowly and a person emerged. Greg, one of the magazine's college interns, was incredibly tall—at least six foot six—and carried not a spare ounce of flesh.

"Greg! What's the word? How did my pictures turn out? Any good enough to use in the magazine?" The shots I'd posted on the blog had been fine by my standards, but I figured we'd only use the best of the lot in print.

Moving slowly over to a work table near one wall he began in a matter-of-fact fashion, "You've got a few blurry ones, but not too many. A couple looked pretty good. Here, judge for yourself." He gave me a manila envelope thick with prints. Had I really taken so many pictures? Had he printed out every one? Elaine would be proud of me.

As I fumbled with the clasp, Greg gave one of the desk chairs a shove in my direction and I sank down onto the edge of it.

Flipping through the stack of glossy paper, I glanced briefly at each shot, looking for the pictures I'd taken at Tikal. As I rifled through the others, I had quick impressions of the colors. Green in the forest, blue on the sea. The deep, dark navy of the Blue Hole. Rainbow hues while we were in the marketplace.

At last, the pictures turned black and grey, the colors of the ruins. Slowing my shuffle, I paused to examine each picture. I had to suppress a shudder at the sight of the temple and its narrow, dangerous steps. Closing my eyes, I drove away the memory of my mysterious "accident" and put that particular picture face down on the counter in front of me.

The next picture was the one I'd been waiting for. Clark and the native were clearly visible, deep in conversation against the backdrop of the forest. Clark was facing the camera, the native was in profile.

"Drat!" I muttered, wondering if the authorities would be able to identify the man from the picture.

"Well, I don't know," Greg spoke over my shoulder. "That's not a bad shot. Not blurry. Not too dark or light."

"What?" It took me a moment to realize he was judging the photograph's quality, not its content. "I was hoping for a better view of these two," I told him, pointing at the men and thinking out loud.

"If you want an enlargement, Allison, let me know. If that would help." He leaned closer, scrutinizing it with a technical eye. After a moment, he straightened up.

"Thanks, Greg. I'll let you know." I stuffed the pictures back in their envelope and carried them upstairs to my desk.

It took a few minutes to spread all the Tikal shots out on my desktop. Then, I fished in my purse for the packet of pictures Dan had given me.

These were a humorous lot. Obviously, both of the Underwoods liked to clown for the camera. The pictures featuring either one of them were posed to be amusing—Elaine in an oversized straw hat at the marketplace, Dan "balancing" one of the temples in the palm of his hand.

I laughed out loud, wondering how our readers would like them, then set those aside. I was looking for Dan's pictures from Tikal, hoping to find some sort of clue. Another incriminating shot of Clark, perhaps.

"Or better yet," I mumbled, "a picture of Clark carrying a big box labeled 'DRUGS' and with money sticking out of his pockets."

Mart might think Clark wouldn't get actively involved with criminal activities, but he had also been the one to tell me about Clark's profit motive. Mart might think I was jumping to conclusions, but I wasn't. I was investigating.

Ah! Here it was! A nice picture capturing the grassy plaza at Tikal, this snapshot was populated by trekkers. I bent close, searching the tiny figures for my own. Sure enough! There I was, just a blot on the landscape like everyone else.

I scooted my chair closer to my desk, rested my elbows on the edge and brought the picture close to my nose. Where was Clark? After a few minutes of careful scrutiny, I gave up. Maybe he just wasn't in the shot.

He was in the next one, though, lecturing to a little knot of trekkers. It wasn't a flattering picture. He'd been caught in mid-sentence, mouth open, arms gesturing. The people around him were a study, as well, their expressions varying from boredom to intense interest. Dan, in the foreground of the shot, was rolling his eyes at the camera. After attending four or five zoo treks, he must have had his fill of Clark's lectures.

A few more snaps of the ruins and monuments followed. Then, it became more evident Elaine had taken the camera on her climb up the temple. There were many stunning views of the rain forest as seen from the top of the structure.

At last, I held only one picture and the moment I saw it, I felt a chill. It was just another shot from the top of the temple, crowded with tourists. I recognized a few of the faces from our group, but it was the person at the edge of the shot who intrigued me.

It was a man in native dress, colorful patterned shirt, dark shorts, sandals. He was turning away from the camera, not as if he were deliberately avoiding it, but as if he'd been caught in mid-movement.

Was it? Could it be?

I flipped through the stack of my own pictures, searching for the one of Clark in the jungle. All the other pictures fell from my hands when I found it and there was a rushing sound in my ears. Sweeping away a clear spot on my desk, I set the two pictures side by side: Clark and the Guatemalan in the jungle, Elaine's tourist shot on the temple.

Yes!

It was the same man. With Clark. On the temple.

I gasped, my hands clenching into fists. It's one thing to suspect a truth. It's another to hold the evidence in your hands, to see it right before your eyes. Irrefutable.

I'd been spotted leaving the jungle and Clark's Guatemalan buddy followed me to the temple. He'd seen me begin my clumsy ascent. Had charged at me, knocking me down, then continued pell-mell to the top, where Elaine accidentally caught him on film.

"I could have been killed," I whispered, remembering my fall down rough stone.

Oh, things were looking worse for Clark with every moment. If I had been killed in the fall, he would have been responsible for my death. He was dealing with drug traffickers and it was clear they put a very low price on human life.

If Clark's ultimate goal was the lofty one Mart originally claimed—to find Tommy Mendoza's killer—he had a dangerous way of pursuing it. If his goal was something other—well, then I'm sure Clark would tell me the ends justified the means.

I shuffled all the pictures together and put them carefully into the big manila envelope. When the metal clasp held the package securely closed, I reached for the telephone.

"May I speak to Mart Lawler, please?"

Chapter Twenty-Four

Within the space of a few heavy heartbeats, Mart was on the line. The sound of his voice made me feel better almost immediately and I unburdened myself. I told him about my pictures and Elaine's shot showing the same man.

"Well, that confirms why he broke into your room for the camera," Mart said when I'd finished. He was quiet a moment and it was easy to picture his handsome face serious in thought. "When are you coming out here to the zoo for your series?" he asked.

I shrugged. "I thought tomorrow morning. Although how I can face Clark knowing he nearly got me killed—"

"Allison," Mart's voice held a calming note, which I ignored.

"Oh, come on, Mart!" I exclaimed, my volume increasing. "Maybe Clark started out wearing a white hat, trying to find Tommy Mendoza's killer, but somewhere along the line, he changed hats. I can't believe he's still trying to track a criminal. In fact, I don't think I've ever believed that. You want to know what I think? I'll tell you! I'm convinced Clark's taken over where Tommy left off. I know, I know," I rushed on when Mart began to sputter, "I said it before, but I'm serious now!"

"Allison! Allison!" Mart broke in when I stopped for breath. "Will you hang on for just a minute and listen? I wasn't going to tell you you're wrong."

I'd been staring at the envelope on my desk and had to blink a few times as his words registered. "You weren't?"

"No. I wasn't. You aren't the only one gathering information today, although I don't quite know what to make of mine."

"What? What? Tell me."

"I can't now, over the phone. Anyone could walk in and I don't want to be overheard."

"When, then?" I pressed.

"Tomorrow morning, when you come here. We can talk then."

The hours stretched long between now and then. Plenty of time for nail biting and pacing. "Why not tonight? Come to my place. Or I'll come to yours," I suggested.

He hesitated. "No, no. I can't tonight. I've got another obligation."

"More important than this?" I questioned in disbelief.

"It's unavoidable. I'm sorry. Look, I'll see you tomorrow, first thing, okay?"

"But—"

"I've got to go. Bye."

The receiver buzzed into my ear.

*

The ticket taker waved my car through into the zoo parking lot. Since it was early, I got a spot near the entrance.

I'd dressed with extra care, knowing if I thought I looked good—cool and professional—I'd have a better chance of coming off that way to Clark, as well. Still, as I clutched my folder and marched resolutely toward the zoo gate, even my best coatdress in deep berry wasn't up to the task.

How could I face a man whom I suspected of such crimes? How could I smile and be friendly without betraying what I was really thinking? I was a journalist, not an actress. But right now, I knew I'd have to be both.

I moved through the entrance and was immediately assaulted by the smell of the concession stands getting ready for business. Even on a cool spring day, crowds were evidently expected. Popcorn, hot dogs, and cotton candy were the items closest at hand. At ten in the morning, the very idea made my already-nervous stomach churn. I turned away, wondering where the administrative offices were located.

Signs and posters cluttered this area, directing visitors to the gift shop, the petting zoo, and the dolphin show. Others trumpeted the Mardi

Gras gala, just a few days away. I'd heard about this event at work, and would be covering it for the society page. A big fundraiser for the zoo, it would be attended by all the social luminaries, decked out in satin ball gowns and tuxedos. Briefly, I wondered what Mart would look like in a tuxedo. I could almost imagine it. It was even easier to imagine him with the bow tie undone and a few buttons open. I blinked, dispelling that inviting image and focusing on my surroundings.

Wending my way past the gift shop, I could also imagine his reaction to this commercialization. With his emphasis on naturalism and recreating the wild, the existence of dolphin shows and petting areas must be especially grating. I marveled at his ability to tolerate it, recalling his statement about change and how it will never come from those content with old ways and old ideas. He was a strong individual, no doubt about it.

Off to the side of the path was a wooden sign shaped like a penguin. One flipper pointed to the left and was labeled "Offices." I followed the direction.

The secretary kept me waiting a full ten minutes before I was finally able to see Clark. Was he deliberately putting me off, or was I being paranoid? The stagnant time merely increased my apprehension and it took conscious efforts to keep from tapping my toes or some other fidgety motion. I did dog-ear the cover of the magazine I was holding, I'm afraid.

Lost in my thoughts, I jumped when my name was called.

Clark's office was dark. Dark wood, dark wallpaper, dark green drapes at the windows. When I entered, he rose from behind a huge, curved desk, extending a hand and smiling what looked like a genuine smile. He was dressed just as he'd been on the trip—pseudo-safari—a thing which seemed odd since we were back home now, surrounded by indoor plumbing and automobiles and all the other things that make us civilized.

"Miss Belsar, hello!" he greeted me. "Good to see you again so soon. Have a seat!"

"Hello, Clark."

He waved me into a deep leather chair and I perched on the edge uncomfortably.

"I'm here to continue my series, as you know."

He nodded several times quickly.

"And I'd just like to thank you again for giving me this opportunity."

Reaching into a desk drawer, he produced a packet of cigarettes. I hadn't seen him smoke on the trip.

"I didn't know you smoked," I said. Action man. Fresh air fiend. Smoker?

He shrugged, fumbled with a match and muttered around the cigarette. "Just now and then. Not a habit or anything." He tipped his head back and blew a long column of noxious fumes into the air.

I wrinkled my nose, and hoped for a fast exit. I had no desire to carry the scent of stale tobacco around all day, embedded in the fabric of my favorite dress.

We chatted a few more minutes, him talking up the Mardi Gras, me trying to steer the conversation back to the matter at hand. Which, as far as he was concerned, were the articles on zoos.

"Sylvia's told me all about your plans," he said, taking another puff, and I recalled the conversation she and I had had at Altun Ha. What had she called Mart? Idealistic.

"And there is definitely a place for Mart's vision in the world," Clark went on, surprising me with the admission. "But that doesn't necessarily mean we must throw out the baby with the bathwater. Evolution takes time, my dear. To shift from one model—say, tradition—to another—like Mart's sanctuary, will not be an overnight event. Not by a long shot, as they say."

He smiled in a practiced way.

"What steps is the Rochester zoo taking," I asked, "to pursue a more natural model?"

Clark frowned then leaned forward aggressively. "The most important one. We are raising money. Nothing happens without funding, as I'm sure you know."

And he was back to the Mardi Gras, down to the last detail.

Eventually, he said, "Well, I'm sure you won't mind if I turn you over to Mart. He can tell you all you'll need to know. And then some!" Laughing at his own joke, he stood up, stubbing out the remains of his cigarette in what looked to be—

I sucked in a breath and pointed. "Is that a monkey's paw?"

"What? Oh, yes. It is. Confiscated by wildlife protection officers. They're sold as souvenirs in some countries." He picked it up, cradling the hairy, wrinkled hand in the palm of his own. The fingers curled up in grotesque imitation of life.

"That's . . . that's appalling!" I sputtered, my eyes transfixed by the gruesome sight.

"Yes, it is. That's why I keep it here, in plain view. So others will see tangible evidence of wildlife atrocities."

It seemed to me that by using the artifact, he was condoning the activity, not educating the public, but I didn't say so. Instead, I turned away as he set the "ashtray" back on his desk.

"Good luck, Allison," he said, holding the door for me. "And, if you need me, feel free to stop in any time."

I nodded and scurried out. Out of his office, out of the building, out into the fresh, bracing air of the spring day. I gulped in a large breath, thankful to be away from the smoke in that oppressive room, occupied by that man of questionable motives.

Drawing the collar of my dress closer around me, I shut my eyes on the image of the severed monkey's paw. Had Mart ever seen it?

I started walking, heading in the direction of the education building, where Clark told me Mart could be found. It was a long walk, past several animal enclosures. Many were empty, the animals still inside winter quarters. But I got to see several bears, a tiny herd of moose, and a few whitetail deer.

The education building was new construction and looked it, with a sharply slanting roof and plenty of big windows. Inside, my footsteps echoed in the open space. Glass cases lined several walls, waiting to be filled with eye-catching displays. A little raised area off to one side could serve as a stage, if need be, although a bright red sign clearly indicated the way to a big auditorium.

I saw no signs of life in the building and I called out hesitantly, "Mart?"

A mechanical hum from somewhere close at hand announced the presence of an elevator in operation. I heard the bell ring as the doors slid open and turned to see Mart emerging from an alcove I'd overlooked.

"For a minute there I thought Clark had sent me on another wild goose chase," I said, hurrying over and into his embrace.

He dropped a kiss on my forehead and slipped his arms around my waist. I could feel my heart hammering just because he was near and knew my smile stretched full across my face. For those first few seconds, I forgot all the other reasons I should be glad to see him, all the other things we had to discuss. It was enough to just be held tight in his arms.

"How's it going, Allison?" he asked in a husky tone, nuzzling at my ear.

"Mmm, it's going," I told him, stepping reluctantly away.

"Did you bring the photographs?" His voice dropped low, coming out in a whisper. I half-expected him to shoot nervous glances over each shoulder even though we were obviously alone.

"Yes," I said, my hand going out to close protectively around my purse. "They're here. Do you want to see them now?"

"Um." Now, he did glance around. There was no one in evidence, but apparently, this public area didn't suit him. "Follow me. We'll go to the new aviary. It's under construction. Closed to the public." He took my hand and tugged. Then tugged again.

"Aviary?" My question was simple and immediately understood.

"Oh, Allison, don't worry. I told you it's being built now. All the birds are still in their old quarters. This new one won't be ready for them until summer." He punctuated the last with another firmer tug and I followed with hesitation.

We left the education building and crossed a limestone path, then proceeded up a winding brick walkway to the new aviary. The exterior was completed and labeled in big, bright letters. Using one of the many keys on his ring, Mart opened the door, stepping inside first.

"Mind the cables," he instructed, keeping a guiding hand on my elbow.

It was dim inside since the electricity hadn't been connected and there were no lights. The air was heavy with the dust of construction, the walls blank grey slabs of concrete.

I shivered in the dampness and looked around the eerie interior. Bags of supplies were scattered across the floor and scaffolding rose to the ceiling in the middle of the room. The silence only added to the unreal atmosphere; there were no workers here today.

Mart put his hands on his hips and looked around, surveying the operation with a critical eye. "We're behind schedule on this," he told me, sounding frustrated. "But I guess you have to expect some delays."

He seemed to be merely thinking out loud, so I let him scan the area, turning my attention to the deepest, darkest regions of my purse, where the envelope containing the two pictures was hiding.

By the time he had mentally returned, I had it located, held between fingers that quivered, but just a little. I waved the packet at him.

"Take a look."

Mart slipped the photos out of the envelope and peered at them intently, his head bent low. "Let's go in the other room. The light's better."

We moved slowly across the littered floor, stepping carefully over tools and cords and sacks. I found myself hunching up my shoulders so they wouldn't brush against the dusty wall. We went about ten feet down a hallway, then veered right, into a room at the rear of the building.

The entire back wall was made of thick, double-paned glass, looking out at a heavily wooded area. Here, the sunlight filtered gently in, making this room considerably brighter than the one we'd left.

Mart's footsteps echoed in staccato fashion against the concrete as he hurried over to the window.

My hands were clenched deep in the pockets of my dress and I felt afraid suddenly, watching him as he studied the pictures. The scowl etched into Mart's features gave me a clue, but I questioned him anyway.

"What are you thinking?"

He glanced up at me. "Remember how I told you I had some news?"

Of course I remembered. I'd spent half the night awake and wondering what it could be. I nodded impatiently.

"I got an e-mail yesterday. They've confirmed the identity of the man in your photo." He flapped the picture. "If he's into drug running, it's a new line of work."

He tapped an angry finger at the image on the paper.

"This man's a well-known dealer in illegal animal products."

Chapter Twenty-Five

Our eyes locked and held and I could practically see the thought we shared hanging in the air between us. I knew Mart would never give the idea words and cleared my throat.

"Seems to me there never were any drugs. I think this whole thing all the way back may have been about animal trafficking."

Looking stunned, Mart paced a few steps in one direction, then back again, slapping the envelope containing the pictures against his thigh. "I just can't believe that Clark would be part of something like that! It could be his involvement is all part of his pursuit of Mendoza's killer," he said in a desperate tone, trying unsuccessfully to convince himself. "Maybe the feds—"

"You mean maybe Clark's still got some noble aim?" I shook my head. "I can't buy that anymore."

"He's sworn to protect endangered species, to educate the public about the need to preserve. We—we hold workshops for kids here at the zoo and he conducts them. How? How can he—" he broke off, turning away.

My heart ached for Mart, for the anguish I read in the slump of his shoulders. I sighed and looked around for a place to sit down. My legs had gone all wobbly.

Over against the window, several white sacks labeled MORTAR BOND were stacked about three feet high. They didn't look too dirty, and they were the right height.

As I walked toward them, I said, "This whole thing has gotten so twisted I can't tell up from down anymore. And we're no closer to any conclusion."

Whirling around, he took several rapid steps in my direction. "Are you thinking about the great break this is for you? What a scoop you'll have when you finally get to write the story?"

I held out both hands to ward off this unwarranted verbal attack. Backing up, I bumped into the stack of bags. The top one started to slip and I made a grab for it, my hands catching the end of the bag as it slithered to the floor.

Mart continued to range around the space as I struggled to hoist the heavy sack. It must have gone forty pounds at least, awkward and cumbersome. I lifted the thing into my arms, bent my knees and rose. When I let it down, none too gently, on top of the others, it landed off balance.

"Oh!" I gave a cry of dismay, interrupting Mart's continuing tirade, as all the sacks tilted like the tower of Pisa.

The first one hit the concrete floor with a thud, rapidly followed by the raspy sound of tearing and the clatter of many tiny objects spilling onto the floor.

Mart broke off in mid-sentence, but I couldn't see him as I struggled mightily to keep the other bags from falling as well.

Then he found his voice.

"Oh, no! No, no, no!"

He sounded shocked, horrified, and I straightened up in a rush, hardly noticing when another sack teetered and fell.

Mart was crouched down low, his hands buried deep in a pile of small, ivory items that glowed in the faint light like polished porcelain. I dropped to my knees and put my hand on his shoulder, swiveling around so I could see his face.

Harsh, deep lines had been driven into the set of his mouth. One vertical crevice halved his brow as he frowned. His eyes were rock-hard chips, swimming under a glaze of hot tears.

"Mart! Mart, what is it?" My own heart swelled at the sight of his pain and my question ended on a ragged scrap of breath.

He closed his eyes, heavy lids sinking slowly and staying down. Beneath my hand, his shoulders shook with deep emotion.

I patted him on the back as if he were a colicky baby and waited, feeling utterly and totally powerless. I knew I was watching a man's illusions shatter and it was a terrible sight.

He drew a sharp breath and let the little trinkets flow from his hand. The face he turned to me was strained, incredulous. "Do you know what these are, Allison? Have you any idea?"

I shook my head.

"It's ivory. Genuine, illegal ivory. It comes from elephant tusks and walrus tusks. The animals are killed—by machine gun! Then, their tusks are sawn off their faces. Turned into this!" He spat out the last, pushing at the pile in disgust. "Allison, elephants may be gone from this earth very soon, because of man's greed. Because there is money to be made selling baubles like this."

The plight of elephants wasn't new to me. I'd seen it on television and read about it in national magazines. The images were vivid ones of the huge, rotting corpses with no faces, the bodies picked at by scavengers and covered in bird dung.

"Webster is a monster," Mart went on, his fists clenching. The words barely squeezed out between his gritted teeth. "He's in zoo management. He knows better than anyone what's happening in the wild. He lectures on it! I always knew he was out for a quick buck, but I never suspected he'd stooped this low. Profiting from death!" He broke off, shaking his head in mournful lament.

I covered his hands with my own and leaned closer, moving to kiss him gently on the forehead. "Oh, Mart, I'm so sorry," I whispered. "For the animals. For you."

"I could kill him," he ignored my sympathetic gesture and raged on. "I could march right into that office and strangle him where he stands. The savage!"

The violent talk, stated so coldly, frightened me and I gave him a shake.

"Mart, stop it! It won't help anyone to do something violent and stupid. We have to call the police, have him arrested. We have to stop him and whoever he's working with. Mart, help me. Think!"

He'd been looking out the window into the distance and it was a moment before he blinked and focused on me. He sat back, letting his feet slide out from under him. Oblivious now to dust and scattered nails, I sat, too. Our shoulders touched as we sat contemplating the stack of ivory bits.

How many elephants and walruses? I wondered. How many dead for the sake of these souvenirs? I shuddered in pain and disbelief.

Beside me, Mart gave a sigh, the kind that heralds decision-making and gaining control. "I'll talk to the feds—and to Ricardo. And I'll ask what we can do. How can we pin it on Clark so he can't ever get away. So he ends up behind bars forever."

"What time is it in Belize? Call now," I urged, knowing action would help defuse Mart's justifiable rage.

"Good idea. I will." He spoke absently, as if his mind were already on the conversation to come. When he stood up, he extended a hand, pulling me to my feet beside him. "Let's clean this up. Then, perhaps we could take a raincheck on your tour? I need to get right on this."

I tucked my hair behind my ears and nodded. "Of course."

Mart scooped up the ivory and dropped it handful by handful into the bag I held. His nose wrinkled, as if he smelled something foul and I couldn't help cringing each time another cascade of trinkets slithered into the sack. We propped the broken bag behind the other intact ones. There was no way to secure the torn opening and this worried me.

"Someone will realize we know!" I said, reluctant to leave the scene.

Mart gripped my elbow firmly and steered me away. "Clark may know someone has seen it, but he won't know who. No one saw us come in here. The logical assumption would be that the workmen knocked it over. It's anyone's guess how long Clark's been using this site as a warehouse. I'll bet those bags are gone before the day is out."

I stopped in my tracks. "And we'll have no proof! Mart, we should take a piece of the ivory as evidence. Otherwise, no one will believe—"

He reached in a pocket, extracted one of the polished bits and held it up, grim-faced. "I've already thought of that."

Together, we left the building and began the long walk to the zoo entrance where my car was parked.

"I'll call you later," he promised, as we faced each other over the open car door. "Don't worry about me flying off the handle and doing something foolish. This is too important to botch up because of personal feelings. And, Allison?" He waited for me to answer.

"Yes?"

"I'm sorry about before. About accusing you of wanting a story. It's just—"

Reaching up, I cupped his face in my hands. "I know. I understand." Emotions can be powerful and dangerous.

He smiled, just a bit, and I knew he was still reeling from our discovery. Would keep on reeling for quite a while, too. I wanted to hug him. To comfort him if I could, offering assurance that everything would be okay. But the door was between us now, and his eyes weren't looking at me any longer. He was gazing off at the zoo entrance and I could almost hear the grinding of wheels as he thought. Best if I just cleared off, I decided with a pang of disappointment.

"Right, then," my tone was brisk, covering up what I felt inside. "Talk to you later. I'll be home after five." I smiled. "Waiting with my phone." I tried to sound flippant, but the words were truthful. I'd be very anxious to hear what transpired, what Ricardo and the others instructed.

He was already walking away, waving a hand.

It's a miracle I made it safely back to the office that day. My mind was not on my driving and my eyes kept glazing over as I concentrated on this latest wrinkle. More than once, a horn honked and startled me back into the present, where traffic lights were green and other drivers were impatient.

Chapter Twenty-Six

When the ten o'clock news ended, I snapped off the television and listened hard to the thick silence around me. I hadn't felt this edgy since I was in high school, waiting for the call that would bring my invitation to the prom.

It had been nearly twelve hours since Mart and I made our gruesome discovery. Twelve stomach-churning hours when I pictured Mart in a showdown with Clark. A fist fight. A gunshot. Mart dead on the floor of Clark's office.

I poured myself another cup of tepid coffee and debated. Should I call him rather than wait? It took only a few moments of senseless pondering before I reached for the phone.

"Hello?"

I must have the wrong number, I thought, hearing a low female voice at the other end. Somewhere in the region of my stomach a knot was rapidly forming.

"Is Mart Lawler there, please?" I used my professional voice, flat and brisk.

"Just a minute."

It could be his sister. Or a neighbor. Or the maid. While I waited for Mart to take the phone, my brain worked frantically to produce an explanation which would not result in heartbreak.

"Hello?" It was Mart and my mouth dried up. He tried again. "Hello?"

"Mart, it's Allison." I stopped to clear my throat. "I hope you don't mind me calling," I continued, "but you said you'd call me as soon as you'd heard anything. I've been dying of curiosity. . . ." I let my sentence dangle in the air and nibbled on a fingernail.

"Oh, Allison, I'm sorry! I didn't forget, but it's just been one thing after the next!" he said. He sounded genuinely distressed, which afforded me a little comfort. Surely, though, he couldn't feign such a tone? "I had to keep doing all my regular duties and squeeze this espionage around it," he went on. "I even had to have my department head meeting with Clark this afternoon! It was a short one, let me tell you. It wasn't easy to keep my temper, looking at him and knowing what he is responsible for."

"He does put on quite a different face for the public," I agreed, remembering Clark's lecture on the rain forest. How he'd gone on about the environment and the fate of the planet. The man should be on the stage with such acting.

"So, what happened? What's the word from the authorities?"

"I don't know. I'm just getting to that part now. Ishani said she had some important details for me and she wanted to see the setup here for herself. I just picked her up at the airport an hour ago."

I'd been fiddling with the fringe on the edge of a pillow, but at the mention of the name, my fingers stopped the nervous motion. That voice on the phone had sounded vaguely familiar.

"Ishani? Ishani, the singer from our hotel?" *The one who kissed you goodbye at the airport,* I thought, but didn't say. *The one you seem to know, but never mention. That Ishani?*

"Yes, that's the one. See, she's the federal authority. She works with the government, but in the field."

"Undercover? Ishani is an undercover agent?" This seemed a bit of a stretch. *You'd certainly never suspect her,* I thought, picturing her exotic beauty and remembering her wonderful voice.

"Right. That's why she's in Belize at the hotel. She's been investigating Tommy Mendoza's murder, following the zoo trek link. They've been working flat out to identify the individuals involved and nab them. Nab the whole network."

"Really?" I moved to the kitchen counter where I could find paper and pen. This was too bizarre to be true and, if true, too good to miss.

"Something like that. I haven't gotten too many details, yet."

"Come over," I urged suddenly.

"What, now?"

I nodded, even though he couldn't see the gesture. "Yes, now. Bring Ishani, come over, and let's talk."

"I don't know," he hesitated and I knew he was planning to refuse. "You promised not to use this for a story, Allison. You promised to keep quiet and stay out of it."

My eyes gave just the slightest roll as I replied. "I said at the beginning I wouldn't write about it until it's all resolved and I won't. You have my word on it. But I've been in on this nearly from the beginning, Mart, and I think I can help. Especially now, when I'll be out at the zoo so much with this series. Maybe I can ask questions you can't, just because I'm an outsider."

He was silent, considering this idea. I scurried around the kitchen, tidying up the place, anticipating visitors.

At last, he sighed in resignation. "All right. We'll be there in twenty minutes."

Chapter Twenty-Seven

When I answered the doorbell half an hour later, my apartment looked presentable for a change and a fresh pot of coffee was brewing in the kitchen.

Remembering Ishani and her knockout looks, I'd even found time to dab on some blush and lipstick and had abandoned my sweatshirt for a pastel cotton sweater.

I shouldn't have bothered.

Both Mart and Ishani looked tired and worn out. Mart entered first, his hands grasping my shoulders as he gave me a brief peck on the cheek in greeting. His eyes were shadowed with fatigue and concern. His mouth seemed set in stone.

"Hi, Allison." He moved determinedly past me into the living room and flopped onto the sofa.

I turned to Ishani, waving her in and closing the door.

"Hi," she greeted me, almost shyly, her lips twitching into a self-conscious smile. She looked so different in jeans and a sweater, with her hair bundled up at the back of her neck, I almost didn't believe it was her. Devoid of makeup, she lost that glamorous aura, looking more like the girl next door than a flashy performer.

I stuck out a hand and formally introduced myself.

"Mart told me about your part in all this, Allison," Ishani explained. "And I'm eager to get a better look at those pictures he was telling me about. Do I smell coffee?"

I hurried from the room, returning in a minute with a tray holding the coffee and some cookies.

"Help yourselves," I said, "while I get the photographs."

The pictures had suffered a bit at the aviary, having been dropped and stepped on during our encounter with the ivory. I'd absently stuffed them into my bag after we'd picked up the bits of contraband. Now, I retrieved the snapshots, tapping them into a neat pile.

When I entered the living room after a moment, Ishani was leaning forward with her hands on her knees. Mart had tilted his head back against the sofa cushion and his eyes were shut. He'd stretched his arms in either direction across the back of the sofa and was the picture of exhaustion—physical and emotional.

"I really appreciate your coming over tonight," I told them both sincerely, handing the photos to Ishani. "You didn't have to, any more than you had to include me at all."

Mart opened one eye and regarded me warily. "When we talked on the phone, you didn't give me any choice," he said. "Made me feel like it was my moral duty to drag you in deeper."

I plunked down beside him. "Well, now that you're both here, let's concentrate." I changed the subject. "Ishani, what do the pictures tell you?"

She gave her head a shake, twisting in the chair to hold the pictures directly underneath the lamp. "This man has been definitely identified as Hector Juarez and he is definitely a dealer. But not in drugs. His line, as Mart told you, is animals. Or bits of them."

I shuddered. "You mean he probably sells living animals, as well?"

"Almost certainly. Some people will pay a lot of money to own an endangered species." She flipped through the pictures as she spoke, holding them at an angle into the light. "Others have the animals illegally imported so they can be shot later at what is euphemistically called an exotic game ranch."

"I saw that on television!" I exclaimed. "A man shot a panther as it stepped out of the shipping crate!"

Ishani laid one picture aside and turned her attention to the next. It was Elaine Underwood's shot from the top of the temple. "Well," she concluded after a moment's silence, "it's purely circumstantial evidence, this. But it is Hector and he is certainly capable of murder. I think you had a very close shave that day,

Allison." When she looked up, her eyes were deadly serious, as if she felt she needed to convince me of the danger involved.

"What's your plan of attack, Ishani?" I asked. "How do you want to handle this?"

She tipped her head to one side and pondered.

Mart sat up abruptly, breaking the mood. "Are there more of those cookies?"

"Yep." I pointed him in the direction of the kitchen.

He heaved himself off the couch and headed into the other room.

As soon as he'd gone, I turned to Ishani. An undercover agent. And anything else? Even though Mart had told me there was no blazing romance between them, I wouldn't be normal if I didn't wonder. About those voices I had heard in the room next to mine in Belize. About that goodbye kiss at the airport. I started feeling fidgety and insecure, unfamiliar territory for me.

"You know," I began, unable to stop myself, "I'd never have guessed you were a government agent. You do your job well. No one would ever suspect you."

"That's good," Ishani replied without looking up from the snapshots. "If the wrong people were suspicious, I'd end up dead."

"True enough." I paused, then pushed the tiniest bit. "I thought you were just a singer. Although I did wonder how come Mart seemed to know you."

From the kitchen came the clatter of dishes and the sound of cabinet doors being opened and shut.

If she knew what I was getting at, she didn't let on.

"Oh, we'd talked on the phone and corresponded prior to the zoo trek," Ishani explained. "But we didn't actually meet face to face until your group arrived at the hotel."

I shifted on the sofa. This wasn't getting me the information I wanted. Maybe I should abandon my probe. After all, Mart had said there was nothing. His word should be enough for me, right?

"You know what I thought when I saw you together?" I hurried on, turning to shoot a glance at the doorway. Mart was still nowhere in sight. "I thought you and he were, um, more than casual acquaintances. You know?"

"Did you think I was the hotel hooker?" She did look up, then, the photos dropping into her lap. But she didn't raise an eyebrow, didn't even sound surprised.

"No, not that exactly. But I did think, well, that you were a couple. I guess I was wrong there, too. I mean, you're a professional. Business and pleasure don't mix."

Our eyes met and I knew she knew. Knew I had fallen hard for Mart Lawler.

"Don't they?"

Her words teased me. A professional journalist, more than interested in my subject, I'd combined business and pleasure with Mart on plenty of occasions by now.

I looked away, down to my hands clenched in my lap. "Well, they aren't supposed to," I finished lamely. "Not usually."

She put me out of my misery, laughing in understanding. "You needn't worry, Allison. He's all yours, if you can hold him. He's an attractive man, one I wouldn't mind getting involved with, if I didn't need to be concentrating on my job. Under different circumstances. . . ." She lifted slender shoulders in a shrug. Her eyes seemed to sparkle slightly when she stated in a flat voice, "But, we don't have different circumstances. We only have these." She smiled at me. "Could be you and Mart make a good team."

"I found the cookies." Mart spoke from the doorway, carefully carrying a plate piled high.

He took cautious steps, looking down at his burden, and missed the glance Ishani and I exchanged. She closed one eye in a wink and I visualized her stepping back, out of the way, leaving the field of battle, so to speak.

Mart set the plate on a space I hastily cleared next to the larger tray. Once he'd settled back on the sofa, he directed the conversation. "Okay, then, let's make a plan! Ishani, what's it to be?"

"I'd think it would be good to take a look at your facility, if I may. Specifically this building where you found the ivory. But we need to see if we can determine how the items are moving through the zoo and where they're going from here."

"I think we know how the stuff is getting in," Mart said, telling Ishani about the zoo van we saw at the airport upon our return. "The attendant said shipments come regularly and are picked up at the airport. Of course, anything else we receive for legitimate purposes is usually sent directly to the zoo. And the fact that the director himself was involved in the pickup is suspicious. The man isn't known for taking on extra work—especially something so menial."

Ishani was nodding, as if some of this sounded familiar. "And, of course, I'd like to examine a bit of that ivory, if it's still around."

"I'd be surprised if it remains at the zoo past today. But we can check. In any event, I have samples of it."

He reached awkwardly into the pocket of his jeans and pulled out two of the small pieces. Ishani set down her coffee cup and Mart dropped them into her palm. She turned them over, rubbing her thumb across the smooth surfaces.

"Do you think Clark would recognize you if he saw you?" I asked her, an idea hatching slowly in my brain. "If you wore a disguise—a wig or dark glasses—and slung a camera around your neck, you could come with me as the magazine's photographer."

Ishani pursed her lips in thought. Mart didn't seem to appreciate the idea either. He'd scrunched up his nose and ran a hand uneasily through his hair. The clock against the wall ticked, pacing off the time, emphasizing the silence.

"Maybe. . . ." Ishani said at last, drawing the word out. "It might work. It's worth a shot. Coming in so boldly would certainly divert suspicion."

I grinned, pleased by her approval, and nudged Mart with my elbow.

"If you're willing to risk it," Mart lifted both hands, "I'll go along. You're the expert on this, Ishani."

"That's right. I am and I say let's do it. Allison, when were you scheduled for your next zoo visit?"

"Tomorrow, about ten in the morning. Mart is supposed to give me a tour of the primate house."

"And, then, we can detour back to the aviary and, perhaps, the ivory." Ishani drummed her fingers against her chin, thinking aloud. She'd set the tiny ivory tokens beside the chocolate cookies, where they sat in innocent silence.

Mart shrugged. I was convinced of the plan and Ishani was thinking it over. He raised a hand to his mouth suddenly, stifling a yawn and said, "We may as well try it. Allison can pick you up at your hotel and I'll meet you at the zoo gates at ten. How's that?" He spoke hurriedly, wrapping up our discussion and emphasizing the finality by standing up.

Quick to take a hint, Ishani rose, as well. "I'll call a cab."

I nodded, even as I wondered why Mart didn't just drop her off.

When she went into the kitchen, Mart ranged slowly around the room, his hands shoved deep into his pockets. We could hear Ishani making the call, her voice the only sound in the quiet apartment.

I remained seated, my eyes following Mart's figure as he bent to examine the photographs hung on the wall, then crossed the room to look out into the darkness. For the first time since we'd returned from our trip, the atmosphere between us was strained and I didn't know why. Was he just concerned about the next day and what it might bring? He'd been yawning. Maybe he was drop-dead tired and ready to go home.

"You don't have to stay, Mart. I'll be here with Ishani until her taxi comes," I said, directing my words at his unresponsive back.

His shoulders stiffened and he turned swiftly around. His eyes were wide, startled, his mouth open in surprise. Then, just as quickly, he grinned and said, "Trying to get rid of me, Allison?" His voice was low and husky, and when he took a step toward me, my breath caught in my throat.

Our eyes met and locked as he drew nearer, until he stood before me and I was looking up . . . up . . . up into his eyes. Wordlessly, he held out his hands and I placed mine gently in them.

I could hear Ishani's voice droning on in the distance, but the words were lost in the rushing sound filling my ears. My fingers tingled where he held them tight, their glow radiating up my arm and into my belly. I could feel myself melting under his gaze and longed to melt further, into his arms. Tipping my head back as he sat beside me, I invited his kiss.

His lips on mine were warm and soft. The light scent of coconut came from his skin and I breathed it in deeply. Mart's hands moved to my shoulders, squeezing them in that tender spot just above the collar bone.

Our lips separated, only to join once more. Mart's mouth was a bit more demanding, capturing all of mine.

I slipped my hands around his neck and caressed the warm skin I found there. Both of us had blocked out Ishani's presence, so her voice startled me when it came.

"Okay! The taxi should be here in—" she broke off as we scrambled into an upright position. "Oh, hey, I'm sorry. Didn't mean to interrupt anything." She laughed in embarrassment.

My cheeks burned as I blushed and looked away from her there in the doorway. Mart was unfazed, straightening up with no signs of discomfiture.

"You're all set, then?" he clarified, nodding when she did. "Great." He moved to the rocking chair and set it slowly into motion.

Ishani joined me on the sofa.

"More coffee?" I offered, but there were no takers. After an awkward moment, I asked, "Where do you think this investigation of yours will lead, Ishani? I know the goal must be to round up everyone involved, but will that be possible? It seems like an awfully tall order."

"Oh, it is," she agreed, rubbing at her tired eyes. "Especially now that it seems to have veered off in another direction. I'd been thinking drugs and looking at everything from that angle. Now that we know the crime is wildlife smuggling, I'll have to reevaluate the evidence." Her breath came out in a sigh of something like despair and she massaged her scalp with both hands. "But we'll get that crook, Clark, and all his contacts in Central America. I promise. Tomorrow, we'll check out the zoo. Tomorrow night, I'll go back to Belize and get busy. I've a few favors to call in. Perhaps that will bring me the information I need." Her eyes had gotten that lost-in-thought glaze and I could tell she was planning a strategy.

"Just be careful," I said, even though the words sounded limp and meaningless. "There's no telling what could happen. I mean, those people killed Tommy Mendoza."

"So they wouldn't hesitate to kill again. I know." Ishani stood up as a car horn honked outside. "There's my cab." She collected her coat from the rack near the door and gave me the name of her hotel. "I'll meet you in the lobby," she promised.

I thought I saw her wink at Mart just before the door closed behind her.

Chapter Twenty-Eight

Late the next afternoon we saw Ishani onto her plane. Our day hadn't been very productive or eventful and we were all feeling deflated. We'd started out with such high hopes that morning and had ended up frustrated at every turn. Or so it seemed. Oh, I'd actually gotten some information for my series of articles, but at this point, the magazine was the last thing on my mind.

We had toured the primate house—an appalling and depressing place filled with pacing animals. When they stopped their motion momentarily, putting their hands against the glass that separated us, I couldn't help but think how my hand looked like the chimpanzee's hand. And one of the monkeys bore a striking resemblance to my uncle Richard. *Animals deserve better,* I thought, *than glass-and-tile prison cells.* With a heavy heart, I said as much to Mart.

"Yes, they do. Progressive zoos give them a better environment—much better. A natural one, like we saw in Belize, could give the best of both worlds." And then, he was off, launching into a lengthy depiction of the unstructured surroundings to be found at top zoos, ending up with a description of his planned improvements for Rochester's primates.

"It's not enough," he said, shaking his head and putting his own hand up against the glass cage, "but it's the best we can hope for in these economic times. Things won't get much better any time soon, I'm afraid."

Ishani, "disguised" in a baseball cap and no makeup, had snapped a picture of the monkey's forlorn expression then commented, "But, Mart, if you weren't here, pushing for change, it would be even worse." I didn't know if she'd ever been exposed to Mart's particular vision for Rochester, but I knew that, by now, she'd be up to speed on his thoughts regarding zoos in general. I wondered what she thought of that, compared to the plight of animals who encountered Hector Juarez.

In a solemn procession, we left the primate house, taking one of the paved and marked paths to cross to the farthest corner of the zoo.

My heart picked up its pace as we neared the construction site of the aviary. Would the ivory still be there? I wanted to hurry inside, but we put on a show of snapping more pictures and discussing the new building in case anyone was watching.

A few workmen were here today, laying tile with a steady slap-slap of movement. A radio played as accompaniment to their casual conversation. While Mart took his time, pointing things out to Ishani, I headed directly to the rear of the building.

No one was in the room with the big wall of windows, however. And no bags of ivory trinkets were perched on the floor.

"I knew it!" Mart said, cursing under his breath as he came up behind me. "I knew we'd be too late." He wore his disappointment, the edges of his mouth curved down in frustration.

Ishani took a more philosophical view. "We figured they wouldn't be here. This is just as we anticipated. Obviously, goods must move quickly to escape detection. Let's just see if we can trace their path—at least off the premises." She pointed out the window into the woods. "What's in there? Where does that lead?"

"Just woods there," Mart told her. "They border the zoo property on this side." He gestured to the north.

"And the nearest road?"

"Through the woods. About a quarter mile."

"Mm hmm. Mm hmm." Ishani stepped up to the glass, peering out at the trees.

"Do you think they use a path through the woods to the road?" I asked.

"Yes, that's exactly what I think."

"No one maintains anything in there so those woods are pretty thick," Mart said. "But there are a few dirt paths. Narrow ones. Overgrown."

Within minutes we were outside, poking quietly through the underbrush, looking for a smuggler's trail. Having so recently tromped through the rain forest, this work felt familiar. Off in the distance, I could hear children's laughter and the steady calls of their parents. We were too far from the concession area to smell popcorn and instead picked up only the scent of the earth, with an occasional whiff of car exhaust carried on the wind.

I didn't know what to look for on the path, but Ishani did. Trampled patches, broken branches, the slightest gap in the trees. With Mart bringing up the rear we followed the sketchy path to where it came out on a seldom-used service road owned by the utility company. It felt like the middle of nowhere, which surprised me. We were so close to the hubbub of the zoo and the hum of the city. Yet, the area was deserted.

Standing in the middle of the narrow blacktop, her hands on her slim hips, Ishani surveyed the area. "Perfect spot," she declared, echoing my thoughts. "At night, it would be black as pitch. No street lights. No houses nearby. Why, you could do anything here and be undetected."

"So, now what? Do we have a stakeout?" I asked. I didn't mean to sound dramatic, but I must have because she laughed.

"You watch too much television, I think," she told me, slipping an arm around my shoulders in a hug. Then she sobered. "What we'll need to do is find out when the next shipment will go through. That's when we have our stakeout."

She stepped away from me, walking up the road a ways to see where it led. Mart was already following her, so I fell into line.

"How will we find that out?" I asked.

"I've got to go back tonight, at least for a few days, so I'm afraid I won't be much help around here. You two will have to keep your eyes open. Watch for anything suspicious."

"Follow Clark?" I volunteered.

"Too dangerous, Allison. You're not trained in this. I am, so believe me. That's too dangerous for amateurs." At my stricken look she went on. "Mind you, I don't think Clark is foolish enough to cause you harm on his own turf. But off his turf, who can say?"

"So what if we find something out while you're gone?" Mart asked. "What then?" He brought one hand up to shield his eyes from the sun.

"Before I go, I'll speak with my local counterparts, apprise them of the situation. I'll make sure both of you have their phone numbers, and then, if anything does happen quickly—and I do mean anything—you must get in touch with them at once. At once!" Her voice was stern and emphatic. She further emphasized her concern by putting her hand on my arm. "Take no chances! Follow my instructions. I wouldn't forgive myself if either of you came to harm."

Mart slipped an arm around my waist. The tangle of nerves I'd been harboring in my belly unknotted as our eyes met, his an oasis of calm in this sea of anxiety.

We scouted the service road in both directions, finding that while one way led onto a busy thoroughfare the other came out at the back end of an industrial park.

"Where you would expect to see and hear trucks at all hours of the day or night," Mart concluded.

Turning back, we headed through the woods again and onto zoo property.

Even though we spent the next several hours tramping around the zoo taking photographs and notes, at the end of our day we hadn't added anything else to our list of clues, and nowhere looked as inviting for moving contraband as that path through the woods. Soon the three of us were in Mart's car on the way to the airport. Ishani pulled off her baseball cap and shook her head, sending her dark hair tumbling around her shoulders. Even as she applied lipstick and a dusting of powder, transforming into someone more closely resembling the glamorous lounge singer, she gave us instructions and warnings and phone numbers.

With Ishani's admonishment ringing in our ears, we watched her plane take off, arching south in the sky on its long journey.

Chapter Twenty-Nine

It was after we'd gotten back to the car and were in a line of traffic waiting to leave the parking structure that I spotted the van.

"Mart, look!" My finger pointed at the road we could see running past the garage.

A maroon van, emblazoned with the catchy zoo logo, was pulling onto the same service drive we'd seen—and followed—the day of our return from Belize. It was too far away to make out who was driving, even though I leaned out the window to look.

"Well, that's interesting," Mart said in a calm voice, showing none of my excitement.

"I'll say! Ishani said watch for something suspicious and here it is—already!"

"Clark is supposed to be at a meeting today in Milwaukee. That's two hundred miles from here." Mart's fingers drummed on the steering wheel.

The line of cars inched forward. Soon, we'd be out of the gloomy building. But would it be too late to follow the van?

"Let's follow it," I said. "I mean, this is exactly the kind of thing Ishani told us to watch for and here it is dropped right into our laps!"

Another car pulled out of the garage onto the road and we moved ahead once more. Mart turned away from me to check oncoming traffic. When it was clear, he accelerated sharply, the car sputtering with the effort, and turned in the opposite direction of the van.

"What are you doing?" I demanded of his profile. "We can't miss a chance like this, Mart. We've got to follow—"

"There's a method to my madness," he promised. "Give me a minute and I'll explain."

I sat back against the seat, folding my hands and pressing my lips together until they hurt. We moved down the road at a snail's pace, letting other cars surge around us, speeding off into the day's twilight. After we'd gone half a mile or so, cresting a small hill, Mart pulled onto the gravel shoulder and shut off the engine.

"Okay," he said, turning to face me, "here's my idea. We know where that service road leads. We know where that van is headed. There is only one road out of the airport to the freeway. This one."

"So, when the van goes by on its return journey, we'll just fall in behind," I followed the thought to its logical conclusion and was rewarded with a wink.

"Go to the head of the class," Mart teased. His eyes darted frequently to the rear-view mirror, watching for the van.

It made sense, I conceded, settling down to wait. How long could it take to load up the van and zoom past us back toward the zoo? We'd have to move quickly when it did appear. Darkness was falling rapidly and, if we lost sight of the van, we might never have another chance like this to follow it. Or, at least, never one so convenient.

A stream of cars went past us, our car swaying with each one. The speed limit along this stretch was forty miles per hour, but few drivers observed the regulation.

With neither of us speaking, the silence in the car made my ears ring. I was glad when Mart leaned over and snapped on the radio. The lilting, gravelly voice of a popular country-western singer filled the air and my toes tapped out the rhythm of the song.

Another ten minutes crept by. I'd grown lax in my vigilant watch of the traffic, picking at my fingernail polish as my mind wandered off. I was looking out the window into the field at the side of the road when Mart bolted upright.

"Here we go!" he said, reaching to start the ignition. It caught on the second try.

"You've got to get that checked," I said, shifting my seatbelt.

"Can't get it into the garage until next week," he said, putting the car in gear as a
maroon van passed on the left.

The zoo logo had been obliterated by a magnetic sign advertising a real estate company. I noticed the driver was observing the speed limit. It wouldn't do to get a speeding ticket, I supposed, and invite the scrutiny of police. Our car slipped neatly onto the road, a few discreet car lengths from the van. It was full darkness now, which seemed like a point in our favor at this stage. The driver would be less likely to notice us.

We moved onto the freeway and remained in the slower right lane, following the van to the interchange leading to the zoo—and then beyond it. If Mart was surprised by this, he didn't let on, keeping his eyes firmly on the road.

"Where do you think it's headed?" I asked. "If not the zoo, where?"

"I don't know, Allison. Beats me." He blinked heavily and refocused, humming along to the radio and easing up on the gas as the van slowed at the bypass. It was nerve-racking pursuing the other vehicle, trying to second-guess its movements.

To our mutual surprise, we headed downtown, pulling off the freeway at a busy area of restaurants and overpriced boutiques. The van parallel-parked and we cruised slowly past it, looking for another empty spot.

"There's one!" I pointed across the street a few cars down and Mart executed a swift and risky U-turn to nab it.

"Look, the driver is getting out!"

Mart glanced over at the van as he finished backing into the space and I felt one wheel bump over the curb.

"Well, I'll be!" he exclaimed, straightening us out in a hurry. "That's Kyle Armour, one of the groundskeepers. I was sure it would be Clark behind the wheel."

We watched as the man closed the door of the van and pocketed the keys. Then, he put coins into the parking meter and walked away.

"Should we follow him or stay with the van?" I wondered aloud.

"Stay with the van. That's what we care about." Mart spoke swiftly, without deliberation.

"Then we might be here waiting for hours," I mused.

Just outside, only a sidewalk away, was a little cafe. I could practically smell the coffee and realized I was hungry.

"Mart, I think I'll just pop in there and get a cup of coffee to go. Interested?"

"Um, sure. That sounds good. And maybe a bran muffin?" he suggested, adding. "But make it fast."

Inside of ten minutes, I was back, carrying a paper tray with two cups of hazelnut coffee and a wax paper bag with four jumbo-sized muffins.

"Take your pick, Mart. We've got banana nut, bran, blueberry, and cranberry." When he raised his eyebrows, I said, "There's no telling how long we'll have to sit here. We may as well have a picnic."

He wrinkled his nose at my frivolous choice of words, but tucked into a bran muffin while I broke off big chunks of the blueberry, consuming them slowly.

One hour stretched into two. Mart cracked the windows to bring in some fresh air, but the car's seats became uncomfortable and constricting. My legs felt crampy and the small of my back started to ache. My head kept slipping to one side as I drifted off to sleep, but when it came into contact with the window, I'd jerked upright.

Shifting over, I leaned my head against Mart's shoulder instead and muttered, "It's never like this on television."

Chapter Thirty

"Allison, wake up!" Mart gave my shoulder a jostle. "Allison! Allison, look. Guess who's here?"

I came to with a start, blinking uncertainly. Where was I? Not in bed, that was obvious. Then memory flooded in, filling the gaps, and I pushed myself upright.

Street lights illuminated the scene before us. Clark was clearly visible as he climbed into the van and started the engine. A puff of white smoke from the exhaust billowed out in the cool evening air, then dissipated. Mart had put the car into gear and was checking his mirrors in preparation for another U-turn. He maneuvered quickly. The engine gave only a tiny sputter and a squeal of protest came from the tires. We were in pursuit once more.

Clark drove at a sedate pace three blocks north and eight blocks east. The van turned into a parking structure near the best hotel in town.

We followed almost the whole way before we ran into trouble. With every passing block Mart's car had been losing speed, despite his efforts to punch the gas pedal. Just as Clark made that turn into the structure, we lost power entirely.

Cursing in frustration, Mart steered safely to the curb. If I'd been behind the wheel, I would have pounded it with both fists. But Mart was already getting out of the car and waving me on. I hurried to join him on the sidewalk and we sprinted forward, holding hands.

"Change of plans," he said, sparing time for a sardonic smile.

We were less than a minute behind Clark and there were few vehicles pulling into the garage at such a late hour. It had been after one a.m. the last time I'd checked the clock on Mart's dashboard.

"This could get a bit dicey," he said. "We'll have to be really quiet in here. No talking."

"Got it," I whispered as we scrambled up a flight of dimly lit steps in the far corner of the structure.

Clark's van was just pulling into an empty slot along the shadowy outside wall of the building. A four-foot concrete barrier ran down the middle of the garage separating cars going up from cars going down. If we could reach it unseen we could crouch out of sight on our side of the wall and listen to Clark from just twenty feet away on his. And by peering between the cars parked on his side, we might even be able to see, too.

I pantomimed the idea to Mart with a few gestures and he nodded. Finger to my lips, I led the way, bent over low and running lightly. Any noise from our footsteps was covered by Clark's still-running engine. We were in position, tucked against the wall between a minivan and a sedan just as a sudden silence fell. Clark had killed the engine.

We were both totally alert now as the possibility of action drew nearer. We heard Clark put the van window down and soon caught a whiff of smoke from his cigarette.

Only a few minutes passed before we heard the sound of an engine as another car approached. A big, black, unmarked van pulled into the slot next to Clark and a man promptly got out. The slam of his car door echoed loudly in the night air.

"Who is it?" I hissed as we strained to see.

The silhouette was taller than Clark, with a stocky build like a football player. *Not a man to tangle with*, I thought.

Mart shook his head. "I can't tell," he mouthed.

Clark and the man shook hands and moved to the back of the zoo van. When they opened the door at the rear and stood before it, they blocked our view almost completely for a moment.

"As you can see," Clark said, turning sideways and fumbling with something in his hands, "I have some lovely specimens tonight. Just picked them up this afternoon."

His companion mumbled something low and unintelligible. Mart and I glanced at each other. "Did you catch that?" our eyes asked in silence. Then, we both shook our heads, turning back to the scene.

"No casualties this time," Clark laughed and I felt Mart tense in anger.

"Good. Last time the number was too high." The man's voice was as intimidating as his appearance—gruff with disapproval and scratchy as an old record.

Clark babbled out a sentence of explanation, trying to placate his customer. We could see him gesturing in great animation, turning on his legendary charm. It didn't seem to wash this time and he soon lapsed into silence, taking a step away from the other man.

The bigger man was intent on the contents of a rumpled parcel Clark had just handed over. It looked about a foot long and was rounded off at the edges, making me think of a big submarine sandwich. With careful motions, the man unfurled the covering and bent low over the contents in examination. Clark, hovering nervously nearby, prevented us from seeing what was under inspection and again I heard Mart's murmured oath.

There was no handshake to conclude the deal, just a nod from the big man, who then produced an envelope, presumably filled with cash. Clark made short work of pocketing it then lifted a wooden crate from the back of the van.

Beside me, Mart was quivering with barely suppressed rage and I knew he had to fight for control of his emotions. I placed my hand on his arm and he flinched in reaction, but his eyes never left the scene across the darkened building.

It must be hard for him, I thought, *to sit still when everything inside is shouting: Run over there! Don't let them take that crate away! Save the animals!*

To his credit, Mart repressed that temptation and we watched, motionless, as the transfer was completed. The two men put their heads together and we couldn't make out a word of conversation.

At last, Clark, ever helpful, supplied us with information. Moving around to the driver's side of the zoo van as his cohort climbed into his own vehicle, he confirmed their next rendezvous with a bob of his head and the statement, "Tomorrow."

Mart and I exchanged startled glances. I was surprised the next transaction would take place so soon. Tomorrow night was the big Mardi Gras celebration at the zoo. Naturally, Clark would feature prominently in the festivities. Could he sneak away?

The vans followed each other out of the structure, and the instant the tail lights were gone, Mart sprinted around to where the exchange had taken place, his footfalls ringing on the concrete. I followed.

"What did you see?" I asked, watching as Mart bent low to the concrete. "What are you looking for?"

"Evidence of what was in that crate," he told me. "And here it is."

In the dim light of the shadowed corner, he held up a long thin object I couldn't identify at first. He turned it slowly in the air where it was gently illuminated. Colors appeared, muted, patterned.

Then I knew, too.

Chapter Thirty-One

It was a feather.

The objects trussed up like submarine sandwiches were wild birds. Probably endangered birds. Perhaps an exotic species captured in their native land and smuggled here, to the United States.

"Oh, Mart!" I shuddered, imagining the terror and suffering the animals had endured. "Could they still be alive, wrapped up like that?" It didn't seem likely.

"Clark said they were and I suppose it is possible." He rose slowly, clutching the feather firmly in one hand. Suddenly, he looked ten years older. New creases appeared in his face and his eyes, so expressive, were flat and dull with fatigue and something a lot more serious.

"They said there would be another exchange tomorrow," I said. "With all the excitement and confusion of the Mardi Gras, I suppose it will be easy to pull off the transaction. Who will notice if Clark disappears for a while?"

"Exactly." Mart drew me into his arms and hugged me hard. The unexpected embrace took me by surprise and I knew it was a hug of reassurance, not passion. One of those life-affirming gestures we all need every now and then. I could feel the trembling of his muscles beneath my fingers, the rush of adrenaline that always follows trauma.

After a bit, he stepped back. "Thanks," he said, giving me a timid smile. He dropped a kiss on my forehead.

"Tomorrow," he told me, "I'll get in touch with the authorities Ishani spoke of. Tell them what we saw and heard. Give them this." He handed me the lone feather and I took it reverently.

As I turned it in my fingers, I recalled one of the curious events from Belize. "Mart," I began, thinking out loud. "When Clark got that text message 'airborne' must have referred to the birds who made the journey alive," I reasoned. "Grounded ones were dead. But what about the line 'Uncle visiting'?"

He snapped his fingers. "I bet I know the answer to that. Uncle Sam. Federal inspectors. Perhaps the area the birds were being sent to was due for an inspection. It wouldn't be good to have a shipment of illegally imported birds show up on that day," Mart speculated.

We headed back to his disabled vehicle, where Mart called a tow truck and I called a cab. The taxi showed up first and Mart kissed me soundly before I headed off for home.

At my place, I dropped my shoulder bag onto the nearest flat surface, exhausted in both body and spirit. Every bone in my body ached from the hours spent in the automobile, but I wasn't sure I had the energy to run the tub.

I flopped onto the sofa and covered my eyes with my forearm.

I'll just rest a minute, I told myself. *Then, I'll soak in a tub of hot bubbles.*

When I woke up, the sun was shining.

Chapter Thirty-Two

I made a hot breakfast on Saturday morning. My dreams had been disturbing ones, but none of the details had survived waking. Still, I couldn't shake a distinct feeling of doom and gloom.

As I ate my pancakes, I traced the path of this terrifying plot and my involvement in it. Each little clue and revelation had led to this moment—like the steps leading to the top of the temple. Now, we stood at the precarious summit, seeing the pattern spread before us and recognizing the danger. I stirred a bit of sugar into my tea and wondered what the evening would bring.

To be honest, I'd been looking forward to the Mardi Gras even before our trip to Belize. *Finally,* I'd thought, *I'll have a chance to wear that fabulous gown.*

I'd gotten the dress for a song a few years earlier quite by chance and had never had an occasion to wear it. I knew at the time it was impractical. How much opportunity is there, after all, to wear a full-length, hand-beaded evening gown that shimmers in a breathtaking shade of gold? The creation felt as if it weighed about twenty pounds, thanks to all those beads. But when I tried it on, I felt like a princess, transformed from a plain old working woman to a regal, statuesque glamour girl. Just the thought of it now made my lips curve in pleasure, pushing back the hazardous part of the evening and allowing me to indulge in daydreams of dancing with Mart, looking like a commercial for expensive perfume in our evening finery. I let the fantasy unfold as my tea grew tepid and emerged from that wonderful world only at the insistence of the telephone.

"Allison, it's Mart. Do you have a minute?"

"Sure." I tucked the phone under my ear and moved to the stove, putting more water in the kettle.

"I've talked to those local authorities Ishani named and they've already arranged to be at the Mardi Gras tonight. They'll be watching that service drive closely, but if we spot anything untoward, we're to contact them immediately."

"How many officers will there be?" I asked.

"About half a dozen. Some on the zoo grounds. Some at the deserted road behind the aviary." He stopped, took a breath, went on more slowly. "Allison, you stick close to me tonight, okay? I don't want anything happening to you." His voice was warm with concern and I smiled as a glow of happiness touched my heart.

"Mart," I told him honestly, "I wouldn't want to be anywhere else in the world."

There was silence on the other end of the line for the space of a heartbeat. Then he said, "You know, when this is all over, you and I have to have a talk."

"Oh?" My voice asked the question I couldn't give words to.

"Yes. Somewhere quiet where we won't be interrupted."

The kettle whistled and I poured the steamy water into my cup.

"I'll pick you up tonight around seven," he went on, getting back to the matter at hand.

"Sounds perfect." I was picturing how I'd greet him at the door, my hair upswept, smelling gently of my favorite fragrance, crossing the room elegantly in my high stiletto heels. *Not the outfit for a stake-out*, I thought with a giggle.

"I'll see you then," Mart concluded. "I'd better get back before anyone comes looking for me."

*

When I opened the door at the stroke of seven, my heart was hammering with a heady mixture of anticipation and dread.

The anticipation was fulfilled by the sight of Mart, so handsome and elegant in full evening attire. With his double-breasted tuxedo and jaunty bow tie, he looked rather like a groom in a bridal magazine and I whistled in appreciation.

He did a bit of whistling, too, and I hammed it up, twirling slowly in the snugly fitting gown. Mart followed me into the living room, watching me all the way.

"Zowee!" he crowed. "You look fantastic! I'll have to fight off your admirers all night."

"I hardly think so," I told him, embarrassed by his very vocal attention.

"Oh, I don't know. Come here for a second." He stretched out his arms and took a step toward me.

It was hard to move quickly in the heels, but I managed to evade his grasp. "Now, Mart," I warned, only half in jest. "I spent half an hour on these lips alone." I pointed at my outlined, penciled, and glossed mouth. "Don't muss it up before we even leave the apartment."

"You're right," he stated, dropping his hands in defeat. "Mustn't mess the makeup." He sounded disappointed, even though the light never dimmed in his eyes.

I relented, stepping up to him. With my high heels, I matched him in height and we looked smack into each other's eyes. "One kiss," I said.

"For luck," he agreed.

His hands slipped easily around my waist, pulling me up against his body. One hand slid lower, beyond the small of my back, pressing me closer still. I squirmed in pleasure as our lips met in a fierce exchange.

"You know," Mart whispered in my ear, his breath hot and taunting, "I almost hope nothing happens tonight, so we can get away early. Come back here, maybe?" The suggestion was accompanied by a thorough inspection of each crevice of my ear, traced first with his finger, then with his tongue.

My body was beginning to ache in some places and swell in others. All thoughts of the Mardi Gras had been driven out by his touch and the fate of my lipstick was a foregone conclusion.

"Oh, yes," I sighed, cradling his cheeks in my hands. I kissed the tip of his nose then his mouth.

The slit in the back of my gown that enabled me to walk also made it possible to lift my leg several inches, fitting it tightly against his thigh. I snuggled into his embrace.

"If you're cold now, we're both in deep trouble," Mart quipped, stepping back, knowing if there was one thing I was not, it was cold. "Seriously, Allison, I hope you've got a coat to match. It's a cool evening."

I was already on my way to the closet, reaching for the long black velvet number I'd worn only once before.

"That should do," Mart approved, helping me into it. "And it isn't fur. Good."

"Honestly? Will people wear fur to the zoo fundraiser?" This seemed incredible. "How thoughtless. How—"

"Hypocritical?" he finished my sentence, shaking his head. "Prepare to be astonished, Allison. There will be fur o'plenty."

Chapter Thirty-Three

Standing with a cocktail in hand, I examined the crowd of formally attired people clustered together in the zoo's education building. The Mardi Gras was held at scattered locations throughout the zoo, including a few of the outdoor areas, where folks bundled up to brave the cool spring air. As Mart had predicted, there were many women swathed in fur.

"But it isn't that cold!" I'd protested when I saw the first. Raccoon, or fox, I think.

"Allison, weather has nothing to do with it," Mart told me, his eyes sweeping the room for familiar faces.

We'd spent the early part of our evening mingling, as if our only reason for attending was to socialize. Many of the people from our zoo trek were there. Faith, already looking woozy from drink. Jen, in flaming red. And, of course, the Underwoods. Dan wore a full tuxedo. Elaine was engulfed in blue satin.

I lifted a hand in greeting when they looked my way and Elaine started over to us.

"Oh, great," Mart growled in my ear. "I don't know if I can take these two right now." He'd been edgy all the while, barely responding when people spoke to him, leaving me to make the introductions.

I could tell he was eaten up with concern about the transaction that might be occurring later. My own nerves were pulling tighter by the minute, too. Every tick of the clock brought the event closer. Would we know if the authorities apprehended someone on the path in the woods? Would we hear the news spread rapidly through the crowd, or read about it in the morning papers? I kept my hands occupied, fiddling with my glass so I didn't nibble at my nails. Mart reached frequently in his pocket to make sure his phone was still in place, ready for action. He was like a bomb waiting to go off and I knew the incessant chatter of the Underwoods would do nothing for his mood.

"Why don't you get us another drink?" I suggested as Dan and Elaine drew nearer. "Feel free to take your time." I winked and saw relief flood his features.

"Thanks." He squeezed my elbow, grinned briefly at the Underwoods and took off like a shot.

"Where is your escort off to in such a hurry?" Dan asked. "He shouldn't leave a beautiful woman like you alone for very long. You may not be here when he returns."

My cheeks blushed scarlet at his compliment.

"I'm sure he'll be back soon, dear," Elaine told her husband and I nodded.

"Quite a nice turnout for the event," I made conversation as I scanned the crowd. "It should raise plenty for the zoo."

"I should say!" Elaine agreed. "Clark's really worked wonders since he came here."

At the mention of the man's name, I gave a grimace of distaste that I hoped went unnoticed. The last thing I wanted to discuss was Clark but, here in his domain, such a wish was futile. Elaine went on to recount the fiscal history of the zoo, stressing Clark's contribution to its present tiptop shape.

"Without him," she concluded, "the zoo might have been closed. Then what would happen to all those sweet animals?"

"Why, they'd have to sell them!" Dan stated.

"Sell them?" Elaine sounded horrified. Her hand flew to rest the hollow of her throat and her diamond rings sparkled in the light.

"Would Clark have any objections to that?" I asked, remembering the feather Mart and I had found in the parking lot. Life was cheap. Especially the tiny lives of tiny creatures.

When I glanced at the Underwoods, they both looked puzzled. Elaine's lips were pursed in a pout of disapproval. Dan's expression was more difficult to interpret.

"What do you mean, Allison? Clark loves these animals. Would do anything for them. Even die for them, if he had to!"

Dan protested, each phrase uttered more emphatically than the previous one.

I shifted my weight onto one foot and wiggled the toes which had gone numb from my constricting shoes. This was dangerous territory. If Dan persisted, I'd need to keep a poker face, something which had never been easy for me. No one must know what Clark was involved in. Not yet. Especially here in this crowd of zoo supporters, where a critical comment would travel verbatim to the man in question faster than I could say, "endangered species."

"Yes, well," I stalled, "let's hope it never comes to that." I gave a great smile, hoping to dismiss the topic. "Isn't that band great?" I bobbed my head to the music coming from the stage.

Elaine agreed readily enough, turning my attention to the plaque over the auditorium door that stated: Courtesy of Elaine and Dan Underwood. Dan, however, gave me a lingering look. I could feel his eyes on the back of my head even as I chatted with his wife.

Curse it! I thought, kicking myself for my gaffe. Dan was a nosy old man. He loved a good gossip as much as his wife and I knew it. Still, I reasoned, with all the activity flourishing around us— the band, the dancing, the conversation—he'd soon be distracted. And I hadn't really said anything, I told myself, nodding my head as Elaine prattled on.

Within five minutes, Elaine spotted an old friend and dragged Dan off across the room. As they departed, Dan pulled a comical face, just as I'd seen him do a thousand times. I laughed with more relief than humor and went to find Mart.

As we danced in the crowded area reserved for that purpose, Mart pointed out a tuxedoed gentleman who stood near the entrance.

"He's one of the posse," he told me. "They've got officers behind the aviary, as well as on that service road beyond the woods. A squad is stationed near the zoo gates, but it's hardly likely they would choose such an obvious route," he told me.

"Any word from Ishani?"

"No," he shook his head. "But we weren't expecting any."

"Well, if organization is the key, we should have it handled," I said, wishing I could trust my own words. We turned in a tight circle and Mart spun me out beneath his arm, my heavy gown swirling around my ankles.

Against my back, I could feel Mart's hand clenching and unclenching with nervous energy. He compressed his lips and the creases near his mouth jumped into sharp relief. Then, as if letting go of whatever thought was paining him, he sighed and tipped his head to one side.

Leaning into him, I kissed his cheek and we faltered a step.

"That's very distracting, Allison," he said without scolding.

"Good. It's meant to be. I can't wait for all this to be over. Then we can distract each other a lot more."

"And a lot more frequently." He winked, tightening his grip on my waist and bringing me into solid contact with his body. I teetered on my unaccustomed high heels.

"Mmm," I murmured in his ear, taking the opportunity to nip at the tender skin of his earlobe.

"Let's get out of here, Allison. Let's take a stroll." He took my hand, guiding me off the floor. We didn't stop to retrieve my velvet cloak. Mart assured me he would keep me warm and, if our recent encounter was any indication, he was a man of his word.

The silence of the outdoors assaulted our ears as we left the clamor of the festivities. The evening was a mild one; the wind had shifted and blew gently from the southwest, bringing delicate hints of warmer weather.

Mart's arm went around my shoulder and I cuddled eagerly against him.

We had only walked about a hundred feet when a voice called loudly from behind us, "Mart! Mart! Wait up!"

We stopped in our tracks and turned. On this stretch of the path, trees grew close on the left, casting shadows over the pavement and obscuring the scant light provided by the lamp posts.

The figure coming toward us moved with a slow, halting gait, as if he'd been running to catch up with us and was now gasping for breath. As he drew nearer, he became recognizable.

"Dan!" Mart greeted the elderly man with concern. "What is it? Is something wrong?" His questions sounded a bit frantic to my ears, but I knew what Mart was expecting to hear—bad news about the illegal transaction. *But Dan would hardly be bringing that message,* I thought.

Dan bent forward, placing his hands on his knees, and took a few deep, staggering breaths.

Mart and I exchanged an anxious look. I knew I wouldn't recognize a heart attack, and chances were Mart wouldn't, either.

Stepping up to Dan, I put my hand on his back and leaned over to look into his eyes.

"You okay?" I asked.

He nodded once, twice and stood up slowly. His smile was shaky but his voice was back to normal as he boomed, "Didn't mean to scare you two, but I wanted to catch you, Mart. Clark's looking for you." He paused, furrowing his brow into a frown. "And he didn't look very happy."

My eyes shot to Mart. What could Clark want with him? Had he found out we knew his secret? Giving his head the tiniest shake, Mart warned me to say nothing.

He flashed a wide smile and attempted a chuckle. "Even on my night off, I can't avoid work," he joked.

Abandoning Dan, I moved closer to Mart, unable to shake off my sudden fear. My hand grasped his and I could feel myself quivering. *Don't go!* I thought in desperation. *Don't go!*

"Where is he?"

Dan pointed back the way we had come. "Back at the party headquarters. Near the bandstand." He dropped his voice low and asked, "What's going on? What have you done to get him so angry?"

I gave Mart's hand a tug. My nerves were stretching close to their breaking point.

"Thanks," Mart's voice was steady, ignoring Dan's prying questions. "Let's go, then." We took a few steps, but Dan remained behind.

"Aren't you coming?" I asked over my shoulder.

"Naw. Not just yet. I think . . . I think I wore myself out getting over here. Better rest a bit before I head back." Sagging up against the nearest lamp post, he did look drawn and pale.

I made a sudden decision. "I'll stay here with him, Mart. I wouldn't feel right leaving him alone. What if he had an attack or something?" My words were whispered soft and low, and Mart responded in kind.

"Are you sure? I mean, it's dark here and you don't even have your coat."

"I'm sure." I gave his arm a pat. "He'll be fine in another minute or two and then we'll be right behind you." I tried to make the words convincing, to both of us, and must have succeeded because Mart gave up the argument.

"Okay, but stay here or go back to the education building and wait for me by the refreshment table. I don't want to have to go searching for you," he warned.

"Don't worry. You won't have to, I promise." We kissed briefly then I gave him a gentle shove. "You'd better hurry."

His hands moved up my arms in a slow caress as he asked, "Remember all that while ago when you said you wouldn't write your story until Clark was a hero?"

I nodded as he laughed wryly. "Things have certainly changed," I agreed. "Who would have guessed?" A quiver of horror passed through me at the turn of events and I blinked in quick succession to dispel sudden tears.

One more kiss and he was gone, looking over his shoulder at us until the shadows swallowed him up. I shivered in the air, which seemed much cooler now without his presence, and turned my attention to Dan.

Chapter Thirty-Four

"Feeling any better?" I asked, putting my hand on Dan's arm.

"Yes, yes. A bit." He still leaned against the pole and it seemed his face had lost its pallor. In fact, he looked feverish now—eyes bright, cheeks glistening.

I stepped back rubbing my hands together, then over my arms to ward off the evening chill. "Well, as soon as you're up to it, let's go back," I suggested, trying not to rush him.

"But, Allison," Dan protested, "I was thinking that, since we're so close to it, we could go take a look at the dolphin tank."

"What?" This was the last thing I'd expected. "Why would we want to do that?" I was already shaking my head in refusal. I was anxious enough being separated from Mart these few minutes. I certainly didn't plan any extended tours.

"Oh, c'mon, Allison. Where's your sense of adventure?" Dan asked, straightening up and looking livelier. "You can describe it in your article," he cajoled me.

"I've got plenty for my article, thanks." I went to his side and put my arm through his. He stood rigid as a statue, however, so I gave him a tug. "Dan, I'm getting cold. Let's go."

"Not until we see the dolphins," he whined like a spoiled child.

I pressed my eyes shut. How did Elaine stand it?

"It's warm in there, you know. Elaine and I are so proud. They built that with our money, too."

Oh. That explained his eagerness to show it off, I figured. I looked over my shoulder, at the deserted path leading back to the education building and all those other people. Only the sounds of birds and night creatures competed with the faint booming of the band far away.

I sighed. "How far is it?"

"Not far, Allison. Not far at all." Dan's expression brightened and he stepped off in that direction. "It's just here, beside the aviary."

That nearly stopped my steps. If there was anywhere on earth I didn't want to go right now, it was anywhere within spitting distance of the aviary. What if the smugglers were there at this very moment? And the police? There could be gunfire.

But I could hardly tell that to Dan. We marched along, side by side.

The aviary was dark and deserted-looking now. Was anything happening inside it? Were the police watching? Could they see us go by? My footsteps slowed and I lagged behind, my eyes sweeping quickly over the area.

Almost instantly, Dan was beside me, hurrying me along and telling me plenty of unnecessary details about the dolphin tank and the building that enclosed it.

"Look, you can see it from here. See, there's a pool indoors for winter and outdoors for summer. And there are bleachers for people to watch them do tricks. Two shows a day, Allison. Really packs them in, too."

"I can imagine," I said, picturing Mart's response to the idea of making wild animals perform like Vegas showgirls.

The building looming before us appeared to be constructed entirely of glass. I wondered if it was unlocked.

"I'll bet we can't even get in, Dan," I said, feeling relieved. "This exhibit isn't one of the Mardi Gras sights."

Dan reached into the pocket of his tux, jangling change and keys. "No problem, Allison. I've got a key." He held it up in the moonlight and grinned.

I didn't even wonder where he'd gotten it. *One of the perks of being a big contributor*, I thought vaguely and my heart, already not in this project, plummeted a bit further. I didn't want to be rude to the old man, but this was taking much too long. Besides, it was frightening here.

The glass doors, windows, and walls reflected the night, pressing it in all around us. We seemed to be the last two people on earth, an idea immediately reinforced when Dan pushed open a door and ushered me inside.

The place smelled a bit like the pool at my high school and I knew that must be because of cleaning supplies used on the tiled floors. The ceiling soared far overhead, adding to my sense of isolation. The pool itself stretched the length of the building, glowing faintly under muted artificial lights. Several dark shapes moved within, mere shadows at this distance.

We advanced toward the edge of the water and I got my first look at the long, silvery creatures, watching the pair swim in gentle, synchronized motions.

Dan found a pail filled with dolphin dinner and flipped a few fish bits into the water. We were instantly rewarded with the animals' full attention.

"They like you, Ally. See? They're smiling," Dan said, smiling, too.

I wrinkled my nose at his silly joke, some of my nervous tension dissipated. It must have been from watching the dolphins' smooth, effortless motion. So graceful, so calming.

For several long moments, we stood there, watching in fascination as the dolphins jumped and dove for the tidbits. When the bucket was empty, Dan set it down with a clang and extended both hands.

"All gone!" he told them and they seemed to understand, turning swiftly and racing off to the far end of the pool.

Against one wall, the bleachers Dan spoke of rose twenty feet up. He headed there now, wiping the fish off his hands with a handkerchief. I stayed right at his heels.

"The dolphins are wonderful," I told him sincerely. "And this facility seems marvelous. The zoo is lucky to have patrons like you."

"Gotta do something with my money," he told me, easing down onto the lowest seat.

"I'm glad you shared this with me, Dan, but I think we'd better be getting back," I said. "We've been away a long time. I'm sure Elaine is wondering where you are." I wrung my hands, certain Mart was wondering about me, too. Now that we'd seen the animals, I could pressure Dan to return. "Are you up for the walk back?"

"No, Allison," he shook his head. "No. We're not leaving. At least, you're not." His words were cold and terse, uttered without his characteristic liveliness.

"What? What do you mean?" I asked, pushing down a tiny flame of panic leaping to life inside me. I took a step backward.

Quick as a snake striking its victim, his hand reached out and fastened around my wrist, pulling me down hard onto the wooden bench.

"I mean, dear, that you won't be returning to the party. You aren't going to leave this building."

I jerked my arm, but he held fast, tightening his grasp until I wanted to yelp in pain. "Dan, this isn't funny! Let me go!" I demanded, my words echoing eerily in our glass enclosure.

"I can't let you go, foolish girl. You know. You know, don't you, about Clark and what he's up to?"

I stopped thrashing and stared at him. Was he trying to protect Clark? Was that why he was scaring me this way? My mind whirled as I tried to determine the right answer to his question. Should I say yes? Or no? Which one did he want to hear? In the end, I said nothing.

"You don't have to answer, Allison. I can see it in your eyes. You have lovely eyes. Has Mart told you that?"

"I don't know what you're thinking, Dan," I blustered, "but I'm leaving." I stood up and he did too, still clinging like a limpet to my arm.

Waves of water rippled as the dolphins swam in endless motion. The pool lights reflected the patterns onto the walls behind us and across our faces, making Dan look like a ghastly villain from a bad horror film.

"You're not going to capture Clark and expose him," he told me with certainty, his brows meeting as he scowled with ferocious intensity.

"Your loyalty is admirable," I said, "but you're much too late to save him." I tried to make the statement boastful, to startle him, catch him off guard.

"Save him?" Dan laughed, a hearty, full sound. "I don't care about him. Lock him away forever if you like. The problem with Clark is he's a weak man. If he's pressured, he'll talk."

He paused, but I knew with a flash of insight what he was going to say next. I didn't even blink as he concluded, "And he'll talk about me."

Chapter Thirty-Five

In the stillness following this revelation, the only sound came from the pool, where the dolphins still swam undisturbed. I watched Dan in shock and confusion, not fully understanding the import of his words.

"Yes, if Clark is cornered, he'll crumble," Dan said. "He isn't a strong individual, you know, despite his outward appearances."

"Clark is a criminal," I said slowly, stating a truth. "But, you?" I shrugged my bare shoulders. I wasn't fighting his grasp now. I was too stunned to resist just then and he loosened his hold.

I must have looked as dazed as I felt, because he laughed again, with great amusement. "I guess I owe you an explanation. After all your hard work, you deserve to know, I suppose. It's a short story, really. You see, several years ago, when Elaine and I were on our first zoo trek in Africa, Clark came to me one night in great distress. He told me he was in desperate need of a rather large sum of money and he needed it immediately. Well, naturally, I'm always one to help out a friend and we arranged a loan. I asked him what he needed it for, of course, and his explanation was surprising. It seems he'd gotten involved in a very lucrative but illegal scheme importing protected animals— or parts of them." He grinned and I recoiled, pulling away in shock.

When he gave my arm a painful wrench I went still.

Dan continued, as if my pain or fear was no concern of his. "He'd come up a bit short on this occasion and didn't have enough to pay his partners. Without pay, he knew he'd be killed. There is no honor among thieves, Allison." Dan pursed his lips, shook his head. "No honor. No loyalty."

"And that surprised you?" I asked. It was hard for me to get the words out. My heart was pounding and my breath was coming in short little gasps.

Intent on confessing his sins, Dan ignored my remark and went on. "All my life—my adult life—people have said I made my money by saying 'I do.' They think I married Elaine for her fortune. That I wasn't capable of earning it on my own. And that isn't true! I had a good start on it when I met her. Would have done all right on my own. But, then, there she was. So young, so lovely, and with a substantial fortune, to boot. I won't deny that was part of her charm then, but we were well matched in other ways."

I saw an opportunity to reason with him and jumped at it. "You still are. Anyone can see you two love each other very much."

He nodded. "Yes, yes, we do. I've always wanted to give her everything her heart desires. I've always wanted to prove to us both I could support her. Earn the money she's so used to having." He trailed off, his eyes wandering over my left shoulder as he examined the past.

"You got involved with Clark and his criminal activity to prove a point?" I couldn't keep the astonishment from my voice. If Dan needed to build up his ego, there were plenty of good ways to do it. This didn't make sense!

"I don't expect you to understand, Allison. I expect you to listen. Unless you'd rather I just kill you now?" All traces of the kindly, comically grouchy man I'd known had vanished. In his place was this hardened, brittle bit of humanity, so anxious to prove his own worth to no one but himself. So far gone on his quest for fulfillment, he'd kill to protect it.

"Dan! You're going to kill me?" My entire body was shaking now, quivering with the fear I couldn't hide or control. Even though the building was warm, I felt cold and stiff, literally petrified as reality dawned. He meant it. He would kill me because I knew about the smuggling.

"But I'm not the only person who knows all this," I told him. "Do you plan to go on a spree and kill us all? It wouldn't serve any purpose," I bargained for my life, hoping to make this irrational man see the truth in my words.

"That's what Clark said. He's all in favor of taking the next plane to South America."

"You told Clark you plan to murder me? Is he supposed to be killing Mart now? Is that why he wanted to see him?" I pressed Dan for answers, moving closer to him as concern for Mart flooded me.

"Clark didn't ask to see him. I made that up. I'll deal with Mart later."

A flicker of hope sprung alive within me. We'd left Mart on the path ages ago. He'd had plenty of time to discover Dan's lie and realize Clark really wasn't looking for him. *Surely then,* I thought, *Mart will know something is wrong. Surely he'll come looking for me!* The tiny bit of hope shriveled with my next thought. We were here in the dolphin enclosure, where no one would ever think to look. Until it was too late.

"I'll deal with Mart next," Dan repeated, blinking and bringing his eyes back to focus on me. "Just as I had that greedy Mendoza eliminated."

"You killed Tommy Mendoza?" The revelations were coming fast and furiously.

"No, *I* didn't kill him. I merely arranged it. He stumbled onto our scheme and wanted a part of the action. Too big a part. He wouldn't listen to reason, so. . . ." His shoulders lifted and fell, casually explaining away violent death.

"What about Clark?" I asked. "What are your plans for him?"

"I think it's time Clark left Rochester. Got started somewhere else. Our business can easily switch locations. Demand is limitless, and so is supply."

"Limitless!" I burst out, thinking of the ivory bits and the elephants they had once been part of. "You're crazy! These animals are endangered. They could become extinct. Disappear forever!"

Dan waved a hand in dismissal. "You've been hanging around Mart too much. He's such an alarmist. Clark assured me from the start that all these so-called ecologists were overreacting. Animals are like cabbages, Allison. You can always grow more."

"Clark told you this? The man who leads treks and give lectures on conservation?" I shook my head, sending my earrings dancing. "That's ludicrous!"

"No, lucrative. If you had a demanding gal like Sylvia to support, you'd find this scheme pretty attractive, let me tell you. That girl loves the finer things, you know. Clark is well paid by the zoo, but it's still never enough."

"It's amazing what people can justify for the sake of a buck," I said. I hung my head down and fought back tears. I wasn't thinking of myself then. I was thinking about human nature and all its inherent flaws.

Lost in my dismal thoughts, I didn't hear the door open on the other side of the pool. Didn't realize anyone had come in until the sound of voices reached my ears.

Dan heard them, too, and jerked me to my feet, clapping a hand over my mouth and pushing me toward the wall. I stumbled a bit in my shoes, but Dan's firm grasp around my body kept me upright. Shoving me under scaffolding which made up the underside of the bleachers, Dan joined me in the shadowy darkness.

Something hard poked me in the rib cage and I looked down to see the outline of a gun.

"If you move or make a sound, I'll shoot you," he hissed in my ear, and I knew he meant his words.

In silence, we watched two people move into view, engaged in a heated argument. I nearly fainted dead away when I recognized them.

It was Clark and Sylvia.

Chapter Thirty-Six

I heard Dan draw in a sharp breath beside me as the couple moved further into the room. Sylvia was speaking, her angry gestures accompanying angry words.

"I won't stand for this behavior, Clark! You'll not humiliate me like this again, do you hear me?" She stomped one foot down hard on the floor.

Clark defended himself. "You've got it all wrong," he told her, his voice soothing, as if he were trying to deal with a sulky child. "You know there's no one but you for me. Pumpkin, you must realize that." He reached out, attempting to touch her but she stepped back out of reach.

"Don't you touch me and don't lie! I'm not blind, Clark, although I've certainly done my best to overlook your faults!" She gave him a contemptuous glance, her eyes flicking over him from head to toe. "I saw that woman hanging all over you tonight. Cozying up to you—in front of everyone. And this isn't the first time, either!" Spinning on her heel, she strode to the very edge of the pool, looking down into the depths of the water. The worst of her anger seemed to have flared and abated. Her shoulders slumped in defeat and I thought she might start to cry.

Clark advanced slowly, coming up behind her in silence, as if he were approaching a motion-sensitive explosive. He looked nervous and stricken, his mouth drawn down tight. The flickering light from the water played over his strained features. "Sylvia, that woman didn't mean anything. She's drunk! Couldn't you tell? She didn't know what she was doing."

As he explained, I could picture the scene. A tipsy attendee, in a partying mood, advancing on the object of her affections, Clark. Sylvia, watching from the sidelines, would be doing a slow burn. Looking away, she'd remain in character as hostess of the fete. But inside. . . .

"Well, then why didn't you stop her?" Sylvia wheeled around to face her husband, teetering for a second as her shoes slid on a puddle of water created by the dolphins' splashes. She recovered her balance almost immediately and didn't miss a beat. "Why didn't you tell her to knock it off, instead of just standing there enjoying it?" She waved her arms in accompaniment to her words. "I tell you, Clark, I've had too much of this over the years and it just seems to be getting worse. I'm not along on every one of your blasted trips to God-knows-where to keep an eye on you! What happens when I'm not around? Maybe I don't want to know!"

"Sylvia, you're blowing this way out of proportion." Clark made an attempt at damage control. "Be reasonable, darling. She contributes a lot to the zoo. It wouldn't do to be rude to her, would it?"

"The zoo! The zoo! All you ever think about is this stupid zoo. I'm sick of it! Sick of the politics, the problems, and the smell. Clark, I want out. I want a divorce."

Dan and I had been silent and still, our own horrific tableau frozen as this new one unfolded. At Sylvia's pronouncement, Dan stiffened, as if he'd taken the blow personally.

Shifting around beside me, he was getting nervous, I could tell. He was a jittery old man, emotionally unstable and armed with a lethal weapon. I should have been taking these moments of delay to think and plan. I should have been developing some sort of strategy to try and save my life. But my mind was a blank, dwelling on other details, wondering where Sylvia placed the blame for her own clandestine love affair.

Clark had staggered back a step at her declaration, making me wonder how he really felt toward her. Was it love or security that kept them together? In Belize, at Altun Ha, Dan had said he wasn't sure it was Clark whom Sylvia loved, hinting it could be something else. Prestige? Social standing? Or had he meant someone else? The professor?

Whatever Clark felt, its roots ran deep because he looked truly anguished now. Sylvia's eyes glimmered with unshed tears as she looked at her husband. This was exacting a toll from her, too.

Clark opened his mouth to speak and Sylvia held up a hand to stop him. "No. No discussion. You won't change my mind. Please don't try."

He took another step closer and the assertive action jolted Sylvia past her moment of sadness, bringing her anger back to the surface.

She backed up, standing at the very corner of the pool.

One more step and she'll end up in the water, I thought, realizing how close she was to the edge.

"Leave it, Clark! I'm going back to the party where I will be your dutiful wife one last night. Tomorrow, you'll hear from my attorney."

She made to move around Clark, in the direction of the exit. His hand shot out, grabbing her arm and twisting her around. I gasped and Dan gave me a jab.

"Sylvia, please!" Clark begged, but she was having none of it. He shifted gears. "I won't let you go! I won't let you do this to me." His own violent instincts surfacing, he tightened his hold on her arm.

"Let go of me!" she hissed, squirming and fighting. With one sudden, forceful jerk, she pulled her arm away adding a swift kick at his shin. As she wrenched free, Clark was left off balance, slipping in the same puddle Sylvia had earlier, teetering at the edge of the pool.

Sylvia took off, running for the exit and sobbing loudly. Maybe she never even saw Clark's flailing arms and his attempts to catch himself. She didn't hear the heavy thud as his head collided with the tile floor at the edge of the pool. She didn't see the blood red stain rapidly seeping into the water, turning it pink.

It all happened in the blink of an eye, moving in slow motion to be replayed in my nightmares for weeks to come. Beside me, Dan was stunned and motionless.

Without taking time to think about it, I made my move. Mercilessly, I rammed my left elbow into his paunchy stomach, doubling him over as his breath came out in a rush, and getting that gun away from my side. My stiletto heels, causing me pain all evening, were a blessing now as I brought one down on the top of his foot. He gave a yowl of pain, crumpling even further, and it was almost easy to give him the shove that tipped him over.

I leapt over his body, hiked my dress up with both hands and pelted across the room. My heels skittered on the tiles and, as I passed the pool, I spared a second to glance at Clark's body floating on the surface of the water. The curious dolphins had drawn nearer, swimming in circles around him and making the scene even more unreal.

I hit the door at a run, pushing it open with one hand while the other hand kept my dress above my knees. It was a ridiculous outfit for the situation, heavy, awkward, and incredibly restricting. If I'd been able to remove the shoes rapidly, I would have, but the straps were buckled tight, making it impossible.

The cool night air, such a contrast to the humid dolphin area, made me gasp. But a second later, I recovered, taking a deep, full breath to fill my lungs and using that air to shriek.

"Help!"

Chapter Thirty-Seven

Each step was jarring as I ran flat out along the shadowed path between the dolphin enclosure and the aviary. Over and over, I shouted that single word.

"Help!"

I didn't look behind me or off to either side as I fled, just kept my eyes glued on the tarmac unfolding endlessly before me. I didn't seem to be making any progress and my voice was getting weaker with each exclamation.

I don't know if it was instinct that guided me to the aviary or if some non-terrified part of my brain actually recalled Mart telling me the police would be there. In any event, I headed for its door at a full gallop, my breath catching in my throat on sobs I didn't dare let out.

The door opened, swinging silently inward as I approached. And Mart was there, arms outstretched to catch me, pulling me to a stop. He folded me closely up against his body and I babbled madly into his ear, each word crowding onto the next in the rush to get out.

"Allison! Allison! Calm down. It's okay."

I pulled away in frustration.

"No, no!" I shook my head wildly, looking past him into the dimly lit interior of the unfinished aviary. Several uniformed men stood nearby and just the sight of them—authority figures to end this chaos—made me feel a second of relief.

I took a deep breath. It was important that they listen to me now and believe every word I said. Squaring my shoulders, I began. "Clark is dead. An accident. In the dolphin pool."

"What?" Mart's eyebrows shot up. He directed a glance at the policemen and they drew in around us.

"He and Sylvia had an argument. He grabbed her, she pulled away. Then he fell. Hit his head." My eyes pinched shut at the remembered image. I could hear one of the officers speaking in low tones into his walkie-talkie, giving the information to the voice which squawked back.

"And Sylvia? Where's Sylvia?" Mart asked.

"I don't know. She ran out. She doesn't even know he's dead. But Mart—there's more." I grabbed his arms just below the elbow and his hands tightened around my waist. "It's Dan behind the animal smuggling. Dan's the ring leader!"

Mart's mouth gaped open like a fish; he was speechless.

In halting sentences, I stammered out my story, telling Mart and the officers what Dan had told me. When I got to the part about the gun, Mart's face turned a pasty shade of white and he interrupted my narrative to engulf me in a fierce, protective hug.

"Oh my God, Allison!" he exclaimed and I could feel him shuddering as he held me.

"How did you get away?" he asked me and I finished my tale, ending with my flight from the dolphin enclosure to the aviary.

"So, Dan is still there?" Mart asked and I shrugged.

"I don't know. I doubt it. "

Once more, the officers near us were in action, asking me for details and radioing the information to other authorities on the grounds. For the space of a few moments, all the work fell to them, giving Mart and me a chance to just cling to each other, out of harm's way. An ambulance had been ordered, its siren already sounding shrilly in the evening air. We heard one officer describe Dan, the suspect, as "armed and dangerous."

Truer words were never spoken, I thought.

The policemen bustled around us in an orderly fashion, obviously knowing what needed to be done and doing it with great efficiency.

"We've had some excitement here, too," Mart told me, leading me to a ladder left by the construction crew and perching me carefully on one rung, where I could rest.

"Did you intercept the exchange?" I whispered, my voice still unsteady.

"Yes. At the service road on the other side of the woods. They arrested the man we saw with Clark at the parking garage and Kyle, the groundskeeper. Remember, he drove the van downtown and left it for Clark to pick up?"

He gave me a second to nod before going on.

"Tonight's bit of contraband appears to be some powdered rhino horn." His mouth squared and I remembered him telling me—ages ago, before any of this began—how he'd been part of a rhino relocation program.

I reached for his hands. "Oh, Mart!"

He sighed before continuing. "It's hoped these two will provide the specifics of the operation. But, if what you say is true, they won't have to lead us to the head of the operation."

All I could say was, "It's true."

*

The officers asked us to remain where we were for the time being and a full fifteen minutes went by before we heard a commotion out front, followed by the sound of the door opening and Dan shouting.

"This is absurd! Do you know who I am? Treating me like a criminal. I'll have your badge for this—every one of you!" Hair mussed and clothing rumpled, he was held securely between two uniformed policemen. The federal authority Mart had pointed out earlier was there, as well, his tuxedo giving him the appearance of a real guest at the Mardi Gras.

They'd advanced well into the room before Dan saw me. Unabashedly clinging to Mart, I was doing my best to hide behind him.

"You!" Dan stopped in his tracks and the look he gave me chilled my heart. "What crazy stories have you been telling them? I haven't done anything wrong!"

"You tried to kill me," I stated flatly. "I told them everything you told me. About the wild animal smuggling. About Clark being in on all of it. About you getting involved and taking it over."

"Why, you're out of your mind!" He gave a chuckle and shook his head. "She's got it all wrong," he told the gathering. "I'd never be party to such a thing. How she can even suggest—"

"Can it, Underwood," Mart growled low.

"Hey, it's her word against mine!" Dan declared.

A lump formed in my throat as I realized this was true. No one had heard what he had told me. No one had seen him pull that gun. I groaned.

"No, it isn't." Someone spoke from behind the little cluster of policemen holding Dan.

As they moved to one side, Elaine came into view. She looked awful, haggard and tired. Her lips were white and her eyes appeared sunken and dark. Standing between Dan and me, in the middle of the action like an actor taking center stage, she wrung her hands.

Directing her comment to the officers and pointedly ignoring her husband, she said, "I saw everything. I saw it all!"

Chapter Thirty-Eight

"Elaine, what are you saying?" Dan tried to take a step forward, but was held back by the strong arm of the law.

Slowly, her mouth drawn down in infinite sadness, Elaine looked at her husband. Sounding exhausted, she said simply, "I saw you, Dan. I heard what you told Allison," she paused, gulped a breath, and continued. "I heard you say you'd kill her."

"But, how?" I asked her, puzzled. "We were alone in the building."

"I wasn't in the building," she told me. "I was just outside the door. Your voices carried quite clearly in all that empty space."

"I think I can explain part of this," Mart put in. "After Dan sent me on that wild goose chase looking for Clark, I ran into Elaine back at the education building. She was looking for Dan and I told her he was with you on the path."

"So, I went to meet you two," Elaine took up the story. "But you weren't where Mart said you'd be. I wasn't sure where to look next, so I just kept walking. When I got to the dolphin building, I thought I'd just take a peek. I knew Dan was very interested in the place. It's . . . it's one of his favorite exhibits."

"Elaine, don't do this!" Dan demanded, his eyes pleading with her.

She viewed him dispassionately, as if she was looking at a stranger. "When I got to the door, I heard voices and I looked through the glass. I didn't go in because something didn't seem quite right. Just something about the way you two were standing. I don't really know. But, I just froze there and listened."

"Then what, ma'am?" one of the officers prodded.

"Well, naturally, I couldn't believe what I was hearing. I was utterly stunned. I . . . . I didn't know what to do next. But then there were voices behind me, heading in my direction and I panicked." She looked down at her clasped hands. "I hid in some bushes a few feet away."

"It was Clark and Sylvia. Arguing. They went inside and I snuck back to the doorway. I was sure they'd see you. Save you from Dan." Elaine shook her head. "Sylvia almost knocked me over when she ran by on her way out. Never even saw me, though."

"Why didn't you come inside then?" I asked, my voice sharp with anger. "Why didn't you try to save Clark—and me? You could have gone for help!"

The older woman looked down at her hands, twisted together in a nervous knot. Her tiny shoulders were stooped with fatigue and despair. When she replied, her voice shook with tears. "I didn't know what to do! I couldn't think. I needed time. I've been walking all this while, trying to sort it out." She looked up and met my eyes, saying with great sincerity, "I'm sorry I didn't come sooner, Allison. But I'm here now."

Dan let loose a string of angry exclamations, condemning his wife for turning against him. The officers immediately cut him off, leading him forcibly from the building.

"That will do, Underwood," one officer said. "You'll get your day in court."

Elaine followed slowly behind them. "I'll meet you at the police station," she told them, sounding subdued but brave.

"Should we go with her?" Mart suggested in a whisper, but I shook my head.

"I think she'd rather be alone right now."

*

Hours later, after more interviews and explanations, Mart and I snuggled together on my living room sofa. Our shoes lay in a discarded heap just inside my front door. I nestled my head against his chest and he rested his feet on the coffee table.

"But, how did you come to be at the aviary?" I asked, as the thought came to mind.

Mart took a second to drop a kiss on the top of my head, laying his hand against my hair and tangling his fingers deep within it. "When I realized Clark was nowhere around and obviously wasn't looking for me, I got worried. I was pretty edgy all evening, you know, and I think even the slightest variation from normal would have set me off. Anyway, I decided to check in there. It seemed like the logical spot for trouble. Kyle had just been arrested and it's a good thing we were in the aviary."

"Why is that?"

"Because he was singing like a canary," Mart quipped, chuckling. He sobered as he went on. "Clark was Kyle's boss, but Kyle knew there was someone else at the helm. Wasn't sure of the name, though. When he said it was 'something like Oakwood,' my heart almost stopped. I couldn't be sure, of course, but his statement sent me to the door, in search of you and Dan."

"And there I was, hysterical."

"Yes, there you were." He squeezed me tight, then released the hold, running his hands over me in tender, comforting caresses.

"Clark's dead. Dan will go to prison and the smuggling will stop," I summed up the situation, wriggling closer.

"In Rochester, it will stop. We'll have to count on Ishani and others like her to block the pipeline at the other end," Mart pointed out.

"Won't Ishani be surprised, hmm?" The terrors of the evening were beginning to fade and I was able to think about how the activities at the Mardi Gras would affect others.

"Yes. We'll contact her in the morning." He shifted on the sofa, drawing me closer, pulling my legs across his lap. His hand rested briefly against my cheek and he traced the outline of my lips with his thumb.

"In the morning," I echoed just before our lips met. The kiss kindled fires of love and of passion deep inside me. Warming me, melting me, each emotion fed and enhanced the other, inextricably bound together.

As our lips separated, I opened my mouth to speak, but Mart beat me to it.

"I love you, Allison," he whispered.

Tears formed in my eyes, blurring his sweet, handsome face. "And I love you."

Swinging my legs to the floor I stood up, the skirt of my heavy gown swirling around my ankles. Tugging his hands, I drew him up beside me.

"You know," I said, "we never got to finish our dance tonight."

"Well, then."

Mart gathered me into his arms and we began to move together. His gentle humming was all the music we would ever need.

www.ingramcontent.com/pod-product-compliance
Lightning Source LLC
Chambersburg PA
CBHW010636100726
47900CB00011B/2845